DOMINIC

A DARK MAFIA ROMANCE

NATASHA KNIGHT

A NOTE FROM NATASHA

Dear Reader,

All the while that I was writing Dominic's story, I kept thinking of a line from the song *Ordinary Love*, by U2 about how "*all the beauty that's been lost before wants to find us again*"[1]. I felt like Dominic needed beauty back in his life and although he certainly wasn't searching for it, it found him.

He was probably one of the hardest characters for me to write and you won't think him a hero, not for a long time as you read his story, maybe not ever, but I hope I've told his story as it fits.

Thank you so much for purchasing this book and wanting to read Dominic's story. I dedicate this book to each of my readers and hope you know how grateful I am to you.

Love,
Natasha

———————————————————————

1. U2, Ordinary Love

1

F ear has a distinct smell, something that belongs only to it. Pungent. Acidic. And at the same time, sweet. Alluring, even.

Or maybe only sweet and alluring to a sick fuck like me. Either way, the girl huddled in the corner had it coming off her in waves.

I pulled the skull mask down to cover my face. The room was dark, but I could tell she was awake. Even if she held her breath and didn't move a single muscle, I'd know. It was the scent. That fear. It gave them away every single time.

And I liked it. It was like an adrenaline rush, the anticipation of what was to come.

I liked fucking with them.

I closed the door behind me, blocking off the little bit of light I'd allowed into the small, dark, and rank bedroom. She'd been brought here yesterday to this remote cabin in the woods. So fucking cliché. Cabin in the woods. But that's what it was. That's where I did my best work. The room contained a queen-size bed equipped with restraints, a bedside table, and a locked chest holding any equipment I needed. The attached bathroom had had its door removed before my arrival. Only the bare essentials were there: a toilet, sink, and a shower/bathtub. The bathtub was truly a luxury. Or it became one at some point during the training period.

The windows of both the bedroom and the bathroom had been boarded up long ago, and only slivers of light penetrated through the slats of wood. Both rooms were always cold. Not freezing. I wasn't heartless. Well...I had as much heart as any monster could have. I just kept the rooms at about sixty degrees. Just cool enough that it wouldn't do any damage but it wouldn't be quite comfortable.

I walked over to the crouched form on the floor. She stank. I wondered how long they'd had her. If they'd washed her during that time.

I wondered what else they'd done to her, considering the rule of no fucking on this one. My various employers didn't usually give that order. They didn't give a crap who fucked the girls before auction. It's what they were there for. But this time, Leo—the liaison between the buyer and me—had made certain I understood this particular restriction.

I shoved the thought of rape aside. I didn't do

that. Whatever else I did to them, I didn't do that. Some tiny little piece of my fucked-up brain held on to that, as if I were somehow honorable for it.

Honor?

Fuck.

I had no delusions on that note. Honor was a thing that had never belonged to me. Not then, not when I was Dominic Benedetti, son of a mafia king. So close, so fucking goddamned close to having it all. And it certainly didn't belong to me now. Not now that I knew who I was. Who I *really* was.

More thoughts to shove away, shove so far down they couldn't choke me anymore. Instead they sat like cement, like fucking concrete bricks in my gut.

I stepped purposefully toward the girl, my boots heavy and loud on the old and decrepit wood.

"Wakey, wakey."

She sat with her knees pulled up to her naked chest, her bound wrists wrapped around them, and made the smallest movement, tucking her face deeper into her knees. I noticed she still wore underwear, although it was filthy. That was new. By the time they got to me, they were so used to being buck naked they almost didn't notice anymore.

The three night-lights plugged into outlets around the bedroom allowed me to take her in. Dark hair fell over her shoulders and down her back. So dark, I wondered if it would be black after I washed the dirt and grime from it.

I nudged the toe of my boot under her hip. "You stink."

She made some small sound and dug her fingernails into the flesh of her legs, crouching farther into the corner, folding and withdrawing deeper into herself.

I squatted down, looking at what I could see of her too skinny body. I'd check her for bruises later, once I cleaned her up. Make sure there wasn't anything that needed immediate attention. No festering wounds acquired in transit.

"Did you piss yourself?"

She exhaled an angry breath.

I grinned behind my mask. There we go. That was different.

"Lift your head, so I can see your face."

Nothing.

I lay one of my hands on top of her head. She flinched but otherwise didn't move. I gently stroked her head before gripping the long thick mass of hair and turning my hand around and around, wrapping the length of it tight in my fist before tugging hard, jerking her head back, forcing her to look at me.

She cried out, the sound one of pain and anger combined. They matched the features of her face: eyes narrowed, fear just behind the rebellion in her hate-filled, gleaming green eyes. Her mouth opened when I squeezed my fingers tighter, and a tear fell from the corner of one eye.

"Get your hands off me."

Her voice sounded scratchy, low, like she hadn't spoken in a long time. I looked at her. Heart-shaped face. Full lips. Prominent cheekbones.

Pretty.

No, more than that. Aristocratic almost. Arrogant. Beautiful. Different.

Different than the usual girls.

She scanned my face. I wondered if the skull mask scared her. Fuck, it had scared me the first time I'd put it on. Nothing like death staring you in the face.

"Stand up," I said, dragging her by her hair as I straightened.

She stumbled, but I kept hold of her, tilting her head back, watching her process the pain of my fist in her hair. Teaching her.

Actions spoke louder than words. I always started my training from minute one. No sense in wasting time. She'd learn fast to do as she was told, or she'd pay. She'd learn fast that life as she knew it was over. She was no longer free. No longer human. She was a piece of fucking meat. Owned. Owned by me.

That first lesson was always hardest for them, but I was nothing if not thorough.

I guess you could say I'd found my true calling.

"You're hurting me," she muttered.

She swallowed hard and blinked even harder,

maybe to stop the tears that now leaked from both eyes. This girl was a fighter. She hated weakness. I could see it. I recognized it. This battle, she warred as much with herself as she did me.

"What's the magic word?" I taunted.

She glared, her gaze searching, trying to see through the thin layer of mesh that covered even my eyes. I could tell she was trying not to focus on the mask but rather my eyes. To make me more human, less terrifying.

Fear. It was the one thing you could always count on.

"Fuck you."

She reached up with her bound hands to grab hold of the mask, but before she could tug it off, I jerked her arms away.

"Wrong."

I spun her around and shoved her against the wall, pressing the side of her face against it. She pushed at the cheap, dark-paneled walls with her hands, her bound wrists just in front of her chest. Her breathing came hard, harder than mine.

I looked her over. Even beneath the layers of dirt, I saw the print of a boot turning blue on her side.

I was right. This one was a fighter.

Leaning in close, I let go of her hair and pressed my body against hers, bringing my mouth to her ear. "Try again. Magic word. And remember, I don't usually give second chances."

"Please," she said quickly before a sob broke out that she tried hard to suck back in.

I kept my chest to her back, holding her against the wall. I wondered if she could feel my erection. Hell, she'd have to.

"Gia," I whispered against her ear. I knew her first name, knew it was her real name when she sucked in a breath.

That was all I knew, but I wouldn't tell her that. It was all I wanted to know. Contrary to what my various employers thought, I didn't like training the girls. Or selling them. I wondered if I should. It was one of the things my father had done, my real father. He was a scum-of-the-earth asshole. I'd just been trying to live up to my heritage over the last seven years. Hell, I had to make up for lost time. Twenty-eight fucking years' worth. From the terror on the girl's face, I was doing a good job of it.

I hated myself a little more because of it every day. But that was the point, wasn't it? I didn't deserve any different.

"You belong to me now. You will do as I say, or you will be punished every single time. Understand?"

She didn't answer, but her body began to tremble. She squeezed her eyes shut. I watched as tears rolled down her cheek.

"Understand?" I asked again, trailing my fingernails up her back and splaying them beneath the heavy veil of hair at the base of her skull, ready to grip and tug and hurt.

She nodded quickly.

"Good."

I abruptly stepped back. She almost fell but caught herself. She remained standing as she was, her back to me, her forehead against the wall. Her hands moved, wiping her cheeks.

"Turn around."

It took her a moment. She moved slowly, keeping as much space between us as she could, keeping her bound hands raised so they covered her breasts.

Defiant eyes met mine, the green shining bright in contrast to her dirt-smeared face. There was something about her. Not once in the dozen girls I'd trained had I ever felt anything but emptiness, a space between me and them. The girls, they weren't even human to me. It was easier that way. They were things. A means to an end. That end being me sinking deeper into depravity, so deep I'd never see the light of day again.

I steeled myself and let my gaze roam over her. She shivered, and I knew it wasn't the cold that made her shudder.

"Raise your arms over your head. There's a hook there. There are many throughout the room."

I watched as she scanned the room. Her eyes would have adjusted to the dim light, so she'd see at least the outline of what I was talking about. Chains had been fitted to the ceiling in various spots. Overkill maybe, but like I said earlier, I liked fucking with them, and imagination was often worse than reality. Attached to these chains were large hooks, like meat hooks. When I needed to, I used them to secure the girls.

"You'll have to stand on tiptoe to slide the ring at the center of your restraints onto the hook. Do it."

Her chest moved as her breathing came in short gasps while her gaze traveled around the room again before finally coming to rest on the one over her head.

I walked over to the locked chest and took the key from my pocket. "I already told you, I don't like to repeat myself," I said as I bent to unlock it. I raised the lid, taking out what I needed. This was the usual. Gia was no different than the others. They always had trouble obeying at first.

I put the lid down and held the crop close to my leg so she wouldn't see it. When I reached her, I took one of her wrists and raised both arms to secure her on the hook.

"No."

She immediately started trying to free herself. It was futile, but what the hell. She could wear herself out. I already knew she'd be a slow learner. The fighters always were.

"Yes," I said, moving around her.

She tried to follow me but on tiptoe, she was

slower. I wondered if she even saw the first strike come because at the sound of leather striking flesh —a sound my sick brain loved—she sucked in a breath and went stock-still.

"Do I have your attention?" She tried to turn this way and that, wriggling to lean away. I raised my arm again and this time, struck the side of her hip.

"Stop!" she cried out.

I gripped her arm, turned her to face away from me, and brought it down three more times over her still panty-clad ass.

"Please! It hurts!"

"No shit, Sherlock."

I struck again, this time spinning her to face me and marking the fronts of her thighs.

She screamed. I wondered how much of that was shock, although the crop could sting like a motherfucker, and I wasn't being gentle. No sense in coddling them.

"More?" I asked.

"No!"

I laid one more stripe across her thighs anyway. "No, what?"

"No, please, no!"

"Well, hell. Maybe you're not as slow a learner as I'd pegged you to be." I tossed the crop onto the bed and adjusted the crotch of my pants. Her mouth fell open, and her eyes widened as she watched. "Now don't move."

I looked her over, checking for bruises, finding several, all of which seemed to be a few days old. No fresh cuts, nothing that needed anything other than time to heal. Although time was limited.

Turning her, I touched the imprint of the shoe on her side. She hissed when I pressed. "You must have pissed someone off." I chuckled.

"He didn't appreciate my knee in his crotch."

I laughed outright. "I like a girl with some fire," I said as I slid my fingers into the waistband of her panties. "These have to go."

She struggled violently until I smacked her ass with the flat of my hand. "I said don't fucking move."

"Please."

"That won't work every time, honey." I tugged them off, watching them drop to the floor. Gia squeezed her legs together, clenching her ass as she tried to get away from me.

"Please," she tried again.

I dug my fingernails into her hips to keep her still. "Do you need the crop to stop fucking moving?"

"No! Just don't...please don't—"

I felt her struggle to stop moving, and I knew what she was afraid of. I knew exactly what she was afraid of.

"Still." My voice came as a low, dark warning.

She shuddered in my grasp and hung her head, her breathing loud and uneven.

That was when my thumb rubbed against a thick

scabbing of skin. It was about two inches all around and when I pressed against it, she sucked in a breath. I leaned down to have a closer look. The circular scar stood on the side of her left hip. It was an intentional marking, a burn.

"What's this?"

She just made a sound.

"What is it?" I asked again after smacking her other hip.

"He didn't exactly bother telling me when he fucking branded me." She swallowed a loud sobbing breath.

I straightened. It couldn't have been more than a few days, maybe a week old. I'd see what it was once the scab healed. In the meantime, I had work to do.

When I didn't hold her steady, she wobbled from foot to foot, unable to get any sort of a foothold considering her height. She couldn't be more than five feet five. She'd barely come to the middle of my chest when she'd stood on flat feet. I walked around her a few times, just circling, taking my time as she tried to follow my movements, her eyes watching me closely.

"You really do stink," I said, stopping to face her. "Did you piss yourself, or did they piss on you?" I couldn't help it. One corner of my mouth lifted at the question. At the callousness of it.

The girl's eyes narrowed. A brief look of shame flashed through them.

"Are you going to kill me?" she asked finally. "If you are, just do it. Just get it over with."

She wasn't begging for her freedom, or her life, for that matter. Hadn't offered a single bribe—they usually did. Offered all the money they had. Their families had. They didn't have a clue that what I'd be paid would far exceed what most families of these lost girls could earn in a year.

Lost girls. I'd come to call them that. This one, though, this Gia—she was no lost girl. No. She was different, and I wanted to know what it was that made her so.

"You're not here to die. You're here to train. We only have two weeks, which is less than my usual. And given your...unpleasant disposition"—I let my gaze travel over her—"it'd take anyone else double that time." I looked her in the eye and winked. "But I'm a professional. I'll make it work."

"Train?"

"Teach you how to behave—for the auction, at least. After that, you're not my problem anymore."

"What auction?"

"Slave auction. There's one in two weeks. You'll be there. Guest of honor. At least, one of the guests of honor. Let's get you cleaned up, so I can see what I've got to work with."

I reached up to free her cuffs from the hook, and she sighed in relief when her feet stood flat on the floor again. Holding her by one arm, I wrapped the other around the back of her neck and pulled her close. She planted her hands on my chest, keeping as much distance as she could between us.

"You want the cuffs off?"

She searched my masked face, focusing on my eyes, then nodded.

I reached into my pocket and took out two pills. "Open up."

She eyed them. "What are they?"

I shrugged a shoulder. "They'll help you relax."

She shook her head. "No. I don't want them."

"I don't recall asking you if you wanted them."

She slowly turned her gaze up to mine and gave me a one-sided grin, then opened her mouth.

"Ahhh."

Piece of work, this one. I would administer the sedative a different way next time, and when I did, she'd be begging me to take it orally again. But for now, I brought my hand to her mouth and tilted it. But before the pills could slide in, she opened wide and bit hard into the flesh of my palm, breaking the skin.

"Fuck!" I yanked her off but only after she'd drawn blood. My hand automatically rose to slap her, and she cringed, cowering before me.

In the moment I hesitated, she backed up against the wall, eyes huge, hands up, palms to me.

I lowered my hand and took hold of her arm instead, shoving her to the floor. "Down!"

My blood streaked her skin where I held her. She made a sound when her knees hit the hardwood.

"Pick them up."

She whimpered, muttering something senseless. I squatted beside her and gripped the hair at the back of her neck to force her to look at me.

"Pick. Them. Up."

Her terrified eyes shifted from mine to the two pills lying on the floor and back. Holding my gaze, she felt for them and closed her fist around them.

"Hold them out to me."

She did, her hand trembling, her eyes locked on mine.

"You want to swallow these, or do you want me to shove them up your ass?" I sounded calm, as if I had full control of myself. Little did she know that was when I was at my worst. When rage owned me.

She studied me, perhaps unable to speak.

"Ass it is," I said, making to rise and dragging her with me. But by the time we were standing, those pills had disappeared down her throat, and she gripped my forearm, trying to relieve the pressure on her hair. "Open."

She did, and I turned her head this way and that to make sure she'd swallowed. She had.

I released her, and she stumbled backward.

"I owe you one," I said, referring to a punishment, but from the look on her face, she didn't get it. I headed to the door.

"Wait."

I unlocked it and pulled it open. I'd bandage my hand while the pills did their work.

Gia moved toward me and then stopped.

"Go lay down," I told her.

She'd be out soon. The dosage was probably too high. She was a little thing. I'd guess maybe 115 pounds soaking wet.

"Please let me go," she managed.

I took her by the arm and walked her to the bed, picked her up, and placed her on top of it.

She pulled her knees into her chest, and my eyes fell again on the scab that had formed on her hip. Something about that worried me. I had a feeling I wouldn't like what I found once the wound fully healed.

I met her gaze again. Our eyes locked, hers searching, uncertain.

She reached for the blanket, pulling it toward her. Her fingertips touched mine when I took hold of it and dragged it away.

Warmth was a privilege earned, and she had in no way earned it.

She shivered. "Please. I'm so cold."

I looked at her and shook my head.

"Don't fight me, Gia," I whispered. "You won't win."

2

GIA

I drifted in and out of sleep. There were moments of lucidity, and it seemed I'd just be gone for a while, as if I'd stepped away from the conversation, then picked it up again like it hadn't happened at all, like I hadn't just nodded off. How long did this go on?

I recalled my last night with Victor. I'd sworn to myself that I would not be a victim. I wouldn't allow him to make me one. The memory of it made me shudder.

Shit.

Shit, shit, shit.

Did they think I couldn't hear them? Did they think I couldn't hear the fucking fire crackling?

Mateo had fucked up. God, he'd fucked up so big, and he'd paid. He'd paid big. He was gone. And he'd saved me —he'd made sure I'd live.

They'd made me watch. Victor, fucking Victor, had made me watch. I glared at him sitting there now, all smug, in his perfect three-piece suit, adjusting his perfect cuffs, turning the gold links, that smirk on his face, the one I wanted to permanently wipe off. His hands were the bloodiest of all, even if he never raised a freaking finger to do the actual work of killing.

"Ready, boss," one of his masked soldiers said. I never did see their faces.

A whimper escaped me. I didn't want to make a sound. I didn't want to scream. To give him the satisfaction. But I pulled as far back as I could even though the chains made it impossible to move more than a few inches.

Victor stood.

"Last chance, Gia."

I glanced at the steaming branding iron—I wouldn't let my gaze linger, wouldn't let fear paralyze me. I wouldn't. I couldn't. But the orange glow, the smell, the heat—it scared the fuck out of me.

I turned frantic eyes on Victor. Could I pass out first? Could I piss them off enough that they'd hit me? Knock me out before they did it?

"What do you say?" Victor asked, standing close enough now to lift my face to his.

"Last chance to fuck you?" I asked, a slight tremor to my voice as the man holding the iron came so close I could smell it. And I could imagine the scent of flesh burned away by it. My flesh.

I would be strong. For Mateo. He'd been strong right up until the end.

Victor squatted down beside me and wrapped a tendril of hair around his finger, tugging. "What do you say?" His tone teased. He loved this. The fucking bastard lived for this.

"What do I say?"

He waited.

I looked him straight in the face, knowing I sealed my own fate but drawing all of my courage anyway. I spat. I spat right on his smug killer's face.

"I say, no, thanks. You'll kill me either way."

The back of his hand slammed across my face so hard, stars danced before my eyes, but it wasn't hard enough to render me unconscious.

He stood. "Stupid, arrogant bitch." He nodded to the man holding the iron, and two other sets of hands turned me onto my side.

White-hot pain burned through me, and I opened my mouth and let out a bloodcurdling scream. The sound of the iron sizzling, the scent of charring flesh, were too much to bear.

I never did pass out, not during, not after, not once until Victor slapped me again.

"I'll see you on your knees, Gia. God help me."

The mad grin on his face was the last thing I saw, his words a mystery as I processed pain like I'd never felt before, welcoming the blackness the back of Victor's hand across my cheek finally, thankfully, delivered.

I'd been sure Victor would kill me. Why hadn't he? Did I still have Angus Scava's protection? Angus Scava was the boss of the Scava family. I'd been engaged to his son. I may not have been his first choice for a daughter-in-law, but he'd accepted me, been kind to me even, for his son.

But would he have had me branded and sent me here? To this psychopath? To do what? What had he said? That he would train me. Train me for the slave auction.

Slave auction.

No. Angus Scava would not have ordered this. This was Victor acting alone.

I blinked, trying to turn onto my back but unable to. It was like I was too heavy to move. The pills must have been some sort of muscle relaxer and the dosage too high. I guessed that was his intention, though. To incapacitate me. It would be easier to control me if I couldn't fight back.

I thought of my captor, the man in the mask. That horrible mask. I couldn't even see his eyes apart from a hint of them, a glint of color. Blue or gray. I couldn't tell for sure. I hadn't needed to see them to know the wickedness there, the cruelty. But there was more. When he'd raised his hand to slap me and then had stopped—that was when I'd felt it. Then, and when he'd seen the mark on my hip. A momentary reprieve, a pause in the middle of madness.

I mentally shook my head at myself. I was grasping at straws, needing to hope. The man who had me, he was no better than Victor or any of his soldiers. He was readying me to be sold as a fucking slave. I had no doubt what that entailed.

I'd been afraid he'd rape me. When he'd pulled my panties off, I'd thought that was it. He was going to do it. Victor hadn't. He hadn't let his men do it either. Why? Why not let them? Wasn't that what he wanted? To break me? To—what had he said—*"see me on my knees?"*

Maybe it was his deal with Mateo before he'd killed him that saved me from the horror of rape.

I closed my eyes against the image of Mateo before he'd died, forcing it away. I didn't want to remember my brother that way. I needed to hold on to him as he'd been before—in life. Before he'd ever met Victor. Before everything had happened.

Why hadn't Victor let his men rape me? Why hadn't he done it himself? It made no sense. He wanted me. That was obvious. Had been for the two years I'd had the displeasure of knowing him.

Auction.

Slave.

When I woke next, I could roll onto my back and raise heavy arms just inches off the bed on which I still lay naked.

I had to figure out where I was. Who the man was who currently had me. He was going to train me, so he'd probably been hired by Victor. Train me for what, though? To not fight? I'd never stop. I'd never let them win. I'd never let Victor win.

I wondered if Angus Scava knew what he'd done. He'd kill Victor if he knew, I was sure of it. I'd almost been his daughter-in-law, after all. I'd been engaged to James, his son. James had loved me. No way Angus Scava would ever allow this to happen to me.

I thought back to James. To how good things had been two years ago. Before he'd been killed. Before Victor had come into the picture. I wondered about my mom. Did she know about Mateo yet? Did she know we were missing at least, even if she didn't know he was dead? She was in Palermo, and although we weren't particularly close, surely she'd try to phone.

The deadbolt slid, the sound calling my attention.

For the first time in a very long time, I thought of the man who had promised my father he would protect my family. The man my father had worked for, and for whom he had died. He'd vowed to keep me and Mateo safe. Could he save me from this?

But that was years ago. And a promise to a foot soldier couldn't have meant a whole lot to a crime boss.

The door creaked open.

I blinked, lifting my head as much as I could, and watched as my captor filled the doorway. He was a foot taller than me and strong. I'd never physically be able to take him down. And if he kept me drugged, I wouldn't be able to do much at all.

Light outlined his body from the outside room, creating a sort of halo around his head. I squinted, used to the dark now, and when he closed the door, I saw his face again—saw that mask. A skull. Death. As if he were death.

I made a small sound, and my body instinctively tried to pull back. Tried. Nothing much happened, though. Nothing but him stepping closer, chuckling. He must have seen the attempt. He seemed to see everything.

He sat down on the edge of the bed, and when I saw the bottle of water in his hand, I opened my mouth, realizing how dry it was, how thirsty I was.

I couldn't pull away or cover myself when his gaze raked over me, but when he reached into his pocket and produced a key that he used to unbind my wrists, all I felt was grateful.

"Really need to get you washed."

He twisted the lid off the bottle, and I swallowed in anticipation. But then he brought the bottle to his lips and took a long sip, emptying half of it. I wanted to cry. I may have even, but I couldn't be sure.

"Thirsty?" he asked.

I blinked.

"I like you like this, you know? You're kind of sweet when you're not talking."

Then he raised my head and held it as he brought the water to my lips and gave me two small sips before setting the bottle aside and standing.

"All right."

He tugged his shirt off. It looked strange, his chest bare but him wearing that mask covering his face. In the dimly lit room, I saw he had a tattoo on part of his chest and down one arm. I couldn't make out the shape, though. It was just shadow.

"Let's get you cleaned up."

I barely had a chance to look at him before he hauled me up and carried me into the bathroom. My face bobbed against his muscular chest as he carried me, the skin soft, his scent clean, enticing even—or it would be if I wasn't being held against my will. There was something else too. The scent was almost familiar. Was it an aftershave someone I knew wore? I couldn't place it.

"This is probably going to be a little cold at first."

I gasped when he set me into the freezing tub, but my head lolled to the side, and I lay there, shivering, unable to move. He pulled up a chair from the corner and sat. I watched his eyes as he took me in, traveling over the length of me. I tried to cover myself, managing to place a hand over my mound—or close enough to it I could pretend I shielded myself.

"Now, now."

He turned on the taps. I tried to pull back at the

rush of icy water that gurgled out. It sounded like no one had bathed here in a very long time.

"None of that," he finished, pushing my hand away. "We're going to get very intimate, you and I."

I groaned and half turned on my side. I watched as his gaze again fell on the scab at my hip where Victor had branded me.

The water warmed, and he closed the drain to let the tub fill up. He then picked up a washcloth and a bar of soap that sat on the edge of the tub.

I made some sound of rebellion.

"It's clean," he said, holding up the square of cloth. "Relatively."

I must have made a face because he laughed outright.

"Just kidding. Christ, lighten up, princess."

Princess. Victor had called me that a few times. He'd picked it up from Mateo. But the way he said it made my skin crawl.

"Stop," I said, the word coming out slurred.

"Look at you, got your voice back."

He lathered up the washcloth and started to rub me down. I had to admit the water filling the tub felt good. Warm, almost hot. It was so cold in the other room. Although it made me hiss when it reached the tender wound on my hip.

He raised each arm and scrubbed each finger, not leaving even a tiny square inch of skin untouched, paying special attention to my breasts until my nipples hardened.

"Pretty," he said.

I tried to slap away the cloth but he took my hand and shook his head as if he were chastising a child.

"Be a good girl, and I won't add on to the punishment you've already got coming for biting me."

Goose bumps covered me at his words, and I did as he said. I lay still while he cleaned me, his touch gentler than I expected, especially around the scabby, tender spot at my hip, as if he were taking care of it. Maybe he wanted to be sure he'd be able to read whatever it was.

My captor pushed my legs apart then, and, with his eyes on mine, dragged the soapy cloth between them.

I protested by closing my legs and pushing his hand away, realizing as I did so that I was regaining mobility a little at a time. But it wasn't nearly enough to make any difference when all he did was "tsk" at my efforts. This time, he held one knee wide, wider than he'd spread me before, and cleaned between my legs. My face heated—given he'd turned on the lights in here, I could see through the mesh covering his eyes—and I swear he smiled behind his mask. I hated him for it, hated him for his tender invasion, for the natural response of my body as he rubbed that very delicate spot over and over again, as if wanting to draw that very thing from me.

"There," he said. "Almost done."

And to my utter shame, he turned me on my side and cleaned me in the back too, taking his time again until he felt satisfied, before finally allowing me to lie back as he drained the tub.

"Let's get some clean water in here, so we can wash your hair."

He stood, his gaze sliding the length of me.

I pushed myself up a little, although I still needed the support of the tub, and cleared my throat.

He allowed me to sit up and refilled the tub, taking a seat again as he picked up a half-full bottle of some cheap shampoo. How many girls had been here just like me? How many had he washed like he was washing me? How many had he—I had to swallow hard not to choke on the word—trained? Sold into slavery?

I felt my eyes welling with tears. Was I just fooling myself? I was in so deep. After James, I'd kept out of things and had warned Mateo to do so too. I warned him not to get involved with the mob. With men like Victor Scava. But he had, and he'd paid the ultimate price. Would I now pay that too?

His thumb rubbed across my cheek, and I realized I'd started to cry. I watched his eyes as he wiped away my tears, expecting some rude comment, some sick joke about my future, but all I got was silence.

I turned my head away, and the moment was gone. *Poof.*

"Deep breath."

He had his hand on the top of my head as he said it. He barely gave me time to register the words though before shoving my head down under the surface. Water gurgled in my ears, and my scream turned to bubbles before fingers pulled at my hair and drew me back out.

I sucked in air, suddenly panicked, and all he did was chuckle.

"Nothing like a dunk under water to wake you up, huh?"

I spat water and coughed while he poured shampoo on my head.

"Told you to take a deep breath. Next time, you'll know to do it."

"Why?" I cried out.

"To shampoo your hair, silly."

"Why are you doing this?"

"Oh, that."

He rubbed until he got lather, his fingers digging into my scalp.

"Money. Why else? Why does anyone do anything but for money?"

I looked up at him, wanting to see his face, his eyes. Needing to in order to read him.

"Let me see your face."

He paused. Had he been expecting something else? "Going under again, deep breath."

I barely had time to think, gulping air before he shoved me under then, moments later, pulled me back up.

"Your name, at least tell me your name."

"Shouldn't you be asking different questions?"

He dunked me again, three times more before the suds were gone. He pulled the plug from the drain.

He took one of the two threadbare towels from the rack—again making me think of those who had come before me—and once the water had drained, he draped it over my shoulders and lifted me up to stand. He held on to me when he did so, maybe testing himself how much the drug had worn off. Not nearly enough, considering my knees buckled as soon as I stood upright.

Wrapping one of the towels around me, he carried me back into the bedroom and deposited me on the bed.

"Questions like what's going to happen to me once I'm sold?"

Leaving me there, he went back into the bathroom to return a moment later with a hairbrush. I noticed the hairs stuck in the bristles. Blonde and red and brown. I wanted to throw up.

He opened the towel as if unwrapping a candy

bar and pulled it out from under me, then patted me dry before dropping it on the floor.

Goose bumps rose all over my body, both at the cold temperature in the room on my still damp skin and the thought of my future. Of the fate that awaited me.

"Or who will buy me, and what will my new owner expect of me?"

He sat leaning against the headboard and lifted me up so that he cradled me between his thighs, making me very aware of my naked back against his bare chest. At least he was warm. After towel drying my hair with the second towel, he started to brush it, his touch not quite gentle, but also not cruel. Not purposely at least.

"Will he fuck me himself, or pass me around to a dozen friends to initiate me?"

I wondered if he used that tone—quiet and unaffected—on purpose. If it was meant to scare me. If his breath on my face was to let me know I would have no boundaries. That nothing was mine anymore, not even the air I breathed.

Could he feel the quiet tremors breaking me apart inside?

Would he be so callous if he could?

"Or maybe something as simple as will they use lube?"

He chuckled at that, but there was no joy in his tone. In fact, he grew more and more despondent with each comment he made, his tugs on my hair working out the knots, becoming slightly rougher each time as if he paid less and less attention.

He left me to ponder that last one for a while, and when he was able to pull the brush through without a snag, he lay me back down and stood.

I shifted and rolled onto my side, the sedative slowly loosening its hold on me. The tingling in my limbs told me it was almost over. I'd be free of it soon.

But not soon enough.

"Maybe something more imminent, like what punishment can I expect for my earlier transgression?"

Punishment.

He rolled me onto my belly and pulled me toward the foot of the bed until my legs hung over the edge.

I tried to push myself over or off the bed, but that proved too difficult. When he saw my attempt, he snickered.

"You want to see my face?" he asked, his voice quiet.

He came around to where I lay, my right cheek pressed against the bed.

"I guess it doesn't matter."

He seemed to say that more to himself than to me. He squatted down so he came to eye level.

"Will it make any difference for you?"

He brushed a wet strand of hair off my forehead, the touch of his finger making me shiver.

"For me?"

His voice, his tone—it sounded so utterly hopeless, as if truly, it made no difference at all. As if nothing mattered at all.

"No, not really, not for you. And not really for me." He reached up to tug the mask off his head.

I watched, my eyes widening, and gasped.

Short dark-blond hair stood on end, static taking hold of it, making me think of a kid with a balloon, a boy giggling as his hair fanned out in all directions.

What had I expected? A monster. A terrible, horribly scarred monster. Maybe some deformity? What?

Whatever it was, it wasn't this.

Certainly not this.

He was...beautiful. Beyond beautiful. His face— it belied an innocence that did not belong to him. That I knew in my gut had never belonged to him.

Blue-gray eyes the color of coldest steel softened by the thickest lashes were set in the face of an angel carved in solid, unbending stone. Too beautiful. Too unbearably beautiful. Thick, blond scruff darker than his hair and spotted with gray dusted his hard, square jaw. His lips were full, as if swollen from kissing.

Kissing.

He had the face of a man who'd just stepped

out of a magazine. But it wasn't only that—that cool, easy, deceptive beauty. There was more. So much more. And it hid behind his eyes, in that bottomless abyss of blue-gray. Looking at them now sent a shiver racing down my spine, making every hair on my body stand on end. He had the eyes of a man who'd taken more and who'd lost more than any one human being should. A man who'd learned terrible things. Who'd seen the worst mankind had to offer one another. A man who'd hurt.

No. Much more than hurt.

A man who'd done unspeakable evil.

I shuddered.

And he smiled.

He smiled a smile of pure evil, and the dimple in his right cheek disarmed me, or would have, had I not seen the darkness, the depravity, the cold, cold emptiness inside those steely, beautiful eyes, and I wished—and I knew he knew I wished it in that moment—I wished I could take it back. I wished he had never taken the mask of death from his face. I wished he'd never shown me this, this perfect evil, this perfect, cold beauty.

"You want to know my name?" he asked, rising, breaking into my thoughts.

I shook my head. He patted my hair as if he were a proud parent. He then unbuckled his belt and whipped it out of its loops. The sound made me gasp. He doubled it over, watching me as he set the buckle in the palm of his hand.

He moved behind me.

"I underestimated you."

The first lash of the belt seared my ass, making me scream.

3

I have no delusions about the darkness inside my soul. It is a black abyss, a hole so deep and so dark, it could consume me.

It could swallow me whole. It will if I have anything to say about it.

After leaving Gia's room, I locked the door and set the mask on the kitchen table. I opened the fridge and took out a beer, popping the bottle cap off and drinking half of it down on my way to my bedroom. After whipping Gia's ass, I needed a drink. And a shower. Whipping was hard work. A workout, really.

And it made my dick hard.

Sick fuck.

In my bedroom, I stripped off my boots, jeans, and briefs, finished the rest of the beer, and switched on the shower. I stepped into the icy flow before the water even warmed, the cold not doing anything to alleviate my rock-hard erection.

I'd heard Salvatore describe me once. He'd been talking to Marco, his bodyguard—glorified foot soldier actually, but who was I to judge, considering. I'll never forget the word he used. That one word. *Monster*.

Thing was, he'd been right all along. The golden boy had hit the nail on the fucking head.

I was a monster.

Salvatore thought he must be one to do what he did to Lucia. I snorted at that. He was a fucking white knight compared to me. He did bad things. You couldn't not. I mean, it's the fucking mafia, and he's king. Or would have been, but he handed it all over to our uncle. I could still call Roman uncle. He was a blood relation. That should make me feel better, but it only made me sick.

Fuck them. Fuck the Benedetti assholes. Roman's allegiance was to them—my uncle whom I'd hated because of how well trusted he'd been now sat like king of the family. Well fuck him too.

I was never one of them. I didn't even come close to looking like my brothers or the man I'd believed to be my father for twenty-eight years of my life. Blind and stupid. Hell, I didn't even *look* like my mother except for the eyes. The color at least. The look inside them was all my father: Jake *the Snake* Sapienti. I was Dominic Sapienti, and I looked like my loser father. How in hell could my mother have fallen for him? I mean, once she'd gotten to know him? On the outside, I could see it. But the inside? Black as Satan's soul.

He'd aptly earned his nickname. He slithered from one loyalty to the next. Wherever the payout was, there he was. No friends to speak of, but too many enemies to count. A killer. Ruthless. Hateful. He did the work no one else would do. The jobs that no one wanted to take. Crimes that made even me cringe.

I'd learned from Roman that Franco would have killed him when he found out about me. About his wife's affair. She'd begged him not to, she said she loved him. And Franco loved her too much to hurt the man she loved.

Well, wasn't he the fucking romantic. A regular Romeo.

I turned my thoughts to Gia.

To her face.

Her eyes.

Her fear.

I gripped my cock and began to pump, leaning one hand against the wall while water sprayed my head and shoulders. I fucked my hand at the image of her bent over the bed. The sound of her exhalations, her grunts and screams, her drugged attempts to get out of the way of the belt. I thrust harder into my fist at the memory of her bare ass bouncing with each stroke, the welts turning a deep red. I imagined the heat of her ass if I were to spread her open and plunge into her warm pussy. I wondered if she'd be wet. If she'd be ready for me.

The thought made my cock throb. Some girls got off on it. Not the way I'd done it just now, maybe, but for some of the girls, there was something about getting their ass whipped. It made them wet. And even though I didn't rape them, I made them come after punishing them. It was a power play. That was all. I owned them—owned their pain and their pleasure.

I imagined Gia coming. Imagined kneeling behind her and spreading her open, feasting on her pussy—*fuck*—as she'd beg for me to stop. I threw my head back, water prickling like needles against my face as I blew.

She'd beg. I'd make her beg. I'd hurt, and then I'd make her body yield, make it surrender even as she fought its release, its yielding to me, to a man she would come to hate. I'd watch that betrayal work itself into her brain. I'd fuck with her. And I wouldn't stop. That's what this was. Training. She needed to learn, and pain taught. So did pleasure. It taught you who your master was.

I slumped forward, heart pounding, my cock still throbbing in my fist. I opened my eyes.

What I should have done, though, was come all over her instead of in the shower.

Degradation was a good teacher too.

I had time, though. Not much—two weeks until the auction. It'd have to do.

I washed my hair and scoured my body. I did that a lot now, scrub at my skin to the point it hurt. For the last seven years, it was as though I was trying to claw my way out from inside it. I hated myself. I guess I always had, but now I had a reason. Now I knew the stock I came from. The scum I was.

I climbed out of the shower and grabbed a towel, scratching the rough cloth against my skin as I made my way into the bedroom.

Had I intended to become what I was? A mercenary for hire? Taking the highest paying jobs, no matter the cost to my victims? Not consciously, no. Over the last few years, though, I had done everything I could to live up to my heritage. I was a mercenary. I went where the money was.

I didn't like training women, readying them for something like this. But I was good at it. And I wasn't sure there was another job on earth that would make me feel any lesser trash than this. Taking women and knowingly delivering them into the hands of other monsters like me. Worse than me.

I was well and truly a sick fuck.

I'd started taking these types of jobs two months after the night I'd learned the truth. After that night at Salvatore's house when my world had exploded around me, and left me holding the smoking gun.

When I'd stood over my brother's—half-brother's—dying body.

He didn't die.

But that didn't matter. I'd felt Franco's hate. His revulsion. Had he always felt that way about me?

I sat down on the edge of the bed, as if needing the support.

Had I just always been too fucking stupid to see it? Too cocky? I'd been my mother's favorite. Her little prince. I knew why now. She'd loved my father more than she'd loved Franco Benedetti. And I was the living, breathing result of that love.

I shook my head. What would she think if she saw me now?

My throat closed up, and I stood. I had to forget. I just had to fucking forget. I could try to understand forever, and it wouldn't make any difference. It wouldn't change anything. I just needed to stop thinking about it.

I went to the dresser and opened the top drawer, taking out a fresh pair of underwear, jeans and a long-sleeved, V-neck T-shirt. Black. It was all I wore these days. Underneath was the photo I kept there. Taking it out, I touched the little face. The tiny smiling face. Effie. My little girl. She was eleven now. And I missed her. I'd been in her life off and on for her first three and a half years, but when she and Isabella had moved back to New Jersey, I'd seen her almost daily. I think that's why I missed her so much now, even after so many years had passed.

I was just Dominic to her, though. Not dad.

Dad.

I shook my head. *She's better off, asshole.*

Isabella—for some unknown reason—kept e-mailing me photographs. I printed the ones I was especially fond of. It was strange. I didn't think she'd want me in the picture at all. Did she feel bad?

No. That bitch didn't have a conscience. Or she hadn't until Luke.

She was the only one who knew how to get ahold of me, and I knew she hadn't told a soul. That was confirmation of her lack of conscience. She'd watched her sister and my half-brother search and search for me, and she never said a fucking word.

But even she didn't know about this cabin in the woods.

Even she could not forgive this.

I tucked the photo back into the drawer and got dressed. That was what I needed—to remember all the lowlifes in my life. To remember none of us had a conscience. Well, except maybe Salvatore. And fuck him. I was sick of thinking about him.

In the kitchen, I grabbed another beer and opened it, taking a sip and looking at the food supply. The cabinets would have been stocked before I got here. Part of the setup. I had several contacts, but only one man knew of the location of this cabin. And I only knew him as Leo. He got me my jobs. No one knew they were hiring Dominic Benedetti or Dominic Sapienti. Leo got the cabin ready and delivered the girls. I didn't kidnap them. I was purely a trainer. I spent about six weeks with them. I got them from here to the auction. And I delivered them submissive.

Like I said, I had no delusions about what I was.

I took out the eggs and bacon and switched on a burner. My thoughts went back to the girl. No sound came from the room. All cried out from her whipping, she was probably sleeping off the rest of the drug.

She was different than the others. She fought me; they all did to an extent. But they also begged for their lives. She'd done the opposite. She'd told me to get it over with if I was going to kill her. I wondered where she'd come from. Who'd had her, and who'd branded her. I wondered if her new owner would want that mark cut out. They usually liked them pure. Maybe he'd burn his own brand over top of whatever decorated her hip.

There was one thing that bugged me, though. That kind of nagged at me. When she'd bitten my hand, I'd gone to slap her but stopped. I'd never stopped with any other girl before. It was something in her eyes that had done it. Not the fear, but something else. Something almost familiar.

I lay strips of bacon into the pan and cracked two

eggs beside them, the sizzle and smell making my stomach growl, and wondered who she was. It wasn't just her looks but the look inside her eyes. She was different than the others. She wasn't a random pickup off the street. And I had a feeling she was older than the usual girls by a few years. The girls I trained were between eighteen and twenty-one. I wouldn't take them younger. If I had to guess, I'd say Gia was twenty-four, maybe twenty-five. The buyers usually wanted young flesh.

Sick fucks.

Sicker than you?

I scrambled the eggs and told that voice to fuck off. Once everything was cooked, I plated it and set it on the table, grabbed my laptop out of its bag beside the door, and booted it up. I finished the plate of food as I checked my bank balance for the deposit— ten grand up front, the rest upon sale, the final price determined by the amount the girl brought in. Not bad money. But I guessed human trafficking brought in serious money. The auctions were always interesting. I enjoyed looking at the girls. Who wouldn't? But I more liked watching the buyers, who were mostly men, some couples, and a few single women. The same ones seemed to turn up at every auction. I wondered if they were growing their stable of stolen women or if they needed to replace lost or damaged goods.

That little bit of conscience that gnawed at me

got shoved back down into its box and the lid locked down tight. I thought of the girl—the job—and how I could maximize my earnings. She was good-looking, even if she was older than the usual girl, but she had something most of the others didn't: that arrogance. Nothing like breaking a cocky girl. I just needed to somehow preserve that during her training, make her bow down with just that hint of indignation.

Once I finished, I cleaned up, then grabbed a granola bar and a bottle of water and headed toward Gia's room. The cold inside gave me a chill. I saw how she lay sleeping huddled into herself on the bed. I set the water and the granola bar down on the small bedside table and walked back out. Tomorrow I'd give her a chance to earn back the blanket.

4

GIA

I ate the granola bar and drank the water when I woke up. I couldn't remember the last time I'd had real food. Hot food. I had dreamt of bacon while I slept. I even thought I could smell it right now. It was like a mirage of water in the desert. I must be desperate.

No light came through the slats of the boarded-up window, so I knew it was late. How late, though, I couldn't be sure. And it was cold. Really cold. I was glad to have such dim lighting in the room. Sleeping on the bare mattress and knowing others had been here before me—well, I didn't want to know what I'd find staining it.

I stayed at the window for a while, knowing screaming would be useless. If anyone would have been able to hear me, he would have made sure to gag me anyway. This wasn't the first time he'd done this. I knew that much. But I tried anyway. I cried out the window, not caring if he could hear.

"Hello? Hello, can anyone hear me? Is anyone out there?"

Nothing. Nothing but the sounds of night. I went back to the bed and sat down, rubbing my arms to warm up.

I wish I knew exactly what would happen to me. My captor—what was his name? I decided I would call him Death. He looked like an angel of death. That death mask hid his angel's face.

I needed to find out more information. Try to figure out where I was. How far from civilization. I heard no noise, and trying to look through the window slats had proven useless earlier. The room smelled musty and old, like it hadn't been used in a while. The mattress and pillow—I didn't want to think about what those smelled like. But if I went close to the window, in addition to the freezing-cold draft, I could smell pine. We were in the woods somewhere. Question was, where and how far from civilization?

Death. He'd whipped me so easily. Hadn't even had to hold me down to do it, although he had had to adjust my position a few times. I'd have to figure out how to not swallow the pills next time. I couldn't be so out of control again. I needed to find an opportunity to run. But what if when I got that chance, it turned out there were more men out there? What if he wasn't alone? What if I did manage to get past Death and got out there, only to find a second man? Or third. Victor had so many at his disposal.

But did Death work for Victor? I guessed he'd have to. Victor would have to be making money off this auction. Was he doing this to me to keep his promise to Mateo? How cruelly he kept his word. How easily he twisted it.

Mateo had begged him for my life.

He'd been on his knees when they'd brought me in. He'd been beaten and bloodied, bound and kneeling in the middle of that horrible room with the scent of fresh blood, of death, overwhelming every other sense. When he'd seen me, God, his eyes when he'd seen me. The shock. The horror. Like everything they'd done to him up until that point was moot. Like me seeing him like that, Mateo, my older brother, my hero, the one who always took care of me, who saved *me* every time, me being there to see him on his knees had broken him in a way they hadn't been able to break him before.

He'd begged them, then. I knew he hadn't begged before. Victor said so.

Victor.

Victor had looked so smug upon hearing my brother beg.

I would kill Victor with my bare hands. I would do to him what he'd done to my Mateo.

I wiped hot tears from my face and steeled

myself. But remembering...remembering what he'd made Mateo do to promise to keep me alive. What he'd made me watch.

I leaped off the bed and ran into the bathroom, making it to the toilet just in time as that granola bar made its way back up. I'd had nothing to eat in so long. I didn't even know how long.

When I stopped retching, I opened the medicine cabinet in search of a toothbrush. I did find one, a small travel-size one, but no way was I going to brush my teeth with a used toothbrush. And before he made me do it, I flushed it down the toilet. At least there was a tube of toothpaste. Squeezing some on my finger, I brushed my teeth as best as I could.

I needed to focus. To find some way out.

Using the night-lights, I searched both rooms again, and like the first time, found nothing. The chest where he'd kept the crop was locked tight, but I knew if I could get in there, there might be something for me to use, some sort of weapon. Something to use to escape, or at least to hurt him long enough to get out of here. He had to have a phone. I would take it and make the call to David Lazaro, Mateo's contact. I'd memorized his number. But was he in on it too? Had he set Mateo up?

It didn't matter, not right now. I needed to get out of here first. He had to have a car. I mean, if we were in some remote location—and I knew we must be— he'd need a car to get here. I could take the car. The rest I'd figure out. I just needed to get out of this room.

I didn't know how much time had passed, but I tried the door for the hundredth time, growing so frustrated that this time, I pounded on it with both fists, screaming out for him to let me out.

A light went on in the outer room. I scrambled backward to the bed, climbed on, and waited, my back pressed against the headboard.

The lock slid, and I found myself hugging my knees, hiding my face behind a curtain of hair. When the door opened, I lifted my head. Death stood there without the mask, wearing jeans and a long-sleeved shirt. His damp hair told me he'd recently had a shower. I guess he'd built up a sweat whipping me.

My ass hurt, and I shifted my weight.

He didn't close the door.

Without a word, he entered. I studied him.

He watched me, his gaze as effective as chains keeping me locked to the spot.

Then he changed direction and reached into his pocket for what I knew was the key to the chest. It was like as soon as he looked away, he released me. Like the bonds holding me stupidly to the bed while the door stood open had been broken, and I ran. I bounded up faster than I thought I could move and bolted straight for the door. I didn't trip, I didn't think, I just ran. It wasn't a big room. It would only have taken five or six steps to get to it. But I didn't make it. And I knew from the look in his eyes that he'd expected me to do just what I did. That he'd left the damn door open on purpose, testing me. I knew it the instant he shot his arm out and caught me just before I could set foot outside the door. Just a breath away from that other room, that brightly lit room.

Death wrapped an arm around my middle and slapped my ass hard before hauling me kicking and screaming back to the bed with the bare stained mattress.

"Let me go!"

He threw me with enough force that I bounced. I scrambled to get away from him.

"You're so predictable," he said, his voice calm.

I slid off the bed opposite him and planted my hands on it. I shifted my gaze from him to the door and back.

"Get on the bed."

We both danced from foot to foot, him mimicking my movements as I bounced left then right, looking for the opportunity to run.

"Just let me go! You don't have to do this."

"Get on the fucking bed."

God, he sounded bored of all things. Fucking bored.

"I don't know what you're being paid, but I can pay you more." It was a total lie. I had no money.

I took two steps, then stopped when he matched

them, standing opposite him on the other side of the bed.

"No, you can't. Now get on the bed, and I'll take your obedience into consideration when it's time for your punishment."

My ass throbbed at the word. I shook my head and this time, went for it. I just went right for the door even though I knew I wouldn't make it. He was faster. He was bigger. And he was stronger. So when the door slammed shut almost catching my fingers between it and the frame, I wasn't wholly surprised.

I whirled around, feeling him so close. Close enough to knee? He hadn't locked the door yet. If I could—

But he must have anticipated it because he caught my knee between his thighs and pressed himself up against me, holding me tight against the door. We stood like that, watching each other, breath coming fast, my naked chest heaving against his with the effort to keep taking in air as he squeezed it out of me. I felt this strange sort of pull to him, this sort of...attraction? No, not that. He may be beautiful, but he was evil. He was no better, no different than Victor. The draw, though, I knew he felt it too. I saw it in the way he looked at me, now that he wore no mask.

But sexual attraction was a thing of the bodies, not the mind. Not the heart. If it was that, it was mechanic. That was all.

There was more. Something else. Something different.

Sometimes, things we can't remember carry emotion with them. That feeling—good or bad—it's the thing that's present between two strangers. And we were strangers. It's just, this feeling...no, I was confused. Maybe it was a sort of Stockholm syndrome, although it would be too soon, wouldn't it? When did Stockholm kick in? Maybe because Victor had held me for...how long had he held me? Days? Weeks? Hours? How long ago had I witnessed Mateo's execution?

No, I was confused. There was no emotion. No feeling. There was only confusion. Confusion and hate.

We stayed like that, our eyes locked, and I felt him, I felt his cock at my belly, hard and thick and ready. He was aroused. I knew he'd been aroused before too. After he'd whipped me, I'd seen how tight his jeans had stretched across his crotch.

"You get off on this." I said, my voice somehow a controlled whisper, wanting him to know I despised him. Wanting him to believe I felt repulsed by him. "You like it. You like chasing naked girls around this decrepit room, wearing your little mask."

He grinned and pressed his cock against me once as if to say yes, yes he did.

"I'm not wearing my mask now."

"You like scaring women half your size? Who could never stand a chance against you physically?"

In the next moment, he circled my wrists with his hands and drew my arms overhead. He leaned down, so his forehead rested against mine.

"I do, Gia," he whispered.

His eyes roamed over my face and settled on my mouth.

"I like it very much."

I swallowed and felt the hardening of my nipples against the fabric of his shirt and hated myself for it. Hated my body for it.

"I like a little fight too."

He brought his mouth to my ear, inhaling along my cheek as he did so.

"It makes my cock hard," he whispered.

He leaned his face down to where my pulse throbbed against my throat and slid his tongue over it, one long, drawn-out taste to tell me he knew I was terrified, he knew how my heart pounded, and he knew, despite the bravado in my talk, I was scared shitless.

But he didn't know that didn't mean I was done fighting.

He brought his face to mine again. His right cheek dimpled when the corner of his mouth turned upward as he looked at my slightly parted lips. He thought he'd won. He thought I wanted him. His eyes declared his assumed victory.

He leaned his head in and kissed me. He took my lower lip between his and moaned as he sucked on it, and I stood there, feeling my body go limp against his, letting it, using its traitorous reaction to my advantage. And when I tilted my head back and he kissed me full on the lips and slid his tongue inside my mouth, I struck. Even knowing full well I'd be punished, I struck. I drew my head back and banged it into his nose. A break would be painful enough to give me the second I'd need to get out.

I didn't break it, though. I knew instantly because his grip on my wrists tightened and he slammed them hard against the door.

"You're a bitch."

He lowered my arms and twisted them behind my back into one of his hands, wiping the blood from his nose with the back of his other hand. He turned me so he stood behind me, then walked me toward the chest where, without a word, he unlocked and opened it to take out three sets of leather cuffs similar to the ones that had shackled me when I'd gotten here.

I struggled against him as he led me back to the bed. I didn't ask for freedom. I didn't beg. But I fought because he was right. I was a bitch. And I wasn't going to make this easy. Even if that meant I'd pay.

He didn't speak either, didn't tell me to be still, didn't do anything but keep his steady hold on me, tightening it a little. When we got to the bed, he released my wrists and took hold of one arm, pushing me to sit on the edge. I struggled against him as he drew it out and attached the leather to the wrist before fighting me for the other and binding them together. He met my gaze afterward, and I knew this was a show of who was in charge and just how in charge. And I hated myself for the little scream I let out as he drew me backward on the bed to attach the cuffs to a ring on the headboard. He was nothing if not prepared.

He released my arms and stood, looking down at me.

I tested the bonds, knowing they'd hold but needing to anyway. I don't think I'll ever forget the clanking sound of it, of metal on metal, of my louder scream, of the desperation in it as he took one ankle and stretched it toward one corner of the bed and bound it. His face remained empty of expression as he walked casually to the other side, and I found myself mumbling, muttering pleas as he stretched the other leg out and bound me so I lay spread eagle, exposed, at his mercy.

He stood back and looked down at me, first at my face, my eyes, then down over my breasts and belly and to my sex. There his gaze hovered and when he moved to climb between my legs, I screamed and I begged. I begged for him not to rape me. I begged for my life. I begged for mercy. And he just watched me, watched it, and placed his hands on my inner thighs, softly trailing fingertips up and up until tears streamed down my face. His fingers settled on either side of my pussy and spread me open.

"Please. Please don't."

He stopped then, and his gaze met mine. I thought he'd say something, but he didn't. He just watched me for a long time, as if he wanted me to know he held all the power. That he owned me. That he could do whatever he wanted to do to me. And then he bent his head and licked my pussy. He licked its length slowly and purposefully while his eyes remained locked on mine and my breath caught in my throat. He did it again, taking his time, tasting every inch of me, teasing the hard nub of my clit until I couldn't take anymore, until I felt my back arching, my body moving without my brain's permission. I couldn't look into his eyes because I'd see my shame there, see how my body yielded so quickly, gave itself so easily to this man, my captor. My jailor. My keeper. My tormentor.

I squeezed my eyes shut and lay there while he sucked on my clit and died a little when I heard the moan that came out of my mouth as he teased and taunted and tasted and made me gush, made me come so hard I thought I'd break apart. And maybe I did, maybe, in a way, I did.

He didn't speak when it was over, and I opened my eyes to find his locked on mine as he rose from the bed and wiped his mouth with the back of his hand. We stayed like that for a long time until finally, I blinked, turning away, humiliated, and he walked back out the door and locked it behind him.

I wept silently for so many things. For my brother. For myself. For the shame I felt as cool air dried my pussy, dried where he'd licked me to orgasm. I cried, knowing I'd come under my enemy's tongue, knowing this was only the beginning, knowing there would be so many betrayals, so many concessions. I wondered who I'd be by the end of this. If I survived, that is.

And I hated myself for not wanting to be left alone anymore. Hated myself for my weakness. My fear.

Eating her pussy didn't involve penetration. It wasn't the same as fucking her. Not that I didn't fuck the other girls. I did. Some. Not all. Only if they were virgins in any way. Well, that was *mostly* true. It would be better for them, easier, if I took that from them. I'd never eaten one out, though. I'd never wanted to. I'd played with them, I'd enjoyed fucking the ones I did, but it was just that, a fuck, a piece of ass. This was different. Maybe it was like kissing. Too personal.

And I'd kissed her too. Or tried to. Hell, I should have thanked her for nearly breaking my nose.

I don't even know what made me do it. Yes, my cock was already hard after our little struggle, but hell, that was the norm, and in the last couple of years, I'd gotten to know my fist pretty well. And when I wanted a woman, I paid for it. Anonymous sex, exactly how I liked it.

So why the fuck had I eaten her out?

And why couldn't I stop thinking about how she tasted? How she sounded when she came? How she thrust her hips at me, wanting more, even as she resisted me?

I'd felt it again, that strange sense of familiarity, when I'd walked into the room and she'd been sitting on the bed, watching me like that. It was those damned haunted eyes. Haunted? Or haunting. They'd seen evil. They saw through me and into my evil. She'd survived evil. But would she survive me?

Yet it wasn't just that. I knew those eyes. As ridiculous as it was, they were connected to some distant memory, something brief, something...better than this.

Hell, this was all ridiculous. I just needed to focus here and do my job, and if it meant I fucked her while I was at it—virgin or not—then so be it. Stupid fucking rule anyway, considering I trained them to become sex slaves. What difference would it make for them if I did fuck them? None, that's what. And I needed to remember this was a job. Any nostalgic feelings, any attraction to this girl—it would have to get gone. She was a fucking job. Granted, a job with a restriction: no penetration. But hell, if it happened, it happened. No one would give a fuck, not in the end.

I finished my coffee, closed the shutter letting the too-bright sunshine into the kitchen, and walked into her room. She lay awake, but the moment our eyes met, she blinked and looked away. I closed the door and locked it behind me, walked into the bathroom where I'd left the chair, and brought it into the bedroom. I set the blanket I'd carried in on it.

She eyed it.

"Chilly in here," I said casually.

She searched my face, my eyes.

"I'm thinking you need to use the bathroom?"

She nodded, her gaze settling on a spot just beyond me. I guessed she'd be embarrassed after last night's impromptu session. I hadn't intended to do what I'd done. I'd just meant to fuck with her a little. I'd been reading, and all her racket had been annoying, quite frankly. She had to know I wouldn't keep her somewhere she'd be found so easily, so why the screaming?

"Did you sleep well?" I asked, sitting on the edge of the bed and tracing the edge of one of her ankle cuffs.

"How well do you expect me to sleep in this freezing room bound and naked and fucking humiliated?"

Well, no elephant in this room, then. She was straightforward. I liked that. I brushed a strand of hair from her face, and she shook her head to rid herself of my touch. I gripped her chin and forced her to look at me. "Getting my cock sucked puts me out like a light. The way you came, I'd thought you'd have slept into next week."

Her face grew warm beneath my touch, and I had to smile at the blush creeping up her neck and cheeks.

"The least you can do is thank me."

"I hate you. You're the worst of them all."

"Worse than the men who branded you?" I raised my eyebrows, although truly, I didn't care. Fact was, she was right. I *was* the worst of them all.

"The worst," she spat out.

"Then we have no misunderstandings between us." I undid her ankles first. Then I unhooked her from the ring at the top of the bed but kept her wrists bound. "Go."

"With my hands tied?"

"Call me when you're done. I'll wipe."

I almost laughed when her face got so red I thought she'd explode. Truth was, it was an act, this flat, uninterested tone. Not that I cared, I just...that hint of conscience crept in through the cracks in the fucking walls of my chest. It seeped through the tiniest fissure, and it fucked with me. I didn't like it.

She walked into the bathroom. I noticed the bruises on her ass. I hadn't whipped her too hard, but hard enough they'd serve as a reminder to behave every time she sat down.

While she took care of what she needed to, I

went to the chest, unlocked it, and took out what I needed: the collar and the crop. A few moments later she returned, wiping droplets of water from her face with her hands.

"I need a toothbrush."

"Isn't there one in there?"

She didn't hesitate. "No."

"Funny, I could have sworn..."

Her gaze fell to the things I held, and I could see the effort it took for her to stay in place.

"Would you like to earn a blanket?" I asked. "Maybe get some more water and food?"

"What do I have to do?" The question came out slow and cautious as a crawl.

"Kneel."

She studied me, distrust in her eyes, hesitation in the way she bit her lip. "What are you going to do?"

"Put this collar around your neck." I didn't feel like playing all of a sudden.

I could see her mind working, trying to figure out what to do, what was expected, perhaps what would earn her the least amount of pain. But slowly, she knelt. It surprised me.

I stood motionless, looking at her. She turned her gaze away, distancing herself perhaps. I cleared my throat and walked to her, collar and crop in the same hand. She remained as she was, but she looked at me again, her eyes turned watchful. I circled her once, looking down at the top of her pretty head, at the smooth flesh of her toned if not too skinny body. I'd have to feed her soon. For all I knew, that granola bar was all she'd eaten in days.

When I stopped behind her, she craned her neck to look back.

"Face forward unless you're told otherwise."

She gave me a wary look but did as I said. I smiled. Pain and pleasure, the threat of the former and the shame of the latter. Remarkable teachers, that pair.

I picked up the hairbrush I'd left on the night-stand, sat on the bed behind her, and set the crop and collar down so I could pick up her hair. I brushed the length of it, taking care to work out the knots, appreciating the weight of it, the shine when brushed. Once I finished, I braided it into one long, dark pleat down her back and secured it with an elastic wrapped around the handle of the brush. I got off the bed, squatted behind her, and took her in, appreciating how she knelt so quietly, so obediently, waiting. I wondered how hard her heart pounded, and when I swept the back of my hand over the curve of her neck, she shuddered.

I stilled.

I think we both held our breath.

I forced myself to continue and picked up the collar, raising it over her head to secure around her neck, locking the small lock at the back, one only I had the key to and the one she would wear until she was sold. I stood, with my hand on the top of her head and the crop held in the other, and circled to stand where she could see me.

She lifted her pretty gaze to mine, the green of her eyes bright, the pupils dark, dilated. There was a stillness about her. Her nipples tightened, and a scent—her scent, as I'd come to know it last night—hung in the air between us.

She was aroused.

I turned my hand into a fist and gripped the hair at the back of her head. She flinched but remained as she was, keeping her hands together on her lap. I brought her cheek to me, to the hardness just behind the fabric of the jeans.

"Men will want you." Why did the thought not please me? "They will pay to have you." In fact, the idea of it made the fist in her hair tighten. I only noticed it when the first tear slid from the corner of her eye, but I didn't loosen my hold because right now, all I wanted were her lips around my cock, her tongue licking its length, her sucking me off. What I needed was to shoot down her throat, and when she choked, to come all over her, to mark her as mine, to destroy her. Because that would decimate her, and that was what I needed to do. Take her to the point of breaking, but keep her just on this side of that abyss.

Beauty knelt at my feet.

And I would be the beast who would break her.

The monster who would destroy her.

Better me than another.

She'd be mine then, in a sick, unnatural way. In a sick, unnatural mind.

"What happened to you that you're like this?"

Her quiet voice broke into my thoughts, accused me.

"That you can do this?"

Our gazes locked. I felt the shift in my chest, a flashback of me as I'd once been. As Dominic Benedetti. A man with a place, a home, a reason to live. A man with the whole world at his feet.

And then the realization of how I'd lost it rushed in on the heels of that memory, dampening every-thing else, regret and loss smothering me.

"What?"

I wondered if in that millisecond, she'd seen a flash of emotion cross my face.

I felt hot, sweaty. I felt—

"I changed my mind. I want to know your name."

I blinked to dislodge this hold, this strange, new thing she held over me, but it didn't work.

"Tell me your name," she said.

My fist in her hair went limp. "Why? Why does it matter?"

"I don't want to call you Death."

I must have looked as confused as I felt.

"Your mask. The way you act. You try to be cold,

like you couldn't give a fuck, but I know that's not it. There's something else. There's more there."

I tightened my fist and grinned at her pain. "Don't fool yourself. There's nothing else."

"Then it won't matter if you tell me your name."

"What are you going to do for it?"

"You can make me do whatever you want anyway."

"Making you and you choosing to are two different things."

"I get the feeling you'd like making me."

"You'd be right," I said, then squatted down so my face was inches from hers. I inhaled and searched her eyes, let my gaze drop down to her mouth, then back up. "Don't think my eating your pussy means something. It's just part of the job," I lied, then leaned in closer, close enough to trace the curve of her ear with my tongue. She shuddered. "I smell you, Gia," I whispered. "I smell your sex. And I bet if I slid my hand between your legs, you'd be wet."

She didn't blink, didn't breathe. I watched her, challenging her, and when she remained silent, I rose to stand, feeling victorious.

"If I—" She cleared her throat. "If I sucked your cock, you'd come too. It doesn't matter, doesn't mean you have some power over me. It's physical. That's all."

"You want to suck my cock?" I knew that wasn't what she meant.

"No. I was making a point."

"What point?" I asked callously. "I missed it."

"I hate you." It started out angry, but when she repeated the words, tears glistened in her eyes, and she turned away.

"So you've told me." I looked down at the top of her head, glad she wasn't looking at me anymore, glad she couldn't see my face right then, not until I collected myself. Remembered myself. "You should hate me." The words carried no emotion.

She pressed the heels of her hands against her eyes.

I stepped away and readied the crop. I needed to get my head in the game and move. I was over-thinking things. Overthinking her. "Forward. Hands and knees. Doggy style."

"Wh...what?" The word seemed to trip out of her mouth, caught between tears and a sob.

"Forward!" I raised the crop, and she flinched.

"That's what you do, isn't it? You beat women. You tie them down and beat them until they're so scared and broken, they have no will left. No will to defy you."

I slid my fingers through the space between her collar and her pretty little neck. I hated what she said, but she only spoke the truth. "That's right," I said, tugging so she had to put her hands out in front of her or she'd fall on her face. "It's what I do."

"Fine!"

She tried to pull away, but I held her.

"You want to whip me? Fine. I've had worse. I've survived worse. You're nothing. You can't even tell me your name."

I brought the crop down on her ass, and she bit back a scream. "Crawl," I said, tugging her forward before releasing the collar, sending her scrambling to break her fall and striking again.

"At least I knew who Victor was!" She wept but crawled forward a little, pausing to wipe her face.

"I didn't tell you to stop!" I drew her forward again, and she moved, hurrying to get out of the way of the crop. "Faster!"

"I can't go faster, you sick prick." She fell forward, her bound hands hindering her progress.

"Are you hungry?" I asked sharply as I delivered another stroke.

She glanced at me, and I saw the answer in her eyes, heard it in the way her stomach growled.

"Then you'd better move. Are you cold?"

She sucked back tears and paused again to wipe her face.

I struck, aiming where she'd been branded.

This time, she let go of a scream and fell to her side, protecting her hip, watching me accusingly.

"You'd better get used to this. Get used to being treated like this."

"Like a fucking dog, you mean."

"That's a good way to think of it. This is obedience training, and you're my bitch."

"You're a coward. You hide behind a mask. You carry your weapons, against what? Defenseless, bound women who are half your size?"

"Fuck you, Gia."

"It's what you do. Own it. But you have to own what it makes you too. A fucking coward."

"How'd you get yourself caught, anyway?" I asked, gripping her collar and hauling her up to her knees. She fought like an animal. I leaned down so my face was inches from hers. "I'm getting the feeling you weren't some random pickup."

"Let me go. You're hurting me!"

"How? Tell me."

"I wasn't a random pickup you fucking prick."

She shoved at my chest, but she wasn't nearly strong enough.

"Piss off a boyfriend? He finally get enough of your bitchy mouth?"

Tears pooled in her eyes and spilled over onto her cheeks, a raw and complete pain intensifying the green.

"You don't know anything about me. Not a thing!"

"Tell me!" I shook her hard, lifting her to her feet

and pressing her against the wall. I held her there by her throat.

Her face reddened, and she watched me. I wasn't sure if she was able to speak or not. Rage hotter than hell burned through me, and I squeezed her neck.

"Fucking tell me!"

She choked out a sob, and when I loosened my hold, she began to cough.

"Did he order your branding as punishment?"

"He wasn't my boyfriend," she choked out.

I released her, and she dropped to her hands and knees, still coughing.

"He's a murderer. A monster." She paused, turned her face up, and added: "Like you."

I narrowed my gaze, although we both knew she was right. The room stood strangely quiet, her on her knees at my feet, eyes red, cheeks wet with tears, hate spearing me.

"Just like you," she said again, sitting back on her heels and lowering her gaze, giving herself over to the tears that seemed unending. I watched like the monster she accused me of being. The monster I was. I just stood there and watched her come apart until she quieted, and then I pulled the chair closer and sat down, my gaze still on her, as if I'd never seen this before, never seen a person come unglued.

She sat up and wiped the last of her tears, the look in her eyes telling me hate fueled her now. Hate kept her upright.

"I normally don't give a shit about the girls that pass through here, but you're different. You're like me, Gia. You're filled with hate."

"I'm nothing like you."

I ignored her. "Maybe I won't bother taking you to the auction. Keep you for myself until I wear you out instead. Until there's nothing left."

She stared at me. Was it fear that left her mute? That pushed tears from her eyes?

"That's a scary thought, isn't it?"

"It would be if there was any truth to it, but you're a peon."

Her voice broke, betraying her panic. But she kept going.

"You're a nobody. You work for them. You don't get to decide. You don't get to choose what happens to me."

I swallowed hard. She was right. She was exactly right. She paused, and I wondered if she could read my face. I needed to end this, to take back control.

"You don't know anything about me," I defended.

"I think I do." She sniffled, wiped her nose and eyes. "And you're wrong. We may both hate, but I don't hate myself. I know who I am. I'm not evil. I don't hurt people. You...you're a monster. You hate yourself more than you could ever hate anyone else."

I swallowed hard suddenly, wanting my mask, needing it. She saw me, she saw right through me, and she said the words I was too fucking afraid of, too much of a coward to say myself. The words I was too weak to own.

I stood and kicked the chair out from behind me, sending it crashing against the far wall, making her jump, making her lean away from me.

"Turn around." I ordered.

She eyed the crop, and I saw her tremble as her red, puffy eyes searched mine.

"Turn the fuck around." Quieter now. Had she realized yet I was at my deadliest when I grew calm? I watched her think. I studied this girl who desperately needed humbling. This girl who burrowed too deep under my fucking skin.

Her eyes darted to the crop once more, and I set it aside. I didn't need that. There were other punishments. Pain wasn't the worst I could do.

Her throat worked as she swallowed, but slowly, she turned to face away from me. Her hair had come partially out of the braid. I reached to pull the elastic holding it together out. Gia startled but held her position. I ruffled the braid I'd so carefully pleated until her long hair hung down her back. I picked up the mass of it and set it over one shoulder. She remained tense, shoulders high, arms tight by her sides as I squatted down to trace my fingertips down the length of her spine. Her skin was so soft, her body slender, the lines long and straight, her narrow waist giving way to rounded hips. Her arms were toned, like I'd noticed her legs were. Apart from the bruising and that branding scar, she was flawless. Perfect.

I pulled my hand away like I'd been burned and stood.

"Put your forehead on the floor and raise your hips." My voice held a different tone, quieter, darker. My cock throbbed to life, hard and ready and wanting.

Wanting her.

She turned her head, just glancing behind her but not quite able to hold my gaze.

"Do it."

I didn't know what I would do. I could anticipate what she expected, why her face had twisted, and why she remained silent as she slowly leaned forward, her bound hands sliding along the floor, creating a cushion for her forehead as she did as she was told.

I waited, taking her in, slight and frightened and so fucking erotic. I wanted her. I wanted her surrender, her submission, but more than that. I wanted her in a way that was different. Not like the others. Not like the women before—in my former life.

She raised her hips slowly, and I sucked in a breath.

I'd seen her naked. I'd cleaned her. I'd touched her. I'd tasted her. But this, this presenting of herself to me, even if it was under duress, it felt different. And some part of me, it longed for her.

Longed to have her. Possess her. Break her and own her.

It longed for this surrender, for her submission, to be real.

I don't know how long we stayed like that, her quiet and obedient, me in some trance, under this strange spell, watching like this was the first woman I'd seen like this. Wanting like I'd never wanted before. Feeling something almost pure wash over me, at least momentarily, before she sniffled, and I knew she was crying. Quietly crying. Afraid.

No.

Terrified.

Overpowered.

Breaking.

I took a step back, seeing as if for the first time this filthy floor in this filthy room. This terrible place where I would break her, break this beautiful, perfect creature and make her less. I would take everything away from her. That was what I did. What I had done to so many others.

I stumbled backward some more, misstepped, and caught myself.

Pure. I'd felt something pure washing over me. What a joke. What a sick, fucking joke.

I turned on my heel and walked out the door, slamming it shut behind me, locking it, locking her in. I grabbed my jacket and keys and stalked out of the cabin, breaking my own rule and leaving her behind. I climbed into my truck and drove through the narrow passage in the woods and out onto the open road. I didn't stop at the nearest town like I would have in the past. I didn't want a woman. And I didn't want whiskey. I just wanted to be out of my head. Out of my skin. I wanted to be someone else. Anyone else. Because the lowest scum of the earth had to be better than the filth that was me. Than the aberration that was me. This hateful monster who hurt, who broke, who took beauty that did not belong to him and destroyed it.

She was right. Salvatore had been right.

I was a monster.

I was the worst kind of monster.

6

GIA

He'd left the blanket behind. After washing my face and hands, I grabbed it and wrapped it over my shoulders, not caring how dirty it was, not caring about the stains or the smell. I just held it to me and climbed onto the bed and lay on my side, shivering, knees pulled in to my chest, clutching this foul blanket to me. And no matter how hard I tried, I couldn't make the tears stop. I wept like I had when I'd watched Mateo die. How could there be tears left inside me? How could more come, how could I not be dead of dehydration after all this fucking crying?

They'd shot him in the back of the head after they'd cut out his tongue. They'd made me watch it all. Watch him as he set his face before the block—a fucking tree stump stained with the dried blood of how many others? I'd watched as he had laid his tongue on the stump, his eyes wide, trying hard not to show his fear. Failing. I'd seen Victor's nod in my periphery, giving the order. Watched the ax come down and blood pour and Mateo fall over, a garbled scream coming from him. From my brother. My vital, loving, crazy brother whom I loved so, so fucking much.

He'd done it to save me. To spare me. He'd made Victor promise. He'd made the deal. He'd offered his tongue in exchange for my life.

And then, after, was it a mercy then that they'd hauled him up to his knees and pressed his head back onto the block until he held it there, chin cushioned in his own dismembered tongue, in the pool of his own blood seeping into the stump of the tree. He'd looked at me once more before closing his eyes. That was the moment he'd given up hope. I knew it. I saw it. Victor pushed the barrel of the gun to the back of his head then. This time, the scream was mine.

There had been so much blood, an impossible amount. My brother's blood covered me as he fell over, gone, his savaged, beaten body murdered, his life stolen before my eyes, just inches from me while I stood powerless to save him.

He'd made Victor promise he wouldn't kill me. That was the deal. They'd have cut his tongue out anyway, but maybe they'd have done it after he'd died. Or maybe they'd force him. I didn't know. I didn't care. All I knew was that I'd never forget the sound of the ax coming down, the look on Mateo's face, in his eyes. And then that final, deafening sound of the gun being fired.

I'd read that in real life—as opposed to the movies—it sounded like a pop, but this was no pop. It was an explosion, an ear piercing, deafening explosion. Louder than anything I'd ever heard before. More horrible than anything I'd seen.

I'd never forget that day. I'd never forget what they did to him. And it was the one thing that kept me together now. The thing that had me gathering the pieces of myself. Because if I gave in now, then Mateo's death was for nothing. Victor thought he'd won. That Mateo and I were finished. But he was wrong. I had vowed vengeance for what he'd done. I had promised it silently to Mateo, to myself. And I needed to pull myself together, to collect my strength, because I knew now that I had a chance. I knew it.

I had fully expected Death to rape me. I thought...I thought what else could he want? I had taunted him—hell, maybe I wanted him to kill me, to end it all, to make the decision and take the responsibility of vengeance away from me. But that was weak. I knew that now. Hell, I'd known it then. And he, this man I called Death, he surprised me. He unwittingly gave me hope.

I was different to him. He wanted me. I could see

it in his face, his eyes. He'd made a mistake, taking off that mask. He should never have done that. He didn't know me. He didn't know I would stop at nothing to avenge my brother.

Although he was right about one thing. There was one area where we were alike. We both hated. We'd both been hurt—no, we'd been battered. But neither he nor I had broken, and I wouldn't break now. He wanted to break me. It was his job. I had a suspicion, though, that that wasn't wholly true. His own conflicting emotions weakened him. But it would be good to remember that those exact things made him dangerous. They made him volatile and unpredictable. I needed to control him. I didn't need to search for a how. I knew how. I just had to come to terms with the fact that the idea of it didn't repel me like it should. The thought of his hands on me, his mouth on me, his cock inside me, it didn't turn my stomach. The opposite, actually. And that was what made me sick. That made me question who I was. How I could feel these things, feel this way. How I could not abhor this man.

Because if I did hate him, if I were repelled by him, I would still do what I had to do, and I would hate myself a little less for it. But as it stood now, as I felt now, I knew I had to be some sort of monster to be able to feel attraction for my captor. To come under his tongue. To want it again.

I'd lied when I'd said what I'd said to him about

it being physical. It wasn't physical, not for me. It never could be.

He'd said he had two weeks to train me. To ready me for the auction. Well, I had two weeks, then. Two weeks to get under his skin, to burrow so deep he couldn't let me go. He'd have no choice but to keep me. Perhaps even to help me.

No, that I could not expect. I would kill him as soon as I could. It would be good training for when the time came to kill Victor. Because killing was new to me. I may have been born into a family of foot soldiers, men who'd worked for various crime families for generations, but I'd never even touched a gun, never felt the weight of one in my hands. I would learn, though. Maybe I'd even learn how to wield an ax when it came time to take Victor down.

I let hate fuel me while I gathered my courage and pushed the blanket off. I walked into the bathroom and, with my hands bound, switched on the shower. I didn't wait for the water to warm. Instead, I stepped into the tub and stood beneath a spray of icy water, not thinking about the dirt at my feet, the filth around me. I washed away my fear and willed myself to think of Mateo, of his strength right up until the end. I exchanged fear for strength and let the water wash away any weakness inside me. When I was finished, I returned to my room and waited there, ready for Death to come.

BUT HE DIDN'T COME BACK. NOT FOR THE SPACE OF SIX meals.

A few hours later—I wasn't sure if it was hours, as time seemed to crawl by, so it could have been an hour or a day—when the door opened again, it wasn't Death who entered.

All my resolve, all the courage I'd thought I'd gathered, all the strength and drive I had built up, dissolved when that door opened and another man entered.

The only sound was that of my gasp. He was almost as tall as Death but built differently, his body almost paunchy although still strong. He had dark hair and black spots for eyes, his skin tanned and leathery. I'd guess him to be in his late thirties but for the look in his eyes, which seemed ancient. I couldn't see his face. He had a black bandanna draped over his nose and mouth.

I pulled the blanket to me.

"Don't flatter yourself." He stepped into the room and closed the door behind him, locking it and pocketing the key. He carried a tray of food and two bottles of water.

I started to salivate at the smell of rice and chicken wafting from the takeaway box. I sat up straighter, unable to drag my eyes away from it. My stomach growled, and the man chuckled. As he came closer, I inched away but stayed on the bed with the blanket covering me. His eyes remained hard as they watched me, and he set the tray down on the nightstand.

He then produced a fork. A real fork, not a plastic one. "You get one chance with this. If you think you can try to stab me with it or do anything else stupid, I'll whip your ass and dump your next meal on the floor for you to lick it off, understand?"

I swallowed, wanting the food, my gaze locked on the man's. I nodded.

He held the fork out to me. I hesitated, knowing this was a challenge from the way he raised an eyebrow.

I reached out, intending on grabbing the fork out of his hand without touching him, but he had other plans. As soon as I was close enough, he snatched my wrist and yanked me toward him, twisting my arm as he did.

I cried out in pain.

"I'm not playing fucking games, we clear on that?"

"Yes! You're going to break my arm!"

He tugged once more, smiling as he yanked another cry from me, then released me and set the fork down on the tray.

"Eat it all," he said. He turned around and walked back out the door like our exchange was the most casual thing in the world.

Once the door locked behind him, I picked up the box and fork and opened the lid. Chicken and rice and even a side of broccoli. How thoughtful to give me my veggies. It was bland but warm, and I ate every last rubbery bite, forcing myself to slow down so I wouldn't throw it up. My body needed this fuel. I needed it if I had any hope of surviving.

The stranger threw me. Was Death gone? Had he quit? Could you do that in his line of work?

I almost laughed at that last thought, drained the second bottle of water, and sat back, feeling better for having eaten. When was the last time I'd had something warm? How long had I been here, and how long had Victor kept me prisoner before turning me over to Death? How long ago had Mateo died?

For five more meals, the man with the beady black eyes came, checked that I'd eaten everything, took the trash and left me with new food. By the third delivery, I started to ask questions: what day it was, what time, where was Death? He never answered a single one. It seemed we were getting on a regular schedule, though, with the meals. Maybe two in a twenty-four-hour period? I couldn't be sure, but I was starving between them.

The delivery of the seventh meal changed everything. Just as I was starting to get more comfortable, even considering using my fork to do the very thing he warned me not to do, everything changed.

That was when Death returned.

He came when I was sleeping. It was night. No sunlight penetrated the slats of wood over the windows. I woke to find him inside the room, standing at the foot of the bed, watching me. I startled, screamed, and scrambled as close to the top of the bed as I could, the blanket bunched up in my arms, a barrier between him and me.

He wore his mask again. It took me a minute, but I knew it was him. I knew it from his body, from the way he moved. It was as though he screamed power.

"Didn't meant to startle you."

His voice mocked me. He walked around the bed, and it took all I had not to scream again, not to run to the other side of the room to get away from him. He'd changed. He was different. He was cocky, a bastard, like in the very beginning.

"We're changing how we do things."

He took hold of the blanket and tugged it from me. I fell forward and had to release my hold on the one thing that gave me comfort. But maybe it was good he took it. It gave me a false sense of security. As if somehow, everything would be okay. It would never be okay. Nothing would ever be okay again. How could I ever think it would? How could I ever think I could seduce him? That I could somehow win him over, make him want me enough that he didn't take me to the auction but would instead keep me for himself? That he would help me avenge my brother's murder?

"I heard you've been eating, doing as you're told."

I didn't answer, I couldn't. I just watched him, my gaze glued to that fucking mask as he folded up the blanket and set it on the chair in the corner.

"And that you didn't attack Leo with the fork."

Leo. That was the other man's name. What was Death's name? And why the fuck was he wearing that mask again? It worked as a barrier, shielding him from me, keeping him separate from me. And looking at it terrified me.

"I don't like the mask," I said, my voice coming out small.

"Don't you." It wasn't a question.

He unbuckled his belt and pulled it through the loops, holding it like he had that night he'd whipped me, with the buckle in his palm. He then raised his other hand and curled his finger, motioning for me to go to him.

"Kneel." He pointed to the spot by his feet.

I watched him, beginning to tremble, unable to take my eyes off that terrible mask.

"Gia."

"Take it off. Please, take it off." I gripped the rungs of the headboard when he placed one knee on the bed as if he were going to come get me. "Please, just take it off."

In an instant, he was on the bed, one hand fisting my hair and dragging me off and toward the floor.

"I said fucking kneel!" he roared.

I cowered at his feet, covering my ears as best as I could with my wrists still bound together, my heart hammering against my chest, tears spilling down my cheeks, screaming at the searing burn of the belt across my ass.

"When I say kneel, you fucking kneel!"

He lashed me twice more, his anger a palpable thing, his rage so real, so fucking terrifying, I did more than kneel. I crouched down at his feet, my forehead on the floor, then on his boot. I knew he was punishing me not only for disobeying his first command to kneel, but for the last time he was here, for what had happened then, for how he'd left, for his having stayed away. He was punishing me for his own weakness, his own sin.

When he stepped back, I kept my head down, whimpering, my chest heaving with heavy breath, my back and ass throbbing with the lashes he'd delivered.

"Up on hands and knees."

I obeyed, moving as quickly as I could, not earning a stroke this time. He took two more steps away.

"Crawl to me."

I did, I crawled. I covered the space clumsily with my hands bound, all of my limbs trembling, and when I reached him, he took another two steps back, then another, taking me in circles around the room.

"Now bend over the edge of the bed."

"Please don't whip me anymore. I'm doing as I'm told. Please."

"You're not doing as you're told now, are you?"

I swallowed and glanced at how his hand clutched the belt. I crawled to the foot of the bed and stood, then bent myself over it like the first night I was here when he'd whipped me.

"Spread your legs."

I did as he said, widening my stance while he stood behind me. I didn't know what to expect, didn't know if he'd whip me or fuck me or both.

"Don't turn around, whatever you do."

I didn't speak. I was unable to. It took all I had not to look over my shoulder.

It was quiet forever, and I knew he watched me until, an eternity later, his footsteps broke the silence, and he approached. I held my breath, the tears finally having stopped, and when he lay the belt across my back, I startled at the cool, heavy leather.

Fingertips touched me, hands on my ass, tickling at first, then pulling me open.

"Please," I begged, not sure what I begged for. Not expecting the thing that came, the soft wetness of his tongue on me, on my sex, licking me, tasting me, pulling me wide as one hand snaked toward my clit. He began to rub the hardened nub.

I fisted my hands and bit my lip. His tongue working me expertly, the pleasure unbearable as I fought against it, the battle lost when he slipped his tongue inside me, his fingers rubbing harder. I arched my back and pressed against him, squeezing the muscles of my legs and closing my eyes, drawing blood from my lip in an effort to mute the moan that preceded the orgasm while he sucked and rubbed. I gasped for breath and clawed the mattress, my knees giving out as I began to slide from the bed.

He caught me, and when he did, I turned my head to meet his eyes, discovering that the mask had been discarded somewhere on the floor. Blue-gray eyes shone back at me, the pupils big and dark. With one hand, he kept me pinned to the bed while with the other, he undid his jeans and pushed them and his briefs down. He took himself into his hand, and our gazes locked. He began to pump. I watched his face, his angel's face, his burning eyes, swollen lips parted and glistening with my juices.

"I like how you taste," he said, his body jerking a little.

I turned my gaze to the hand that held his cock, watching him pump hard and fast.

"I told you not to turn around, didn't I?" he asked.

I licked my lips, unable to tear my eyes away and

was ready when he fisted my hair and drew me to my knees before him.

"Suck my cock, Gia." He shook me once. "If you bite, I'll fucking kill you."

I nodded. I had no intention of biting. I opened to take him into my mouth, his taste salty, the skin soft around his thick, hard cock. He pressed back too far too fast, making me choke, but when I tried to push him away, he only held me still and did it again, his eyes on mine, his gaze telling me he was punishing me.

"I told you not to turn around."

He fucked my face now, thrusting deeper and deeper down my throat, cutting off all breath until I thought I'd pass out and releasing me for an instant to draw desperate gulps of air before repeating.

"You'll learn to do as you're told."

His cock thickened impossibly larger inside my mouth, his hand in my hair so tight it drew tears from my eyes.

"Fuck, Gia."

He pushed me backward so my head leaned uncomfortably on the bed, and he stilled. I felt the first stream of cum hit the back of my throat. I choked, not ready, but he held me still, closing his eyes until I couldn't take any more. Then finally he pulled out, his grip on his cock tight as streams of cum covered my chest and my breasts, marking me as his, claiming me, owning me.

Only when he'd emptied did he release me. He pulled up his briefs and jeans and looked at me, his eyes strange, searching. He then reached into one of his pockets and drew out two little pills. I looked at them, at him, and shook my head no, feeling again the buildup of tears, those never-fucking-ending tears.

He only had to raise his eyebrows in warning, and I reached out my hands. He dropped them into my palms and watched me put them into my mouth and swallow. Made me open again so he could make sure I wasn't hiding them, and when he was satisfied, he picked up his belt and the discarded mask and walked back out the door, locking me in my room once again.

7

DOMINIC

I went into my bedroom while I waited for the drug to work. There, from inside the same drawer I kept Effie's photograph, I pulled out a small box and opened it. Inside was my ring, the one I'd worn when I was a Benedetti. The one all the Benedetti men wore. I sat on the bed and studied it, ignoring the desire to slip it on my finger. Shoved away the thought of how much I'd lost. How different my life was meant to be.

Isabella had called me late last night. I'd only spoken to her once after I'd left, when she'd called to tell me Salvatore had handed everything over to our uncle, Roman. She hadn't called when Effie had broken her arm. I'd only found out about that when I saw Effie wearing a hot-pink cast in one of the photos. She also hadn't called to tell me about her engagement to Luke. That too I'd seen when I'd spied the rock on her finger in another photo of my daughter. Not that I cared about her marrying Luke. They deserved each other. Where Isabella was concerned, I had no affection. She was the mother of my child. That was all. We'd always be connected no matter what, but that didn't mean anything more.

No, she'd called to tell me about a body turning up. The body of Mateo Castellano. I'd known Mateo. He'd done some work for my fa—for Franco Benedetti—a few years ago. He'd actually tipped me off about a deal being a trap, which had probably saved my ass, even though I hadn't acknowledged that fact then. Too fucking arrogant. We'd gotten along well. He'd become a friend even. But then he'd disappeared, moved on, I guessed. He, like I was now, was a nobody. He went where the money took him.

I didn't get the reason for her call at first. People in our line of work died all the time. A side effect of mafia life. Hearing about Mateo's death, though, had been a little like when I'd heard my brother Sergio had been killed. It made me pause.

There was more. Isabella said the killer had intended for the body to be found. It had been meant to send a message. Castellano had been worked over, which didn't surprise me, then shot execution-style: bullet to the back of the head. But there was one more thing. Two more things, actually.

His tongue had been cut out. He was a snitch.

I had told her callously that I wasn't totally surprised, considering he'd snitched before when he'd saved my ass. But she'd told me to shut up and listen. There'd been a mark on him. A brand. It was in the middle of his chest. She'd seen a picture of it. How she'd gotten her hands on a photo like that, I had no idea, although she was incredibly resource-ful. Never underestimate Isabella DeMarco. Hadn't I learned that yet?

She thought the mark would be of interest to me. It was to Salvatore, apparently. The brand was a larger version of the Benedetti family crest, a genera-tions-old symbol of power in our world, at least in southern Italy and the northeastern United States. It was an exact copy of the one I held in my hand. Mateo Castellano had been branded before his death, and someone wanted to get two messages out: one, that he was a snitch, and snitches were dealt with mercilessly. Two, that it was a Benedetti who'd done the dealing.

But this wasn't how Roman operated. It wasn't his MO. I wouldn't put it past Franco, but he had a different sort of cruelty. He was just as brutal but not medieval in his torture. I didn't suspect Salvatore for a second.

That's why I'd given Gia the pills.

Mateo was my age, or close to it. He had a kid sister. I'd met her once, a long time ago. I think I'd been seventeen or eighteen. It was at a party, which my father had attended, where a secret meeting had been held. He'd brought me along. When they'd gone to talk, I'd wandered around the property, bored, annoyed at not being invited into the meeting. A little ways from the house, I'd come across a little girl backed against a tree by two boys about twelve, I'd say. They were apparently trying to take something from her, and she'd been putting up a hell of a fight, but she couldn't have been more than seven. I'd told the boys to piss off and leave the kid alone. She'd given me a look. It wasn't a "thanks for saving me" or anything like that. It'd been a glare. She'd been just as pissed at me as she'd been at those boys. I remembered I'd laughed when Mateo had found us there and told her to get back to the house and help their mother with something. She'd spoken to him in Italian and thrown a sideways glance my way before running back house, the flash of her angry green eyes from beneath those thick dark bangs now unsettlingly familiar.

I didn't know Mateo's sister's name. I'd never asked.

And I had a suspicion I wanted gone.

I needed to check the mark on Gia's hip.

She'd be the right age. That party had been seventeen, almost eighteen years ago. If I was right about the little girl being seven, that'd make her twenty-four now.

Did I have Mateo Castellano's *sister* trapped in that room? If so, who the fuck had sent her to me? Did they know they were sending her to me? And why the Benedetti brand? I knew all the workings Franco had his dirty hands in, and human trafficking wasn't part of any of it. He did some bad shit, but he didn't sell stolen women.

That was why I needed her knocked out when I first saw the mark. I couldn't give anything away. She knew who had taken her, and it was personal. I'd never bothered to ask more, because I didn't give a fuck, and I didn't want to know. But now, having heard about the brand on Mateo Castellano, I needed to know.

After putting the ring away, I made myself something to eat, wanting to be sure she was out before I went back in there. After waiting over an hour, I took the key out of my pocket and unlocked the door. Light from the room I was in shone on her motionless form on the bed, tucked tight beneath the blanket. I made my way to the bed to make sure she was out. She was. From the locked chest, I took out a lightbulb and screwed it into the ceiling from where I'd removed it before Gia's arrival. I then switched on the light, not too bright but bright enough. Gia didn't stir.

Sitting on the edge of the bed, I pulled the blanket back, guilt gnawing at me when the scent of sex wafted off her. I hadn't meant to do what I'd done earlier. I'd wanted to let her know I was back, and I was in charge. But then, watching her like that...hell, I had wanted her.

I guessed she hadn't been able to shower before the drug had knocked her out.

She mumbled something and rolled onto her back.

Avoiding what I had to do, I went back to my room and returned with a clean washcloth, towel, and soap. Remembering the toothbrush I'd picked up for her, I set it, still in its packaging, on the edge of the sink in her bathroom. I then ran hot water over the washcloth and rubbed the bar of soap over it until it was sudsy. After ringing the excess moisture out, I went back to her and gently cleaned her face, chest, and belly, rinsing off the cloth twice more as I washed her thighs and her sex until the scent was gone. I patted her dry with the clean towel, all the while watching her.

I could tell myself all I wanted to that it was to make sure she didn't wake up, but I knew it was a lie. In a way, I felt something for her that I hadn't for any of the other unfortunate girls who'd lain in this same bed. I could usually put a wall up between myself and the job—whatever or whoever that job was. With her, though, I couldn't put my finger on any particular reason why that wall wasn't staying up. It had for all of five minutes when I'd entered this room the first time. Maybe it was the physical attraction, the pull I felt toward her. Maybe it was the mark on her hip. Maybe I subconsciously knew already, had felt already, that this was different. I didn't know. I just knew I needed to get on with it and see the damn thing once and for all.

After hanging both the washcloth and towel to dry in the bathroom, I went back into the bedroom and turned her onto her side, eyeing the scab that covered the healing brand. My heart pounded. I touched the rough skin. It had already begun to peel away at the edges, revealing pink skin beneath, a circle to contain the crest. Using my fingernail, I scratched away rough skin, exposing more and more, recognizing the ornamental *F* of *Famiglia*. Because to the Benedetti, family came first.

Fucking joke.

The scab became harder to peel away once the edges were gone, but I didn't need to go too much further. I saw what I needed to see. The ornamental *B* of Benedetti, the tips of the spears crossing at the top, protecting the *famiglia* beneath. I didn't need to see the face of the lion at the center of the crest. His mane took shape around the edges, and I had no doubt once the scar had fully healed, I would see the Benedetti crest branded into her skin.

I stood quickly, looking down at the girl. I squatted down again until my face was an inch from hers. I pushed the hair back from her cheek, tucked it behind her ear, and looked at her. At the pretty, unconscious woman lying in the filthy bed, eyes closed, lips parted, her breath shallow. I tried to remember the little girl from the party, but the only image my mind had held onto was those eyes. Gia had looked at me like that once, her glare from beneath her dark hair burning a hole into me.

But was she Mateo Castellano's kid sister? Had whoever killed him taken her? What had she had to do with anything? Although it wasn't like she needed to be involved at all. This was the Italian mafia, after all. Families thrived together, and they were destroyed together. Was this sleeping woman the girl I'd once saved from two overzealous boys at a party?

I stood abruptly and stepped away.

What did it matter if she was? She was a job. That was all. Just because I'd saved her from some idiot kids years ago, didn't mean we were connected, that I was going to be her savior again. I had to remember I was no longer a Benedetti. I no longer had an army behind me. I was Dominic Sapienti. A nobody. Even if I fucking wanted to protect her, what the hell could I do? It's not like I had the fucking money to buy her outright. I'd blown all the money I'd had when I'd bought Salvatore's mansion, lock, stock, and barrel. Everything in it now belonged to me, and it fucking sat there under seven years' worth of dust because it wasn't like I was ever going back there. I didn't even know why I'd bought it.

And even if I hadn't, what now? Buy her? Keep her?

Keep her.

"You're a fucking imbecile, Dominic," I muttered to myself. I stood, walked the few steps to the center of the room to unscrew the lightbulb from the ceiling, and plunged the room into near darkness again. It took a moment for my eyes to readjust.

Keep her, and do what with her? I'd question her about the brand. Find out who'd done it. Why they'd done it. Then what?

This was the drawback to my line of work. I never knew who hired me, and they never knew who they hired. An anonymous world of monsters.

I reached for the phone in my back pocket, closing the space between me and her, and began to dial a number I hadn't dialed in way too many years. I pulled the blanket back over her, taking in her sweet, innocent face—at least in sleep—and walked out of the room, locking the door behind me. I looked down at the phone display. One digit more and the phone would start ringing. My heart pounded, and my hands felt clammy. I hit End. I wasn't ready for that. Not yet. Instead, I opened up my laptop and took a seat at the kitchen table, where I typed in Mateo Castellano's name on the Google search field, already knowing what I'd find.

L ight filtered through the slats of wood covering the bedroom window. My eyelids felt sticky as I blinked them open, my mouth like cotton, and my head heavy. A combination of the drug and life.

Sitting up, I dragged the blanket up and tucked it around myself. Why did he have to keep the room so cold?

I scratched my head. That was when a small movement near the bed startled me. I gave a little involuntary gasp.

Death sat somber in the chair, no mask, his eyes dark, his gaze heavy upon me. Watching me.

Every hair on my body stood on end, and my heart fell into my stomach. What was he doing here? How long had he been watching me sleep? Why? How would he torture me today?

I curled my fingers around the blanket and waited.

"Who sent you to me?"

I pulled my legs underneath me and sat on my knees, covering as much of myself as I could.

"Who branded you, Gia?"

I had to swallow several times to get my voice to work. "Why?" The question made me sound weak. Vulnerable.

"I know who you are."

I stared at him, at this man who held me prisoner. This cruel captor who gave and took as he pleased, who both scared the hell out of me and also drew me like no other. His face, an angel's face, was etched into the hardest stone, his eyes of steel, colder now, the pleasure he took in mocking me no longer glowing like embers of a dying fire. An anger, a hatred replaced it, and that fire was burning bright, ready to consume. To obliterate.

It was a terrifying thing to see.

"What does it matter, who I am?" I asked, my heart pounding, knowing the thin ice I walked on, waiting, watching to see what this brought.

His expression didn't change.

"Who sent you to me?"

It was as though he held his breath.

"Victor Scava."

This seemed to surprise him, because it took him a minute to continue.

"Did he brand you?"

I nodded.

"Under orders from whom?"

"I don't know. I don't know that he took orders from anyone."

"Why did he do it?"

Emotion coursed through me, memory and feeling and loss. Before me sat one of the men responsible for my suffering. I didn't know if he was involved with Mateo's torture or death, but I did know I owed him nothing.

Gathering my courage, I raised my head high.

"Why do you care? Why do you get to ask any question you like, when you won't even answer the one I've asked you?"

"You still want to know my name? It's that important to you?"

Maybe he was right. Maybe I should have been asking a different question. But I nodded and narrowed my gaze.

"Dominic. My name is Dominic"—hesitation, then—"Sapienti."

Even in the dim light, I saw his eyes shift when he said his last name, and I knew it was a lie.

"Dominic Sapienti," I said, watching him closely.

He nodded once, blinking as he did, and I felt sure I was right.

"He branded me because I wouldn't fuck him."

That seemed to catch him off guard. His forehead furrowed, and a crease formed between his eyebrows as he processed my information and waited for me to continue.

I raised my own eyebrows. "You seem to enjoy eating my pussy. I guess he wanted to too. So does it make you more of a monster, since you took it without my permission, when he could have but chose not to?"

"He chose to brand you instead. To mark you permanently. He then sent you to me, knowing what I'd do to you, what you'd have to go through before being sold to some animal. I'd say his actions trump mine in the monster arena."

"Fuck you."

"Besides, I don't recall you shoving me off. In fact, if memory serves, and it does, you were pushing your ass into my face for more."

I turned away. He was right.

He got up, approached the bed, and stood over me, his body a warning in itself. Taking my chin, he forced me to face him.

"I could have taken more. I may yet."

I wanted to say something, to challenge him, but every warning bell inside me went off, and I lowered my lashes instead. I had to be smart, and goading this man into hurting me was not smart.

"Tell me about your brother."

He released me and sat back down in the chair.

I snapped my gaze to his. How did he know

about Mateo? What did he know? Was this part of his "training?" Fucking with my head now, because hurting me physically, making me hate myself for my reactions to him, wasn't enough?

"Is that why you're doing this? Why your boss sent me to you?"

"I don't work for Victor Scava," he quickly clarified, his lip curling in disgust.

"Then I don't understand. Why would he send me to you if you don't work for him?"

"I'm an independent contractor. Now tell me about your brother, Gia. Tell me what Mateo did to get himself killed. To get you into the kind of trouble you're in."

I studied him, hearing the change in his tone, his words, his whole way of being toward me. I didn't understand. "My brother was a good person who got involved with bad people, and when he tried to get out of it, they killed him."

"His tongue was cut out. That means one thing in our world."

My heart hurt at the mention. Would I ever think of Mateo and not remember that?

"*Your* world."

"No. *Our* world."

I looked down at my lap, exhaling. He was right. This was our world.

"How do you know what happened to Mateo?"

"His body turned up yesterday. It was left where

it could be found. Whoever killed him is sending a message. Now tell me why they executed him."

"Why do you care?"

He stood, ran his hand through his hair, and looked away, shaking his head as if he were having some conversation, an internal argument. He then turned back to me.

"Just fucking tell me."

"Because he'd gone to the feds about exactly what you're doing to me now. He'd started to do some work for Victor. I'd told him not to. Told him Victor was bad news. He found out the hard way, and when he tried to do the right thing, they killed him. They tortured him, and they made me fucking watch." My voice broke, and I wiped away a rogue tear. "I think that was the part that broke him."

The room fell silent, and when I looked up, I found Dominic's gaze steady on mine, affected but silent.

"Did you have anything to do with that? With Mateo going to the feds?"

I shook my head. "I didn't know what Victor was doing. I didn't know he was selling girls, not until my brother told me."

"Why didn't Victor kill you?"

"Because he's a sick fuck?" I tried to make light of it, but a sob caught in my throat.

The buzz of a cell-phone message interrupted,

and Dominic reached into his pocket to retrieve his phone, his gaze on me.

"You were engaged to Angus Scava's son, James?"

I nodded. "When he died, Victor came into the picture. He was next in line, since Mr. Scava didn't have any other kids."

"Mr. Scava? You say that with some tenderness, Gia. Scava is not a nice man."

"He was always kind to me."

Dominic shook his head as if what I said were unbelievable.

"How can you be so sure he didn't order this?" He gestured around the room.

"No. No way. James loved me, and he loved James. He wouldn't do this to me."

"You're a fool."

"You have no heart, no soul. I wouldn't expect you to understand love like that, a father's love."

Dominic recoiled as if I'd stabbed him with a knife. It took him a moment to recover.

"Love is changeable. Disposable. It's not everlasting, not in our world. Only a fool believes in happily-ever-after, Gia."

He turned his attention to his phone then. His face changed. Confusion and then alarm crossed over his features as he read the message.

"I'm going to kill him. I'm going to put a bullet in Victor Scava's head," I said.

He looked at me, his forehead creased, eyes dark.

Then, without a word, he walked out the door and locked me inside, leaving me once again in this dark, dank room, confused but also, somehow, hopeful.

Mateo's body had been found. It had been left where it could be found. And its discovery had rattled my jailor.

Rumor has it one of Roman's men killed Castellano. Franco's pissed. He'd sworn to protect the Castellano kids or some shit. Can you believe it?

I had to read Isabella's message twice to understand. To remember.

Mateo's father had worked for Franco. He'd taken a bullet for him. He'd died saving Franco's life. I remembered now. I'd heard it later, heard him talking to Roman about it, about taking care of the Castellano family. Making sure everyone knew they were under his protection.

And Roman had Mateo Castellano killed? Why in hell would he have branded him? Why advertise that? Franco would fucking kill him. It made zero sense. If what Gia told me was true, did that mean he'd had his hands in human trafficking? Did the Benedetti family now sell women on the black market?

I took a seat at the kitchen table and pulled up Salvatore's number. It was time. Hell, it was past time.

I hit Send and listened to it ring. It took everything I had to not hit the End button this time. And when he picked up, his voice so familiar even after all these years, it took me a minute to reply. It took me that minute to get my heart to stop pounding, to get my voice working.

"Salvatore," I said and waited.

Silence on his end now. Then: "Dominic? Is that you?"

Hearing his voice, fuck, it brought back so many memories. So many emotions. "It's me," I said flatly.

"Jesus!"

If ever I could say I heard the sound of relief, now would be the time. As if he gave a shit.

"Where the fuck have you been? I've been looking for you for seven fucking years."

"I'm here. I'm fine." I paused. "How are you?" It was polite to ask, and I needed to be polite. I needed information.

"Fine. Good."

"I heard you have two brats running around and a third on the way."

"You've been keeping tabs?"

"Yeah."

"Two little girls. A boy due in six weeks." He paused. "They should meet their uncle sometime."

"Nah." Fuck. I stood, gritting my teeth. "Better this way."

"Better for whom?"

I ignored his question.

"And Effie?" he asked.

"Better for her too."

"No, not fucking better. Where are you? Are you okay?"

I hated the tone of his voice. The authenticity in what he said.

"I'm around, and I'm okay. I needed to go figure out who the hell I was."

"You're my fucking brother, that's who you are."

"Not so simple."

"I thought you were dead," Salvatore said.

"After what happened, I wanted to be." A long silence followed. The words *I'm sorry* may have fit here nicely. *I'm sorry for almost killing you.* Hell, they might even be true, but I couldn't go there. I hated the Benedetti family. I hated all of them. And that had to include Salvatore.

Quiet.

"I heard they found a body. Mateo Castellano. Did Roman order the killing?"

Salvatore sighed. "I think it's pretty obvious, don't you?"

"I thought the Castellano family was under Franco's protection."

"Me too. Father's pissed. Not sure how Roman will survive this."

Snakes always slithered out just when you thought you had them cornered. But this time, I was sure it wasn't Roman. "He's not being set up?"

"I don't know. I talked to him, but I can't be sure."

"Do you know any details?"

"I don't care about the details. That's why I'm here, in Florida, out of that life. Keeping my family out of that life. I've already been brought in for questioning twice, and I'll tell you what I told them. Roman and I talk twice a year. I called him about this for my own peace of mind. He claims it wasn't him."

"Do you believe him?"

He sighed and took a moment to answer. "Look, I'm not involved anymore. Period. And now I'm telling you that neither are you. Best thing you did was getting the hell away from our father."

"*Your* father."

"Yeah, well, maybe you should count your lucky fucking stars."

"It was a brutal killing."

"I know you and Mateo were friends once, but

you can't get involved. You can't get back into it. Let Franco handle it."

Salvatore always had this way of beating you over the head with shit, especially if he thought he was doing it for your own good. That hadn't changed, apparently.

"I'm not really out of it, Salvatore."

"What the fuck are you talking about?"

"Mateo has a sister."

"Who disappeared a few days after he did, and who's probably dead."

"No, she's not."

"Shit, Dominic. What are you talking about?"

"Look, I just needed to know if Roman ordered the killing. Is he covering his ass now that the body's been found? Because that opens up a whole other can of worms."

"What can?" he asked tightly.

I knew he was waiting for me to fill in the blanks. I wondered if he knew I hadn't talked to Roman in over five years. And how did I tell him how I knew Gia Castellano was alive and that I had her here?

"I know for a fact it was Victor Scava who put the bullet in Mateo Castellano's head," I said.

"Scava? Angus Scava's nephew? What the hell would he have had to do with anything? The brand on Castellano's chest is the Benedetti family crest."

"Then you believe it was our uncle who ordered it?"

"I don't know what I believe, and I'm tired of thinking about it. I'm sorry Mateo was killed, but nothing will bring him back, and my knowing—or *your* knowing—won't change that. Stay out of it, Dominic."

"Victor Scava is involved in human trafficking. Mateo was going to turn over evidence. That's why he was silenced. Made an example of."

"Stay the fuck out of it," Salvatore repeated.

"Too fucking late for that."

"What are you talking about? How do you know all this?"

"I've got Gia Castellano. She witnessed the murder. Scava branded her too. Same mark." I paused, but I needed to tell him everything now. In a way, it was a sort of confession. Although I had no hopes of redemption. Hell, wasn't I way beyond wanting it? "She's due to go to auction in a week."

"Due to go to auction? What the hell does that even mean?"

He knew what it meant. It was the one thing the Benedetti were not involved in. One thing where Franco, his father before him, and his father before him, had put their foot down on. No human trafficking.

Fucking saints, the lot of them.

"Any chance Roman could be involved with Victor Scava in something like this?" I pushed.

"Human trafficking? No. No way. Where exactly are you, and why do you have the girl?"

"If he's not involved, then why would Mateo have been branded with the Benedetti mark? Why not quietly kill him and get rid of the body? I mean, we all know how to get rid of a fucking body if that's what we want to do. Scava was sending a message. I want to know what that message is, and how the Benedettis are involved."

"This is fucked up, Dominic."

"No shit."

"Roman knows—"

"And he doesn't give a shit. He's king now. You made him that, remember?"

"If he betrayed our father—"

I closed my eyes and pinched the bridge of my nose, counting to ten. I'd let this one slide.

The pause told me he realized his mistake. "Where are you, and where's the girl?" he asked.

"Vermont."

"Vermont? You hate the cold."

"I'm surviving." What, were we going to make fucking small talk?

"What do you mean with taking her to auction? You can't be involved in anything like that."

"I'm already involved." Nearly a dozen girls involved.

Salvatore sighed. "Tell me about the auction."

"Ten, maybe twelve girls. Enough buyers invited to make the bidding interesting."

"Jesus."

I snorted.

"Do you know who'll be attending?"

"No."

"Can you find out?"

"There isn't exactly a guest list to these sort of events."

Salvatore paused at my remark. "Has our uncle been to one before?" he asked, a note of caution to his question.

"Why buy the product when he's the supplier?" The more I thought about it, the guiltier Roman grew. The more I saw how he was always there, watching, silent, having earned Franco's trust like no one else had, not even his sons.

"No. No way. He's our fucking uncle, Dominic. Better than our father ever was to us."

"Your father. *Your* fucking father."

"Let it go already."

"You try finding out you're not who you thought you were for twenty-eight fucking years then *let it go already*."

Another long silence filled the space, "I'm sorry." He sighed. "Exactly how much do you know about the auction?"

"It's not my first."

"Are you buying girls?"

"Providing trained girls."

"Jesus."

Fuck. I hung my head, shaking it. What the fuck was I doing? How many lives had I destroyed? How many more would I crush? All to prove to myself and the world the scum I was? God. Fuck. Putting a bullet in my own head would have been better than this.

"Dominic?"

"Yeah," I said, wiping the back of my hand across my nose.

"We have to do something about the auction."

I heard the *we*. And I knew what I needed to do.

I stood.

"No. Not we. *Me.* You're not involved, not anymore, remember? You did good, getting yourself and Lucia out. Keep her safe now. Keep your family safe. Don't tempt fate twice." It had started out spiteful, but that last part, I meant it.

He paused, and I could almost hear him preparing to argue with me. But he didn't. His family came first. Just like it should.

"What are you going to do?"

"I don't know. I'm going to find out if Roman's involved first."

"It doesn't make sense, Dominic. He wouldn't be involved in something like this. You've already tried and convicted him in your mind. And you're on your own, remember that."

Meaning I had no backing. None.

"I won't be on my own."

"What does that mean?"

"Mateo's sister. She knows at least some of what's going on. And she wants revenge for her brother's murder."

"She's a woman. Untrained. Innocent, maybe. She's a victim. You can't involve her any more than she already is."

"Haven't you learned not to underestimate women with an agenda?" Isabella DeMarco's name didn't need to be said.

"Be careful with Roman," Salvatore said soberly. "He's different now. Harder."

"He was always like that. You just never saw it."

"I'll talk to dad," Salvatore said.

"How is he?" The question came before I could stop it.

"He's sorry," Salvatore said quietly. "He writes to me, and every time he says how sorry he is about how he told you. How he lost both his sons that night."

I bit my tongue not to speak. I didn't give a fuck. I. Did. Not. Give. A. Fuck.

Salvatore sighed. "He's older. Weaker. But he's Franco Benedetti. He'll outlive all of us. But if this is true, he'll skin Roman alive." He paused. "Do you have a safe place to go, to take her?"

"Yeah."

"Don't tell me where."

"I wasn't going to. I have to go."

"Check in with me. Please. And if you need me—"

"I won't. Go be with your family."

"I love you, brother."

Fuck. How could those words impact me now? Seven years later?

"I have to go." I disconnected the call before I said something stupid. Before I had to eat the words I'd fed Gia and stand the fool.

FIRST THING I NEEDED TO DO WAS GET GIA OUT OF there.

I had no delusions about what that would mean for me. I was stealing from Victor Scava. Possibly from his uncle, Angus, the head of the Scava family. Either would kill me for what I was about to do.

But according to what Gia told me, Victor at least knew where we were. He'd sent us here to this cabin. I'd used it before. Eight times, to be precise. So he'd been the one who'd hired me all those times. But did he know I was once Dominic Benedetti? If he did, would he have sent Gia to me with our brand marking her body? Or was it just that? Had he sent her, intending for me to find it?

For a moment I entertained the idea of taking

her to Franco. Of reminding him of his pledge to keep her and her family safe. But then, I live in the real world. Family comes before any pledge and ultimately, Roman was family. He was his brother-in-law. Gia was the daughter of a dead foot soldier and the sister of a snitch.

Either Victor Scava branded and killed Mateo Castellano and left it to look like Roman's work, or he'd taken the order from Roman to kill him. Would Victor take an order from Roman? No. No fucking way. And no way Roman would tell him to brand his fucking name on the dead man. He was much too clever for that.

The two families didn't deal with each other. There wasn't a rivalry; they didn't share territory. But was there some sort of allegiance? A secret pact? And had something gone wrong for Victor to want Roman out badly enough he'd send a message that could make Roman's own family turn on him?

Ultimately, Roman wasn't head of the Benedetti family. How could he be if he wasn't even a Benedetti? When I'd found out Salvatore had handed the entire operation over to him, I'd felt so angry. The Benedetti throne did not belong to him. Hell, it belonged less to him than me. He was the usurper.

Then what the hell was I if he was that? I was cut from the same cloth. It'd be good for me to remember that. The Benedetti name did not belong to me either. And ultimately, I'd bring it down. I wanted to end the Benedetti crime family. End their rule. Shove their noses into the dirt.

But I had to admit, it still burned. The thought that he, my uncle, was head of the family I'd so wanted to rule. It fucking burned.

After packing my few things into a duffel bag, I chose a hoodie and a pair of sweatpants for Gia to wear on the drive. She'd swim in the clothes, but it was better than being naked. I'd get her something that fit as soon as I could. Right now, we had to move. I didn't know if Scava would come for her early. Take her to auction himself. Hell, fucking put a bullet in her head for all I knew. Victor Scava was a son of a bitch.

I entered her room and found her standing by the window, trying to peer out from between the slats.

She turned to face me, pressing her back against the wall when she did so, panic widening her eyes like it did every time I walked in. I studied her, trying to keep my attention on her face, not wanting to remember the things I'd done to her. Trying instead to focus on her eyes, her defiant, beautiful, sad, terrified eyes.

"Get dressed." I tossed the clothes on the bed. "We're leaving."

It took her a minute to comprehend what I'd said.

"Where are we going?"

"Away from here. Hurry up."

"Why?"

"Because I said so."

"I...is it time? Is the two weeks up?"

I was confused for a moment, then realized she thought it was time to go to auction. "No. We're leaving this place. I'm not taking you to the auction."

"Then where are you taking me?"

"Somewhere safe."

She studied me, uncertain.

"Let's go. Unless you want to stay here and wait for someone to come find you. It could be today or a few days from now when you don't show up at auction, but they will come, and I don't want to be here when they do. Now I don't mind you naked—in fact, I prefer it—but you might be more comfortable wearing clothes, seeing as how it's freezing out there."

"Why would you help me?"

She moved toward the clothes on the bed. I met her there and uncuffed her wrists, taking the restraints. She pulled the hoodie over her head. I watched it fall almost to her knees.

"Because you're going to help me. I don't like Victor Scava, and I think he's playing games." I left out the part about the games being played against my family. I did that for two reasons. First, I didn't want her to know who I was, and second, I couldn't figure out why I still considered the Benedetti family as my own.

Gia put the pants on and pulled them up. She had to bunch them up and hold them in place so they wouldn't slide off. She then stood there, looking at me, waiting.

"These will be too big, but it's just until we get to the truck."

She slid into the pair of boots I set on the floor. She looked a little ridiculous, but I liked her in my clothes.

I stepped aside and gestured for her to follow.

She moved, uncertainly at first, then more assuredly, in a hurry to get out of the room. Just as she passed me, I grabbed her arm and made her stop.

"Just one thing. You do as you're told or else. You need me to survive right now. I'm the only person who can keep you safe from Scava. Don't fuck with me. We clear?"

"I don't like you, Dominic, and I trust you even less, but I do know you hold the key to my freedom, so I promise not to fuck with you, okay?" she said, trying to free herself.

I tugged harder and leaned in close, close enough that the scruff on my jaw brushed against her soft cheek as I inhaled, then cupped her face so we stood nose to nose. "You've got a smart mouth, but I like it better put to other uses."

She jerked her face from my hand.

"Don't mistake me for a pussy, Gia," I said, shaking her once. "I'm doing this for me, not for you."

I grabbed the duffel bag with my clothes and computer, and we walked out of the cabin.

Dominic drove the SUV with its black-tinted windows through a narrow opening out of the woods, leaving the cabin behind us. I looked back at it as we bounced along, shuddering at the feeling it gave me, like a decrepit, abandoned, haunted place. Maybe it was haunted. Maybe the ghosts of the girls who'd gone before me lingered in that terrible cabin.

I physically shook. Dominic glanced at me, his expression looking as if he were deep in thought, so deep my involuntary movement seemed to surprise him.

"The heating will kick in soon," he said, returning his attention to the dirt road.

He thought I shook with cold. No. It was terror that still gripped me with its long, icy fingers.

"What's changed?" I asked. What had happened

between yesterday and today? And was he stealing from Victor now by taking me away from the cabin? What did that mean for him? For me? What use could he possibly have for me?

"What do you mean?"

"Why are we leaving? Why are you helping me?"

"I'm not. I'm helping myself."

"What game is Victor playing with you?"

"I don't know just yet."

"I don't understand."

"You don't need to understand. You just need to be grateful."

"Where are we going?"

"You ask a lot of questions."

"If you answer one, maybe I'll stop asking."

"Smart-ass."

"Bully."

"New Jersey. We're going somewhere Victor won't think to look for you. Because when he finds out you're gone, he's going to come looking for both of us."

"And he'll find out when I don't show up at auction?"

He nodded and turned the SUV onto a lonely paved road. I saw a sign for a highway twenty-six miles away.

"Franco Benedetti promised my father he would protect Mateo and I when my father died."

"Did he?"

Dominic didn't sound surprised. "Maybe I should go to him."

"Because he did a bang-up job protecting your brother?"

"You have a point." I was silent for a moment. "How many days until I would have gone to auction?"

"Eight."

"What's the date?" I didn't even know that.

"Eleventh of January."

"They killed Mateo the day after Christmas." They'd come for me that same morning. That meant I'd been held captive for more than two weeks.

Dominic didn't respond. We rode in silence, both of us lost in our own thoughts, until we merged onto the highway. It was still early morning, and there were only a few other cars on the road besides us. A sign told me there was a McDonald's at the next rest stop.

"I'm really hungry," I said. "Can we get some food?"

He glanced at me like food was the last thing on his mind.

"Please?"

He put on his blinker, and we took the exit. He rode slowly up to the drive-through window.

"If you try anything, Gia—"

"I won't. I already told you at the cabin. I want Victor Scava. I'm not fool enough to believe I can get to him on my own." It was true. I had to be realistic. Dominic's hatred of Victor meant we had a common enemy. He was taking me away from Victor. I didn't fool myself into thinking Dominic was good, not by any means, but as long as our goals lined up, Dominic was the lesser of two evils.

He nodded. "What do you want?" he asked when we got to the menu board.

"Everything." I felt greedy as I scanned the options. "But I'll settle for a sausage egg McMuffin and a big cup of coffee."

Dominic ordered, taking a sandwich and a coffee for himself as well. He gave me one more warning glance as we drove to the drive-through pick-up window.

I just held up my two hands and shook my head. I wouldn't do anything. Getting away from him may have been smart—getting to the police even smarter—but if I wanted revenge for Mateo's death, I needed to stick this out. I needed Dominic.

I watched the girl in the window when she saw him. Saw how her eyes widened and her smile grew, and for reasons I could not understand, I felt a jealousy in my core. An anger at her boldness. But when Dominic then began to flirt with her that anger boiled. I roughly grabbed the bags from him, and he made a joke to the girl as she handed him our coffees.

"I don't mess with her when she's hungry."

He winked at her as she gave me a sideways glance.

"She has sharp teeth and a sharper tongue."

The girl giggled like a fool. I only glared at him. Finally, we drove off.

"Why did you flirt with her?"

He bit into his sandwich. "Why do you care?"

"I don't. I just don't like being made fun of."

He shrugged a shoulder. "This is good. I haven't had McDonald's since I was a kid. My mother only allowed it when we went on vacations."

I glanced at him. It was hard to imagine him as a kid with a mother. The SUV bounced over a dip in the road just as I brought the cup to my mouth. The scalding liquid burned my tongue. Damn.

"How many girls have you sent to auction?"

He only glanced my way but didn't answer. Instead, he turned his attention back to the road.

"Let me ask you something else. This isn't Victor's first time hiring you, is it?"

He shook his head.

"Does his uncle know?"

"I don't know."

"He doesn't like him much." He didn't. Angus Scava could hardly stand Victor, but he had to put up with him. There was no one else to take over the family reins. "He'd been readying James to take over the family. But then James was killed."

"He was shot, correct?"

I nodded. "On his way home from a meeting he'd gone to in place of his father."

Dominic's eyebrows seemed locked in a permanent furrow, but he seemed to be a man used to shielding his thoughts. The momentary flash of vulnerability I saw in his eyes was gone like it had never been there in the first place.

"The Scava's are a powerful family. James' grandfather was killed much the same way as he was. He had a sister who died in a car crash. I know Mrs. Scava had miscarried twice. James was the only direct survivor. Bad luck."

"Not bad luck. They're a leading crime family. They have enemies. The more powerful you are the more hated you are."

"You seem to know a lot about this."

He glanced my way. "I've been around. What about your family?"

"The men have been foot soldiers for as long as I can remember. I don't think many make it past fifty. So fucking stupid. Such a waste."

"How did you meet James Scava?"

"At a party being used as cover for a meeting. My father had gone as Mr. Benedetti's bodyguard. I'd been invited to come along. Mateo hadn't been there. He'd been at school. He was getting out of the life, making a new start."

"Go on." he said.

I realized I'd stopped talking. I didn't know when

I'd stopped missing James. He'd been so good, so caring, so protective of me.

"I'd just turned twenty. His birthday was one day after mine. He was thirty, older than I usually dated, but we hit it off."

"And you knew who he was, what he did, and still fell for him?"

"He shielded me from that side of things. So had my father. I never saw it. And it's easy to pretend it's not happening when it's someone you love whose hands are bloodied."

Dominic took a bite of his sandwich. "They never found his killer."

"How do you know so much?"

"It was in the news."

"Mr. Scava believed it was a rival family, but I wouldn't be surprised if Victor had his dirty hands in it."

"That's quite the accusation."

"It's not an accusation if it's truth."

"Be careful, Gia."

"It's a little late for that, isn't it?"

"Tell me how Mateo got involved with Victor."

"When my dad was killed, Mateo came back for mom and me. He wanted to be sure we were cared for, protected. He didn't listen to me when I told him to go back to school, that we'd be fine. And then he started to work for Victor. I wasn't sure at first. If I'd known what Victor was up to, I would have gone to Mr. Scava, but I didn't know until it was too late."

"Are you sure Angus Scava isn't already involved?"

"I'm telling you, he wouldn't have done this to me. He would never have let Victor..." I broke off, remembering those nights when Victor tormented me, scared the fuck out of me.

"Your mom, where is she now?"

"She was spending time with her sister near Palermo. I don't know how much she knows. I need to talk to her."

"No."

"What do you mean, no?"

"It's too dangerous."

"But—"

"Not now, Gia. Let me think this through. I'm sure she doesn't want two dead kids to bury."

That made me stop. He was right. "Victor was always jealous of James. I'd go so far as to say he hated him." I drank the last of the now lukewarm coffee and turned to him. "How long is the drive?" I didn't want to talk about this anymore.

"A few more hours."

"Then what?"

"Then I'm going to find out what the hell is going on."

"What about me?"

"You do as you're told, Gia, and I won't have to hurt you."

"Did you know Mateo?" I asked out of the blue, remembering that sense of familiarity, that moment I'd thought I'd met him before.

"No."

He wouldn't look at me. Why didn't I believe him? And why would he lie?

"You won't hurt me," I said, not sure why I said it.

"Sharing a common enemy does not make us friends."

"You won't."

"How do you know I'm not taking you to the auction? Don't you think it'd be easier for me to transport a cooperative *slave*?"

He gave me a moment to process that before continuing.

"Quiet now. I need to think."

Fine. I needed to think too. I needed to figure out how I would proceed. As much as I wanted to kill Victor outright, wasn't it smarter for me to use the evidence Mateo had collected and turn it over to the feds? I still knew where the copy of the recorded conversations were: safe and sound in plain sight. What then, though? Go into witness protection and live in hiding for the rest of my life? Could I trust Mateo's contact? Should I go to Angus Scava, or was Dominic right? That he could be involved too? That he could have ordered Mateo's murder, my kidnapping? Was I naive to think he'd stand by me rather than his own family, even if he did hate Victor? What was I to him? Nothing. Not now that James was gone.

I needed to think. To figure out what to do. How to proceed. How to make Victor pay and stay alive in the process.

I needed to figure out how to manage my captor, how to align his goals to mine, and ultimately, I'd need to figure out how to escape him. I had no doubt his hands were as bloody as Victor's, and I couldn't forget that, no matter how attracted I was to him.

DOMINIC

Gia fell asleep sometime in the next hour, leaving me in blessed silence as I drove toward Salvatore's house.

My house.

All my thoughts led to the same place: I needed to figure out the extent of Roman's involvement, and he *was* involved. Everything in my gut told me so. Every instinct told me he and Victor were partners in this secret endeavor, at least to some degree.

But I needed to remember he was my mother's brother. He'd loved her. Franco trusted him. Sergio had too. Salvatore didn't trust anyone, and it sounded like the last seven years had only put distance between him and the Benedetti family. Me? Roman and I had a strange relationship. He'd known all along who I was—and who I was not. He'd been decent to me, to some extent. Roman was always good to Roman first, though. But hell, same could be said of any of us. Except maybe Salvatore.

Roman had helped to organize the buying of Salvatore's house, helped me sell off the cars and much of the furniture. He'd made sure the house was maintained, even though no one lived there. Why? Why would he help me after that night, when I was out, finished? When I was no longer a threat? One more Benedetti son out of the picture.

Why not, though? Why raise my suspicions by denying me help? And couldn't he then keep better track of me? Keep me in my place, which was far from his.

I thought back to those years and wondered if he'd been a friend to any of us, really. Or did he manage each of us, his eyes on the prize all along— becoming head of the Benedetti crime family.

No, that seemed too far-fetched. Too impossible.

But maybe it wasn't. To be so close to the kind of power Franco Benedetti wielded and sit impotent at his side for so many years? I knew how that felt. I knew what it made of me.

Power corrupted. And Roman was corrupt. I'd bet my fucking life on it.

I slowed as I drove the final mile toward the mansion. Night had fallen, and a crescent moon illuminated a thousand stars in the clear night. Gia stirred beside me.

"Are we there?"

"Yes."

She rubbed her eyes and leaned forward to get a better look as we got close enough for the lights of the SUV to shine on the gates protecting the property.

I slowed the vehicle, and she took it all in.

The last few miles I'd been tense. Now, that tension had reached a new level. I hadn't been back since that night. I hadn't been in the dining room since the shooting, and I was about to face it all now.

"Stay inside," I told her, climbing out to punch in the code. I watched the gates slide open. The single change I'd made to the property after buying it was to have all the locks changed and a keyless entry system put in.

Once the gates opened, I drove the SUV through, then stopped again to watch them close behind us. I'd change the code tomorrow. Roman also knew it. I hadn't thought twice about him having it, not back then.

Gia sat awestruck at what she saw as we drove the long drive toward the front door.

"What is this?"

"My house," I said, realizing it was. I'd taken over Salvatore's home, kept some of his furniture. And he didn't even know it.

I didn't bother trying to figure out my own twisted motivation.

"Your house?"

"Mercenary life pays."

"Can't pay this much."

I parked the car. Gia climbed out. I walked ahead to the front door and punched in the code. The number combination registered, and a click signaled the unlocking of the door. I pushed it open, memory of that last night flooding all of my senses as I stood on the threshold, gripping the doorknob to remain upright as the wave crashed over me, then, slowly, way too slowly, passed. I swallowed hard and reached a shaky hand to switch on the lights. The hallway illuminated immediately, and I moved aside to allow Gia to enter.

"Wow."

It was all she said while she turned around in a circle, her gaze up on the vaulted, frescoed ceiling. Salvatore had tacky taste if you asked me, but watching her take it in, to see her in awe, made me strangely, stupidly proud.

I cleared my throat and pushed the door closed, hearing the lock engage when I did. I moved swiftly through the house, turning on lights as I went, seeing the layers of dust covering the sheets protecting the remaining furniture.

"It'll need to be cleaned," I said, trying to avoid looking at the closed door that led into the dining room. Trying not to think of that night. Of what I'd find there. That was the one room I hadn't allowed to be cleaned. I wondered now how it would look—

glasses left on the table now filled with dust, the whiskey having long since evaporated. Would the blood have seeped into the obnoxious marble floors? Splattered and stained the walls with permanent reminders? Would it take me back in time to that night, that terrible night, when I'd learned the truth and lost everything in the process?

"This room is off-limits," I told Gia, gesturing to the closed dining-room door.

She shifted her weight onto one leg and narrowed her eyes. She looked like she was about to say something smart, but then her expression changed, like she knew this was serious. Like she knew not to fuck with me on this. She nodded.

I walked over to the liquor cabinet and found a bottle of unopened whiskey. I took it and found a glass. She followed me into the kitchen, where I turned on the gurgling tap and waited until the water ran clear before rinsing the glass. I filled it halfway with the liquor. I held it out to her.

She hesitated but then took it and sipped, squeezing her eyes shut. I guessed it scorched the back of her throat. She then handed it back. I drank a long swallow and refilled the glass, appreciating the burn. Salvatore had good taste.

"Can I have a proper shower?"

I nodded and finished the glass, then led the way upstairs to Lucia's old room.

"Who's room was this?" she asked, eyeing the

abandoned makeup, the lipstick on the vanity with its lid off, the discarded pair of shoes lying beside the bed.

"My brother's wife's room."

She looked at me, confused.

"It was my brother's house. He left it seven years ago. I took it over."

She searched my face, my eyes. Had she heard the story of the Benedetti brothers? Of how the one almost killed the other? No one knew what transpired that night, at least as far as the why of it. No one knew the secret Franco had told. No one but those who were here. As far as the mafia world was concerned, Dominic Benedetti was alive and well and had left after a family argument.

"Bathroom's in there. You'll have to deal with the dust. I need to make a call. Do I need to lock you in the bedroom, or will you stay put?"

"Lock me in?" She rested her hands on her hips, and her eyebrows rose high on her forehead.

I nodded. I didn't have time to deal with her right now. I needed to make a call. I needed to find out where Roman stood.

"I'll stay," she said, her tone irritated. "And I want this off," she pointed to the collar.

"Maybe we need to revisit some things." I went to her, took her by the collar, and walked her backward until her back hit the wall. She pressed against my chest, but I pulled upward, forcing her chin up. Her eyes went wide, angry but also fearful, like they'd looked in the cabin.

"You're still mine, you're still owned. When I took you out of the cabin, I stole you from Victor Scava. I did not release you. You do not give orders. You obey them. Understand?"

I felt her throat work as she swallowed. Her lips tightened, and her little hands fisted at my chest.

"I asked you if you understood."

"Yes," she bit out.

I gave her a grin. "Good." I released her. She took a full breath of air and stood against the wall as I left. I didn't lock the door behind me. I went downstairs to Salvatore's study. *My study*. There, I switched on the light and dragged the sheets off the chair and desk and sat down. Using my cell phone, I scrolled down to Roman's number and hit Send.

He answered on the second ring. "Dominic?"

"It's been a while, Uncle."

He exhaled deeply. "Yes, it has."

I hadn't seen him in almost seven years, and his voice told me Salvatore was right. He'd hardened in that time.

"I heard about the body," I said, getting right to business.

Silence, then, "And you want to know if I ordered Mateo Castellano's killing."

"I am curious why you'd mark him for everyone and their fucking grandmother to know it was you."

I played dumb. Even if Salvatore had spoken with him after our call—which I doubted—he wouldn't betray me.

"I have enemies, Dominic. You know how it is for us. And snitches aren't tolerated. Period." He sounded stern, unmoved, like a real head of the family.

But he still didn't answer my question.

"He'd done work for us in the past. His father was a friend to Franco."

"Business is business. Where are you, Dominic?"

"West." I wasn't giving him anything. The more I thought about it, the guiltier Roman became.

"Do you need money? I can send you something. Franco won't know."

My lip twitched at his charity. His giving away the Benedetti money like it was his.

"No, Uncle. I don't need money." I could hear the hostility in my tone. Surely he could too.

Silence. "You're well, then? Do you want me to do anything with the house? Will you be coming back?"

"No. I just grew curious when I heard about the murder, the brand. It didn't seem like you."

"The body shouldn't have been found," he said flatly.

Again, not taking responsibility, although not quite denying it either.

"But it was left where it could be. Seems like quite the oversight."

"I need to meet with Franco, Dominic. Good to hear from you."

"Tell him I said hello." I hung up and leaned back in my chair. I had eight days until the auction. Eight days—at the most—until Scava would come looking for Gia and me. Eight days to figure out how Roman was involved.

A clanging sound stole my attention, and I stood. We were locked in the house. No one was here but us, no one knew about this place but Roman, and he didn't know where I was. I'd left my pistol in the SUV, but checking Salvatore's desk drawers, I found one there along with some ammunition. I loaded the handgun and opened the study door, listening. Another sound came, this time from the kitchen. I walked that way, scanning the large, open space as I went, the ghostlike lumps beneath the dustcovers eerie in the darkness of night.

The kitchen light was on. I could see it from beneath the door. Just before I kicked it open, I heard Gia mutter a curse from the other side.

I opened the door and shook my head. She stood beside the counter, sucking on the tip of her finger. She froze too, her gaze falling from my eyes to the pistol I held. I put the safety on and tucked it into the back of my jeans, then cleared my throat. I scanned her from head to toe.

"I found the clothes in the closet."

She wore an oversize lavender sweater that fell

off the shoulder and a short, hip-hugging black skirt. On her feet she had on a pair of calf-length sheep-skin boots that accentuated her slender, toned legs. She'd wound her long dark hair up into a messy, wet bun, and her face had been scrubbed of all the dirt from the last few days.

Gia shuffled her weight to her other foot and stuck the tip of her finger back in her mouth. "I guess I forgot how to use a can opener."

She looked so different than she had in the cabin. Everything about her seemed changed, now that she had proper clothes, a shower, a freedom of sorts. She looked confident. And fucking beautiful.

I cleared my throat. "There's probably a first-aid kit somewhere, knowing Salvatore." I started opening cupboards and drawers to search for it, doing anything possible to not look at her.

"Salvatore?"

I stopped. I'd given too much away. "My brother."

"And his wife, Lucia."

I looked at her sharply. "How did you know?"

"She likes to write her name in her books," Gia said with a smile. Then that smile vanished. "You're not lying, are you? She wasn't…a slave…"

I thought about Salvatore and Lucia's relation-ship, how it had started, how it was meant to be, how it had turned out. "No." Simple answer. "They're married and have two kids, a third on the way. They love each other," I added, confused why I added that last part.

I knew what lay beneath my anger over how things had been way back when, how I was last in line, the one who would only inherit upon the death of my two older brothers. I always knew, I just had never admitted it—not to myself, not to anyone— but I was jealous. I'd always been jealous, especially of Salvatore.

"Here it is," I said, finding the kit, unable to meet her gaze until I got the expression on my face under control. Too much fucking emotion in this house. Too much memory.

I held it out to her, and she took it, an awkward silence between us. I looked at what was on the counter. She'd cleaned the space and found pasta, an unopened bottle of olive oil, and a can of tuna. A pot of water rumbled to a boil on the stove top.

"Think tuna fish is still good after seven years?"

I shrugged a shoulder. "I guess we'll find out."

"The pantry's stocked. Mostly expired food, though," she said, sticking the edge of a bandage in her mouth to tear it open.

I took it from her and stripped off the wrapper, then took her hand, ignoring the almost electrical charge upon touching her, denying its pull, and held the bloodied finger under the water to clean it. After drying it, I wrapped the bandage over it. "There." I released her as quickly as possible.

"Thanks." She cleared her throat and busied herself with the pasta.

"You didn't stay in your room." I picked up the can of tuna and opened it.

"I was hungry. And don't worry. When I heard you talking, I walked on by and didn't go into the room you don't want me to go into." She rolled her eyes.

I peeked into the pantry to check it out. She was right. There was a lot of food, most of which would have to be thrown away, but it'd do for a couple of days. At least while I figured out what I was doing.

Reaching into a cupboard where dishes were stacked, I took two, washed them, and set them on the counter.

"Do you know what information Mateo had on Victor Scava?"

She glanced at me but returned her attention to the pot when she answered. That's how I knew she was lying. Women tried to look busy when they told lies.

"No. Not specifically."

I sniffed the tuna. "I don't think I want to take a chance with this." I dumped the can with its contents into the trash can. Gia kept her gaze on the pasta. I washed my hands and dried them, then turned to her. "You don't mind?"

She gave me a nervous glance. "No, you're probably right."

I took her wrist, squeezed a little, and made her look at me.

"What information did Mateo have on Victor Scava?"

She studied me, her expression cool, hiding any pain she felt behind her clever eyes as she weighed her options.

"He'd worn a wire and recorded some conversations."

"Why did you lie when I first asked you?" I softened my grip and turned her arm over to look at the soft inside of her wrist, so small and delicate, then returned my gaze to hers.

I squeezed again, hurting her.

She flinched.

"Why did you lie?"

"I don't know."

We locked gazes while water boiled over in the pot. "Do you have access to the recordings?"

Her jaw tightened, and I twisted her arm behind her back, standing so close our bodies touched, hers small and soft, mine wanting.

"Yes."

I waited, twisting again so that she cried out.

"You're hurting me!"

"Where?" My voice came clear and calm compared to her panicked cry.

"At the library where I volunteer."

"You volunteer at the library?"

"I like to read."

"Where exactly?"

Water spilled out from under the lid of the pasta, hissing as it fell to the stove top.

"Mateo saved the file on one of the computers. A public computer. No one will find it."

I smiled. "Clever."

"You're really hurting me."

As if I needed a reminder. Hell, she was the one who needed one. "I told you I would."

She didn't have a comeback for that. I released her, and she stepped back, rubbing her arm. I turned down the burner.

"Did you listen to the recordings?" I asked.

She shook her head. "He'd only done it the day before he disappeared. I found out the next morning when I went in for my shift and found an envelope tucked under the keyboard at my workstation with my name on the front. I recognized Mateo's handwriting and looked when I got a chance. It was a scribbled note with a file path. That's all. I didn't have time to download it."

"Why didn't you tell me before?"

"You didn't ask me."

"Omission is lying."

"This is a fucked-up situation. I don't know left from right, and you go from torturing me to...to..." she gestured around the kitchen. "To fucking playing house."

"We're not fucking playing house."

"No fucking joke. My brother is dead. He died because of what was on that recording. Excuse me if I don't give it up without a second thought to a man I called Death!"

I backed off, filled a glass with water from the tap, and drank, forcing myself to breathe, to calm the fuck down. "What were you going to do with the file?" I finally asked.

She shrugged a shoulder. "Depended on what was on it. I guess turn them over, get Victor arrested, sent to prison."

"That's naive."

"You think I don't know that?"

I know she tried to sound hateful, clever, but she didn't. She just sounded sad and a little lost, actually.

I shook my head and took the pot of pasta off the burner.

"Don't lie to me again," I said without looking at her.

She stood back while I drained then plated the pasta and poured olive oil over it. After wiping down the kitchen table, I carried them over and set them down.

"Utensils are in there." I pointed.

She looked as though she wasn't sure if the conversation was over or not.

I went into the living room and found a bottle of wine, picked it up, and took it and two glasses back into the kitchen. Gia was sitting by then, silent, her gaze on me.

"Hope you like red." After rinsing the glasses, I sat at the table, poured the wine, and started to eat.

Gia ate too, each of us silent, the clanking of forks and knives on the plates the only sound breaking the heavy silence.

"What now?" she asked when we'd finished. "I don't want to hide."

"I need to listen to those conversations. Where's this library?"

"Philadelphia."

"We'll go tomorrow. Does Victor know about the recordings? Does he know that you know about them?"

"I don't think he knows there's a copy. I know he had a flash drive he destroyed. He's dumb enough to think that's the only copy. When he questioned me, he didn't ask me outright about it, so I think Mateo told him I wasn't involved and knew nothing."

"Don't underestimate him." I didn't think Victor was a stupid man. An asshole, but not stupid. Although arrogance tended to give one blinders. I'd learned that myself. Maybe his arrogance would get him caught.

After eating, Gia took the dishes to the sink and began to wash them. I watched her as I finished the wine. Neither of us spoke.

"I'm sleeping in Lucia's room?" she asked once she'd finished and wiped her hands clean.

I nodded.

"Where are you sleeping?"

"Not in your bed. Don't worry."

She gave me a smirk. "I'm going up to bed, then."

I watched her walk to the swinging door. "Gia," I called once she'd opened it.

She turned.

"Don't go anywhere else."

"Like where do you think I would go?" she asked, a hand on her hip.

I crossed one leg over the other and smiled, tilted my chair, and balanced on its back legs. "Like don't do anything stupid," I said, mimicking her.

"I wouldn't dream of it." She turned on her heel and left the room. I laughed outright, knowing she would do exactly what I told her not to.

I followed Gia upstairs half an hour later and walked into Salvatore's old bedroom. I had a shower then put on a fresh pair of briefs, opened the bedroom door a crack, pulled the cover off the bed, remade it with fresh sheets, and climbed in to wait. I hadn't locked Gia's door on purpose. I wanted to see what she'd do. She didn't trust me, which was wise, but I still needed her, and letting her go out there on her own would only get her in trouble. She most likely didn't believe that, but she didn't know this world like I knew it. Victor wouldn't just let her go.

And if Roman was involved, he was not one to leave loose ends. Gia was most definitely a loose end.

I leaned my head back against the pillow and closed my eyes. I was tired and had just drifted off to sleep when I heard it: the whine of a door unused for too long opening. I blinked my eyes open and listened. She walked softly, but the house was old, and it creaked. A lot. I waited until she was on the stairs before throwing the covers back and getting out of bed. I didn't bother pulling pants on and left the pistol on the bedside table. Instead, I crept out of the bedroom and watched her in the dark. She stumbled once, righted herself, and moved toward the front door. She picked up the keys to the SUV I'd stupidly left on the hallway table, and when I saw her punch in the code I'd used to get us inside—sneaky little thing; she'd been watching—I sprinted down the stairs.

Gia turned at the sudden noise, and that second was what I needed. I caught up to her by the time she'd stepped outside the door. Catching her around the middle, I almost fell on top of her as we stumbled forward.

"Never put anything past a woman with an agenda," I said, hauling her back inside.

"Let me go!" she screamed. "You fucking asshole, let me go!"

She kicked and punched. I turned her, tossed her over my shoulder, and slapped her ass. The door banged shut behind us as I carried a fighting Gia up the stairs and into my bedroom, where I tossed her down on the bed. Looking at her flushed face, her hair splaying out on my pillow, her eyes wild with fury—wild like a feral cat—it made me fucking crazy.

She lay still for all of a second, then tried to push me off. I flattened a hand on her chest and shoved her backward, climbed on top of her, and with one knee between her legs, trapped one of her thighs between mine. I laid my weight on her, caught her wrists, and transferred them to one hand. I then lightly tapped her face twice with the other.

"Like I said before, you're so fucking predictable."

"I was out the fucking door before you got to me!"

I gripped her chin, pressed my knee against her crotch, and watched her eyes darken. "Not far enough, though, considering you're in my bed now. You play, you pay, Gia."

She tried again to escape with her free leg, her torso, battling against me with every part of her she could move before I closed my mouth over hers for a quick kiss. I broke it long enough to warn her. "Don't fucking bite me again." I kissed her hard, devouring her, liking the taste of her, the fight in her. I forced her lips apart and bit down on one, not too hard but hard enough to taste the sweet, metallic taste of blood. I sucked.

Gia made some sound beneath me and, still keeping both of her wrists in one of my hands, I pushed the hoodie she had on up and cupped a breast, pinching her nipple through the bra and kissing her again, eating up her moan, my own, as I pressed my cock against her and slid my hand down to unbutton the jeans she must have switched into to make her getaway. I shoved them down, needing to free her wrists to grip the tight jeans with both hands and get them over her hips.

She pulled at my hair, but her eyes were closed and her mouth open, taking my tongue. I pushed my briefs halfway down my hips and gripped my cock, positioning myself between her spread legs, pulling back once to look down at her, at her pretty face, her lustful, panting mouth.

Her hands held onto my head, her fingers tangling in my hair, and when I fisted one handful of her dark mass and tilted her stubborn chin up, she reached to kiss me back, giving as good as she took, biting, her little teeth sharp as I brought my cock to her wet, hot entrance and met her gaze. I pushed into her, to the hilt in one thrust, eliciting a cry of pain from her, her fingers pulling at my hair again. I closed my eyes and kissed her again, moving inside her, her passage tight.

She tilted her hips, wrapping both legs around

me, and when I opened my eyes again, I found her watching me, her eyes dark and pupils dilated, biting her own lip as her pussy clenched around me, squeezing her pleasure from me. It took all I had to hold on until she released the vice-like grip of her thighs around my waist. I pulled out, my breath tight as I came on her belly, my cock throbbing between us, emptying, and finally, falling heavy on top of her, holding her beneath me, both of us spent, our breathing shallow gasps, her shuddering as I rolled off onto my back, one hand around her wrist, neither of us speaking.

Fuck.

    I looked over at him. Dominic watched the ceiling, his breathing slowing down. Sweat covered his brow. His hard and damp tattooed chest rose and fell. I studied the artwork. Intricate drawings in color and black-and-white spanned his right-side upper chest and arm ending just below his elbow. I knew it wrapped around back too. Over his shoulder. I'd glimpsed the edges earlier.

    Central to the design was a clock. Three-thirty-three. Heavy chains circled it, and a skull, a grim reaper, trapped a rosary between its grotesque teeth. Beneath it an eye, the blue-like crystal, watched, and around it, intricate dark designs of which I did not know the meanings bordered both clock and reaper. Within these were carved dates. The whole thing gave off a sense of regret. Of time having run out. Of doom and damnation.

Seeing this, the name I'd given him when I hadn't known his name fit.

Death.

And I'd just fucked him.

Or he'd just fucked me. Hell, we'd fucked each other. He hadn't had to make me. I'd spread my legs wide and gripped him hard, taking my pleasure from him, liking the taste of him, wanting it. Wanting him. Needing him inside me. Making sure he knew he wasn't taking anything from me.

I would not be a fucking victim. Not again. Not ever again.

Dominic turned to me, his gaze on my face.

"You fuck like you fight."

What was I supposed to say? Truth was, I'd never been like this with anyone else. And as much as I tried to convince myself that I did it in order to not give him power over me, I'd never wanted anyone like I wanted him. His darkness drew me as much as it should have repelled me. His loneliness, his secrets—they all worked like a magnet, making it impossible to ignore.

He slid off the bed and dropped his briefs on the floor. I couldn't help it; I let my gaze roam all over his body, his perfectly sculpted, powerful body.

"Up." He held out his hand.

I sat up, then stood, attempting to pull my jeans

over my hips as I did, feeling the smear of him leak down my belly beneath this stranger's hoodie I'd found in the closet.

"No," he said, pulling my hand away. "Take it off. Take everything off."

I gritted my teeth, but my belly fluttered at the command.

"Off, Gia. Now."

I stripped, angry, pushing my jeans down and stepping out of them and yanking the hoodie up and over my head. There was nothing erotic in my disrobing as I tugged the panties off and threw them on the floor as I unhooked my bra, dropping it onto the soiled pile. This man had seen me naked more often than clothed.

Dominic looked me over. Having his eyes on me, as much as I despised myself for it, only made me want. They made my pussy ache. Again.

But they also made me want to understand the darkness behind them.

"You look good wearing my cum."

"I hate you."

He closed his hand around the back of my neck and brought his face to mine.

"I don't care," he whispered.

I believed him. He did not care what I thought, what I felt. I wasn't sure he cared about much at all.

A shudder ran through me. He moved, leading me by my neck into his bathroom. It was similar to

mine but bigger, and for all the white in mine, his
was black. Droplets of water clung to the glass wall
and door of the shower. He reached in and turned
on the water.

"In."

I stepped into the stall, my belly to the spray.
That was when I felt him behind me, his naked body
touching mine.

I turned, panicked.

"What?"

He casually ran his gaze down to my ass, his
hands gripping my hips. He leaned down, his mouth
at my ear.

"I liked fucking you."

I froze when I felt him harden behind me again,
and when he rubbed himself against me as he
leaned over me to pick up the bottle of body wash, I
stopped breathing altogether.

"I think you liked it too."

He squeezed some out onto his palm and began
to rub it over my belly, my breasts, down to my sex
then back up as I sucked in air. He turned my face
and kissed me, his fingers finding my nipples as he
did so, the soap slippery as he kneaded them. His
tongue dipped inside my mouth, swallowing my
moan whole.

He turned me so my back pressed against the
wall, looked down at me, and spread my arms out to
either side. His cock lay thick and hard and ready

between us. God forgive me, but I wanted to touch it, to touch him, to kiss him, to feel him inside me.

"You're fucking beautiful."

He dipped his head to kiss my face, my neck, as the water of the shower rained down on us. He released one of my hands, and I brought it to his chest. He slid his hand down between my legs to first rub, then pinch my clit hard. Holding on to it, he leaned back to watch my face.

I grunted, an involuntary sound, and tried to reach up to kiss him, but he moved so his nose touched mine while he twisted and squeezed my clit.

"I should punish you for trying to run off."

He reached down and bite-kissed my lower lip.

"You won't," I said, closing my eyes as he squeezed harder. "Fuck."

"You like that?"

I curled my hand around the back of his neck and looked up at him, watching him watch me, knowing my vulnerability, knowing he saw it, the fact making me hotter. "Fuck, I'm going to come."

And beneath his gaze, I did, his fingers working as I panted and moaned, knees giving way so that he had to keep me upright, the orgasm quick after what we'd just done, and when he released my clit, I cried out, my eyes flying open to watch him lift me up only to impale me on his thick shaft.

It seemed the only word I could say was fuck again and again and again. Dominic chuckled, but his face grew serious as he took both of my wrists up over my head and brought his mouth to mine, his eyes wide open, fucking me harder, faster, until we both cried out with the release, my third, his second, the walls of my pussy clenching around the throbbing of his cock before he pulled out, again covering me with his cum.

I don't remember the rest of the shower. All I know is that by the time he tucked me into his bed and climbed in beside me, I was half gone, exhausted, thoroughly spent and empty. And when he turned to wrap his body around mine, I drifted off to the deepest, most restful sleep I'd ever had.

WHEN I WOKE THE NEXT MORNING, DOMINIC WAS already gone. I got out of bed, shamefaced at the soreness between my legs, the memory of the previous night at once humiliating and arousing.

I'd wanted him. I'd wanted every inch of him. And I'd had it.

I picked up the clothes I'd worn on my getaway attempt—which had almost succeeded—and crept out the door and down the hallway to my bedroom. Mine at least for the moment. I chose clothes out of Lucia's closet, thanking my lucky stars she and I were similar in size so most things fit well enough. It felt weird wearing a stranger's underwear, but I did anyway. After choosing today's outfit, I went into the bathroom to dress. I wanted to check how the brand was healing, since the scabs had started to peel off.

Standing at the mirror, I turned to my side and looked at my hip, picking at the crusted, raised skin, hating the mark, this permanent brand Victor had burned into me. It would remind me always of that night. Of his power over me. I knew it was stupid to think of it as weakness. Me alone against him and several of his men? I'd had no chance. I'd fought anyway, though, knowing I'd lose. Knowing I'd pay. That's what had earned me all the bruises, which were mostly faded by now. Victor was a bully. A thug. But it didn't mean I didn't feel shame every time I looked at the damned brand.

It was a circle containing what appeared to be a family crest maybe. I half expected it to be the Scava family crest, actually, and was surprised when it wasn't. I knew their symbol. It had been on a necklace James had given me after we'd been dating for a month. This wasn't it.

A *B* stood at the center of this mark, large and decorative. Spears protected that B and the *Famiglia* beneath. A lion's mane acted as backdrop and anchor of the design.

I leaned down to have a closer look, confused. What the hell kind of mark was this?

Would Dominic know? He seemed to know a lot about the mafia world. He'd called it "our world." He was an insider. I had assumed a foot soldier at first, then maybe a mercenary later, after I had gotten to know him a little more. He'd know what it was.

"Gia?" Dominic called out sharply from the bedroom.

I startled, grabbing a nearby towel and holding it up against me when he came into the bathroom, fully dressed in jeans and a tight-fitting, black-cashmere sweater. My eyes fell to the edges of the tattoo the V-neck left exposed. He stopped when he saw me, his blue-gray gaze sliding over me then rising to meet mine.

"What?" I asked once I could get my voice to work. I sounded annoyed, like him. It was an act, though. Was it an act for him? Did he act tough and cruel when he wasn't?

No. It would be a stupid mistake to think that.

"I want to go," he said, walking inside. He stopped, and it seemed to me he had to force himself to keep his gaze on mine even though he wanted to act like he didn't give a damn. Like he was unaffected. I knew he felt it too, this insane physical pull charged and sparking like a live wire between us.

"I just have to get dressed. Give me a minute."

His eyes narrowed a little, and I turned as he moved, keeping myself covered as best as I could, realizing the mirror exposed everything to him when his gaze slid to it.

"Please," I said, no longer able to help the dropping of my head. I needed to manage this, to figure out how to be around him. Fucking like we had last night, it didn't help. Only blurred the already fuzzy line.

He nodded, but I noticed how his gaze settled on my hip as if he too were trying to get a good look. I could ask him. I should. He'd know. But I pulled the towel over it instead. He turned to walk out the door, giving me room, letting me breathe as if he stole all the oxygen out of any room he entered.

I dressed quickly, brushed out the mess of my hair, pulled it into a ponytail, and headed out, stopping at the vanity in the bedroom to smear lip gloss on my lips and mascara on my lashes, not sure why I did. Not like I was trying to look good for him. He was my jailor. It'd be good if I could fucking remember that at some point.

Dominic stood in the hallway, keys in hand, impatience clear on his face.

"Can I eat something first?"

"You eat a lot."

"It's breakfast time."

He sighed, but his stance relaxed a little.

"I saw granola bars. They stay good forever, right? I'll just grab a couple." I walked away before he could stop me.

"Fine. Hurry up," he called out to my back.

In the pantry, I found the bars—dark chocolate and sea salt, my favorite—took two, grabbed two bottles of water, and went back out into the foyer, where I found him holding the door open for me. I walked toward the SUV. Dominic followed.

"I changed the code, so don't bother with another escape attempt."

"Wow, I warrant you having to change your security codes." I went to pull the SUV door open, but he pushed it shut, making me jump, making my heartbeat pick up. I looked up at him looming inches from me.

"I could just chain you to the bed if you prefer? Maybe I will, when we're back."

He stayed like that, his gaze burning into mine until I had to look away, conceding his win. Dominic pulled my door open and walked around to the other side without waiting for me to climb in. Once we were settled, he started the engine. A momentary panic came over me.

"What if someone's there? They see me?"

"Scava thinks you're at the cabin. No one's looking for you. I called already. Told them all was well. That we were on schedule."

I nodded as he drove out of the driveway, but my fear of Victor Scava—as nauseous as it made me to know I feared that man—was very real.

"Why didn't he kill me? Wouldn't that have been smart, in case I did know something?"

"You make a mistake if you think Victor Scava smart."

He made light of it, but then his face grew serious.

"He didn't want you fucked during the training either. The liaison was very specific."

"What?"

Dominic glanced at me as he navigated around the still opening gate. "What I said. And from what you told me, he didn't rape you. Did his men touch you?"

I shook my head. "He wouldn't let them."

"Why?"

"He was jealous of James. Maybe he wanted me for himself? He offered to spare me the branding if I fucked him. When I said no, he didn't force himself on me."

"And he sent you to me to train and sell off?"

"Maybe he planned on buying me himself."

"Sick fuck. I wouldn't put it past him. It would certainly return you...humbled."

"Let's talk about something else."

"Library address."

I gave it to him, and he programmed it into the GPS, studied the map, then turned the little machine off.

"I know where it is. It'll be a little over an hour."

I unwrapped one of the two bars.

"One of those for me?"

"No." As I brought the one to my mouth, he reached over and took it, biting into it himself.

"Don't be fucking rude, Gia."

"Fuck you, Dominic."

He grinned and shoved the rest of the bar into his mouth. "Shit. This is old."

I smiled, but my stomach fluttered, and my face heated. I had to turn and watch the passing scenery out the side window, unable to take his intense gaze. It felt like he read me like a damned book.

I focused on something else. On my mom. I wondered if she was planning Mateo's funeral. Wondered how worried she was about me. I didn't know if they'd trashed my apartment. They'd taken me when I'd walked out of a café after work. Did she even know I was missing? She had to by now, now that she knew about Mateo. She would get in touch with Angus Scava when she couldn't find me. It'd be the first place she'd go.

I almost asked Dominic about calling her but stopped myself. He'd say no. But this wasn't up to him. I'd make sure to get ahold of her or at least get a message to her that I was alive. I'd tell her to go back to Sicily. Hell, she was safer there than here.

At that, the thought that Victor would have hurt her crept into my mind.

No, he wouldn't have done that. He wouldn't have involved her. There was no reason to.

"Did he hurt my mother? Do you know?"

Dominic looked at me as if he hadn't heard my question. I repeated it.

"I haven't heard anything, but I haven't been looking for news. I'll make a call and find out."

To my surprise, he took out his phone and dialed a number then and there. It was to his brother, Salvatore. They spoke for a few minutes, Dominic asking for information and Salvatore, I assumed, promising to call back as soon as he found out.

"Thanks," I said. But that wasn't going to be enough for me. I'd make some calls myself once we got to the library and he was busy copying files.

13

By the time we found parking and walked into the beautiful old library building on Vine Street, it was late morning. Traffic sucked, and parking was always an issue. I held Gia's hand. To anyone who glanced our way, we looked like a normal couple walking into the building.

Gia's hand felt clammy in mine, and I knew she was nervous. I didn't think she had any reason to be, although if anything did happen, we'd be unarmed, since I'd left my pistol in the SUV, assuming I'd have to pass through a metal detector.

"Lead the way," I said casually even though I looked at every single person in the place as we headed toward the long row of public-use computers.

"Hey, Gia. You missed your shift the other day."

A man came toward us, his face beaming at

Gia. A frown replaced that stupid smile, though, when I moved in closer and put my arm around her waist, feeling much more possessive than I maybe should.

Of course she'd run into people she knew. She fucking volunteered here.

Gia tensed beside me.

"Smile," I told her.

"Hi, Ron," she said, her voice tight. "I wasn't feeling well. I asked my friend to call. She must have forgotten."

Ron's gaze kept shifting to me, and I almost laughed at his struggle to keep smiling.

"No, she never did. I covered for you. No worries."

"Thanks, Ron."

I cleared my throat. "Aren't you going to introduce me, honey?" I had to bite my tongue not to laugh outright at the look on Gia's face.

"Um, Ron this is...um...Donnie."

She recovered fast and relaxed. Even smiled. At least for a minute.

"Her boyfriend," I said, gripping her tighter and pulling her close. *Donnie? WTF?*

"Oh, uh, nice to meet you. I guess. I didn't know you had a boyfriend," Ron said, trying not to look at me.

"Yep," I chimed in. "Haven't been together long, but once you get a taste of Gia, well, nothing quite like it..." I winked at her mortified face. "We're on a tight schedule, though," I said, checking my watch.

"Nice to see you, Ron," Gia said, walking stiffly toward the public-use computers.

"Nice to see you," Ron called out.

It took all I had not to flip him off.

"What was that?" she asked in a sharp whisper. "How could you say that?"

"Donnie? What the fuck kind of name is *Donnie*?"

She stopped and turned to me, one hand on her hip, one eyebrow lifted.

"Did you want me to tell him your real name?"

"You couldn't come up with anything better than *Donnie*?"

She only grinned. "That one," she said, dropping the conversation as an elderly woman vacated a computer.

"Let's go." Someone else tried to take the seat, but I shoved Gia ahead and onto the chair.

"I have been waiting!" the woman said.

"Us too." Ignoring her, I watched Gia pick up the mouse and navigate to the file. Mateo had hidden it well while keeping it in plain sight.

"Here, this is it," she said.

I took the thumb drive out of my pocket and handed it to her. "Copy it."

She stood. "I have to use the bathroom. You copy it, and I'll be right back."

Before I could argue, she was gone. The woman we'd butted in front of was pointing at us and talking to the man at the counter, so I knew we had limited time. I took over, copying the file onto my thumb drive, hoping Gia wouldn't be dumb enough to try to run off. I didn't think she would, though. Not with this evidence in my hands now, not knowing I could copy then delete the file. Although I wouldn't. It was my backup.

"Sir."

The man who worked at the library approached my seat with the woman just as the file finished copying.

"That's him. He just butted right in front of me!"

I ignored them both, double-checked the complete file had copied onto my thumb drive, and ejected it.

"I'm done," I said, heading in the direction Gia had gone while looking for signs to the bathrooms.

But I didn't find her at the bathrooms. Muttering a curse under my breath, I walked fast up and down the aisles looking for her. I was going to kill her. My temper grew hotter and hotter with every step I took. And then I saw her. Talking to fucking Ron behind a desk, a phone tucked between her neck and shoulder.

"Gia!"

All heads turned. Someone 'shushed' me and I sped toward her, walking fast without breaking into a run. I wanted to slap the phone away. I saw her talking and reached her just as she hung up.

"Donnie! There you are. Are you done? I couldn't find you."

"Yeah, I'm done. We're done," I said, grabbing her arm as she moved around the counter. "Let's go."

"Gia?" Ron called out.

"What the fuck was that?" I hissed through gritted teeth.

"I needed to call my mom. I knew if I asked, you wouldn't let me, so I didn't bother asking! She's worried sick!"

"Did you tell her where you were?"

"I don't even know where the house is, and no, I didn't mention the library. She's planning my brother's funeral, Dominic! I know you don't have a heart, but try, just try to be fucking human for a minute!" She wiped a tear from her face as we reached the car.

I bit my lip, wanting to shake her but feeling sorry for her and hating her—or wanting to hate her —for what she said. I mean, she was right. It's not like I had a fucking heart. Monsters didn't have hearts.

So why the fuck did her words sting? Why did I give a crap?

I slammed her door shut and took a minute, my fingernails digging into my palms as I got hold of my anger. I climbed into the driver's seat and pulled the

SUV out of the garage, still so fucking mad I could hardly breathe. Gia sat staring straight ahead, and I could see her eyes glisten. She was trying not to cry.

"That was a stupid thing to do."

She didn't answer.

"Fucking stupid, Gia."

Nothing.

We drove in silence all the way back. Once we were back in the house, Gia slipped from my grip and ran upstairs to her room, slamming the door behind her. Fine. That was just fine. She wasn't going anywhere; we were locked in tight. I'd deal with her later. I wanted to listen to the recordings first, and I wanted to do it without her.

After grabbing my laptop out of the duffel bag, I headed into the study and closed the door behind me. I plugged the thumb drive into the port, hit the button to play and leaned over my computer, listening.

The quality was shit, grainy as fuck. Mateo's equipment either sucked, or he wasn't wired right. I could make out Victor Scava's voice, his laugh grating on me, his mood swings in the span of a few minutes giving me whiplash. The man was insane, clearly. He'd say one thing, then the exact opposite just a few minutes later.

Much of the conversation was useless, at least for my purposes. He talked about moving drugs. Moving money. I didn't care about those things. I wanted to know about the trafficking. I wanted to hear Roman's voice.

Mateo must have been recording for a good month. I wondered how they'd figured out he was wired. I thought of how they'd killed him. Right then, Victor laughed again. I fisted my hands.

"Sadistic motherfucker."

How are you different?

I shut down that voice and listened, replaying a piece here or there. It was only toward the end that things got interesting.

I never did hear Roman's voice. There was one time Victor talked on the phone with someone. Victor was pissed after that call. The conversation was about moving product. This particular product, I figured out, was living and breathing. Whoever he was talking to was tearing Victor a new one. Victor had fucked up apparently. Typical. After he hung up was when I knew who it was.

"That fucking asshole thinks he's the boss of me! Fucking imposter. He thinks he can tell me what to do. First old man Scava and now him."

"Take him out, boss?"

Static.

"No. Can't do that, not yet."

Silence. Static.

"If my pussy uncle found out—"

Static cut off the rest of the sentence. When

Victor came back in, he was laughing and someone was getting hit.

"I have a much better idea. The fucker's gonna die, but it's not gonna be me to do it."

A struggle, someone grunting. More punches followed, the sound of furniture breaking.

I thought of Mateo watching the beating, maybe administering it. I wondered what had gone through his head then. He had to know what would happen to him if Victor found the wire.

"The Benedetti imposter's gonna get what's coming to him. I'll let my uncle be the one to do it, though."

"How, boss?"

"Thinks I'm fucking stupid. Thinks I don't know he's keeping me on as his fall guy, treating me like some fucking foot soldier and taking over what I started. What rightfully belongs to me!"

My heart raced. Static cut him off, but I had everything I needed.

"I'll let my uncle dig his and that asshole's grave."

Static again, then laughter.

"Two birds, one stone, and all that shit."

I checked the date on that recording. It was the twenty-third of December. Not a full twenty-four hours before Mateo had disappeared.

Victor Scava killed Mateo because he was a snitch, but he used Mateo's death to start a war. A war within the Benedetti family. He wanted Roman out.

Well, I guess that was one thing he and I could agree on.

With Roman out and no more Benedetti sons to take over, Victor Scava could move into Benedetti territory. Take it over. Hell, maybe he'd overthrow his own uncle in the process.

But if he thought I'd stand by and watch, he had another thing coming.

14

I sat in my room, waiting out Dominic's anger, figuring it was smart to just stay out of his way, at least for now. I picked through Lucia's closet, feeling like some sort of criminal to be looking through her things, snooping almost. She had a lot of books. I could read for a while.

I chose one from her shelf and sat on the bed, flipping it open. I didn't get very far, though. Not past the first blank page, where she'd made a sketch she'd then crossed out in angry lines. I recognized the drawing, but it took me a minute to realize why I knew it. I stared at it for a long time, knowing it was a drawing of the mark on my hip. I read the words *Benedetti Killers* she'd written beneath the drawing. I wondered about her. Those weren't the words of a wife in love. Had Dominic lied to me about that? Was Lucia as much a victim as I?

I didn't need to compare the sketch to my mark. I'd studied it. Hell, I'd memorized it. I knew it was the same. I just needed to figure out the connection.

Growing up, my father had shielded me from his work, but being the daughter of a foot soldier, there was only so much you could keep from your family. We were kids, Mateo and I, but we had eyes. We saw.

Mateo's introduction to the world our father lived in came on his eighteenth birthday. My family had a big birthday party for him, a gathering for extended family and friends we hadn't seen in years. There must have been three hundred people at our house that day with Franco Benedetti at the top of the guest list. In fact, he'd taken the opportunity to meet with several men, including my father, during the party.

I obviously hadn't been invited to the meeting, not only for the fact of my gender, but I was only seven. My father introduced Mateo to Franco Benedetti that day. Mateo had been given his first-ever job; something small, thank goodness. I remember how proud he'd been. How excited.

Franco Benedetti liked my father for some reason. He treated him differently than his other soldiers. My father considered it a promotion when he became one of Franco's personal body guards, traveling with him everywhere, coming home less and less often. Mateo had begged to join him so many times, looking at Franco like he was God almighty. He'd never been allowed, though.

It was during one of these trips that my father was killed. He died protecting Franco Benedetti. He'd saved Benedetti's life by sacrificing his own. That was why Franco had promised to take care of Mateo, me, and our mother.

I hadn't known Mateo was at the meeting, and I'd gone looking for him during the party. I wanted cake, but my mother said we needed to wait for Mateo to sing "Happy Birthday" first, so I'd decided to go get him myself. I remember I'd taken the envelope Mr. Benedetti had dropped off for him, Mateo's birthday gift. My mother had commented on its thickness, knowing it contained cash. She'd put it on the top of the refrigerator for safekeeping, but I'd climbed up on a chair and gotten it down, wanting to take it to Mateo, knowing how happy he'd be. I loved him. He was the best big brother. He was protective and even humored me by playing with my dolls when I begged.

Well, I hadn't found him and had wandered farther from the property, not realizing two older boys had seen me with the envelope and were following. They cornered me when we were far enough away that no one would hear and told me to give it up, give them Mateo's birthday gift.

No way I was doing that, and I told them so.

Well, they didn't exactly take no for an answer,

and I realized that day how powerless I was without Mateo to save me. It pissed me off, actually and I readied to fight, knowing I'd lose, refusing to return to the house empty-handed. At least Mateo would know I'd fought for him.

But I hadn't had to because another boy had been there too. An older one, a friend of Mateo's. Or at least someone I'd seen with Mateo a couple of times.

That boy...I stopped breathing.

That's why I'd felt something, some sort of safety or protection around Dominic at the cabin. That's why the strange feeling of familiarity.

He'd been there that day. He'd been at my house. At my brother's birthday party.

Dominic Sapienti was Dominic Benedetti.

Dominic Benedetti had told those boys to take a hike and had given me the envelope back.

He had saved me that day, and later, his father had vowed to keep my family safe. Dominic knew this. If he didn't, I'd told him on the drive from the cabin to this house, and he'd said nothing. And now, I wore his family's brand on my hip, forever marked. They'd burned it into Mateo's chest before they'd killed him. Dominic Benedetti or his family had killed Mateo. They had ordered my kidnapping, sending me to be sold as a sex slave. This from the man for whom my father had given his life.

I went downstairs to confront him, assuming he

was behind the closed doors of the one room he'd told me I didn't have permission to enter. When I opened those doors, though, I stopped dead at what I saw. The splattering of blood on the walls, the residue of red where blood had seeped into the marble floor. The bottle of half-drunk liquor on the table. Glasses with the residue of whiskey and dust as if someone were drinking now. As if that room had been frozen in time.

I realized nothing was covered in the dining room. No dustcloths, nothing. Two chairs lay on their sides, evidence of a night I knew about. Of the night that brought on the decline of the great Benedetti family. The night when one brother had almost killed the other.

I looked around the room and ran a hand through my hair, trying to make sense of this. I saw the large glass case to the side, and inside it, displayed and dusty, sat a book, the large, heavy tome of the Benedetti family. I opened the glass door and took it out, touching the carving of the family crest on the cover made of wood. I traced each of the grooves, every hair on my body standing on end. It took me a moment to open the book.

Generations of Benedetti were pictured inside. I didn't care about those long gone, though. I turned the pages, working toward the end of the book, noticing the binding, knowing it was a book that would grow with time, adding more and more members as old generations died and new were born. I saw ancient-looking certificates of birth, of marriage, of lineage. I recognized names, unions made to bind families together, making the Benedetti one of the most powerful, if not the most powerful, crime family in America.

At least the most powerful until that night. Until Franco witnessed the battle between his sons and nearly died himself from a heart attack.

That was when things began to fall apart for the Benedetti family.

I turned the book over, laying it so I could get to the later pages. I saw the photograph of Sergio in his parents' arms. Saw the family grow with Salvatore's birth, Sergio as a toddler.

Knowing what I would find on the next page, I flipped past it, not wanting to see just yet. I got to the photograph of Sergio and his wife on their wedding day. She'd been laughing so hard her eyes were screwed shut in the picture. Then came the date he'd died. Then the one announcing his son's birth just months after his death.

He'd never even seen his son.

I flipped back the few pages I'd skipped, my heart racing, blood pounding against my ears, the noise unbearable. I found the page that pictured the third son. Dominic. His parents smiled, but I saw the strain in their faces, the effort it took. They didn't look like they had with the other two births.

The most recent photograph of Dominic had to be at least ten years ago. He'd have been twenty-five. He stood beside his father at a party, his arm around his father's shoulder, his grin cocky, everything about him carefree, as if he were the boy who would have it all. The girl by his side stared up at him, enamored with him, when he seemed barely aware of her presence.

Dominic Benedetti with his father, Franco. The man who'd pledged to take care of my family. Did Victor work for him? Was it a sort of rebellion against Angus Scava? He knew Angus didn't like him. But did that mean Victor did Franco Benedetti's bidding? It made sense. The brand screamed the truth. Mateo and I had been branded with the Benedetti family crest, not the Scava mark. Franco Benedetti had fucked us over, had promised my father he'd protect us then killed my brother and taken me prisoner. Dominic, a man I thought my ally in some strange way, was his son. I wore on my hip Dominic Benedetti's mark as if I were branded cattle, a thing owned, not a human life at all.

He'd lied to me.

He'd told me Victor was playing a game, but Dominic was the master game maker.

Fury raged inside me.

I'd been fooled.

I'd been played.

I'd fucked my enemy. I'd slept beside him, clinging to him, and I felt sick for it.

I picked up the first thing I saw and screamed, sending it crashing into the bloodstained wall, watching the glass shatter into shards on the marble.

I didn't stop.

15

Something crashed to the floor in the other room. Gia screamed. I grabbed the pistol and jumped to my feet, running through the living room toward the open dining-room doors, where the sound of something else shattering had me cocking my gun, ready to fire.

Her scream came again, but I didn't hear fear in it.

I turned the corner and kicked one of the double doors open all the way to find Gia standing in the middle of the bloodstained floor, shattered glass all around her, her face the image of fury.

"You!"

She sneered at me, her lip curled, her eyes hard. No fear, not at seeing me. Not at seeing the pistol I held cocked and ready to kill.

"It was you."

She picked up the bottle that still sat on the dining-room table from that night. Franco and Roman had been drinking it. She raised it.

"What's going on, Gia?" I asked, holding out one hand, palm flat, while I de-cocked the gun and slid it into the back waistband of my jeans.

Déjà vu.

Except I hadn't disarmed the pistol that night.

She threw the bottle at me, rage burning her face as I sprang to the right. Glass shattered at my feet, sticky liquid staining my jeans.

"Calm down. What's going on?"

"He was your friend." She looked around the room for the next thing she'd chuck.

I moved toward her slowly, watching her take aim with one of the crystal tumblers on the table.

"My father took a bullet for yours. He was supposed to protect us! He pledged it the day my father died *for him*!"

She threw it. I sidestepped, and the glass smashed against the wall behind me.

"And you...you were Mateo's friend."

"Gia." I kept my voice calm, moving in closer, trying not to look at the stain on the marble floor, the splatters on the wall I'd ordered no one to clean.

"You like your little masks, don't you?" she asked, looking around the room, finding nothing left to throw and facing me again. "Tell me, was it you who branded Mateo? Was it you who branded me?" She sucked in a breath and pressed the heels of her hands to her eyes. "I never saw your faces. Everyone but Victor wore a mask." She looked at me again. "You sick fucking asshole."

"Gia," I said, close enough now to take her wrists as she tried to hit me. "Gia, stop."

"Did you kill him?"

"No."

"Were you there? Did you hold him down? Did you—"

A sob cut off her words, and she bowed her head into my chest.

"Did you chop off his tongue?"

"No." *Christ. She'd seen that?*

"I know who you are. I know."

I let go of her.

She sank to the floor, her face in her hands.

"Gia." I crouched down.

"Don't touch me."

She shoved me away and sat with her back leaning against the blood-splattered wall. I sat across from her, watching her come apart.

"Don't..." she started, but her words trailed off to nothing.

"The brand was a setup. Part of Victor's plan, Gia."

"Mateo was trying to do the right thing."

She shook her head, not hearing me at all, her face scrunched up in confusion.

I noticed the book on the floor beside her then. The book of the great Benedetti family. Our family crest—no, not fucking ours! When the fuck would I get that into my head? When the fuck would I stop calling it mine?

"You knew all along," she muttered. She looked up, her eyes red and puffy.

But I had to look at the book again. At the open page. At Franco and my mother, standing there holding their second born, Salvatore. Sergio standing beside them, his hand in his father's. Dark wood paneled the background, and above it a painting of the damned crest. Franco stood taller, straighter, his face beaming, so fucking proud. The perfect fucking family.

"The blood, it's when you tried to kill your brother."

Her words broke into my thoughts. Forced me to hear.

"You think no one knows, but we all know. I should have recognized the names."

I turned my gaze to hers. I had no defense.

"You must have thought me pretty stupid, huh?" she asked.

"No."

"You're sick, Dominic. You're a sick, sick bastard."

I felt myself go still, my chest tightening. She was right. Every word she said, truth. My guilt must have been etched on my face, because Gia reached out a hand to shove me backward.

"You're a hate-filled monster."

She rose onto unsteady feet, and I followed, shaking my head but unable to speak, stepping closer to her as she pounded a fist against my chest.

"Sick."

I shoved her against the wall and closed my mouth over hers. It wasn't a kiss, it was to shut her up. I would eat her words, so I wouldn't have to hear them. Because what she said was true. I didn't deny the facts. But to have someone say them. To have *her* say them—

Her hands came to either side of my head, and she tugged at my hair, her body yielding just a little even as she tried to push me off. She turned her face to the side and spit, as if the taste of me repulsed her.

"You're a murderer."

I gripped her jaw and forced her face back to mine, looking at her, holding it tight enough she couldn't speak. I then wrapped one hand around her waist and lifted her, carrying her the few steps to the table, laying her on her back.

"Shut up," I said as I moved my hands to undo the buttons of her jeans.

"You betrayed your family."

"I said shut the fuck up." I tugged them and her panties down.

She grunted, pushing herself upright. Her hand came up, and she slapped me hard.

"What do they do to those who betray their own family?" she hissed. "A snitch loses his tongue. What do you lose?"

Everything. Every fucking thing.

I gripped a handful of her hair, tasting my own blood. I'd bit my lip.

"Again," I said.

She slapped me again, this time with the back of her hand. She was the only person to speak the truth out loud. To tell me what I was without fear of me.

My cock grew harder watching her, watching the raw fury burn her eyes.

"Again."

She obeyed, her palm open, colliding with my cheek. Blood splattered onto her face, but she didn't flinch and she didn't stop and I stood there letting her. Holding her in place by her hair, letting her slap my face until it went numb, until she grunted with the effort, until her hand tired. She stopped slapping and dragged her fingernails down both cheeks, drawing more blood. I smashed my mouth against hers again, set the pistol on the table, and unzipped my own jeans, pushing them down, trying to get between her legs, unable to with her tight jeans at midthigh.

"I hate you," she said against my mouth.

I licked her lips, then took one into my mouth and devoured it, devoured her, sliding her off the table to flip her onto her stomach and push her down over it.

"I hate you," she repeated when I gripped her hips and spread her open, bringing my cock to her wet pussy and thrusting into her.

I grunted, needing this, needing to possess her, desperate to be inside her, connected with her. Her breathing hitched as she said something else, something I couldn't make out, and with a hand in her hair I turned her face to the side and leaned down over her back, my mouth to her cheek, to the side of her mouth.

"Hurt me, Gia," I whispered, close to release.

She shook her head as much as my grip allowed. "No. I'm not going to hurt you. I'm going to *kill* you," she said, her eyes closing momentarily as her pussy tightened around my cock. "I'm going to fucking kill you, Dominic Benedetti."

"Do it. Kill me," I whispered as she sucked my lip into her mouth, then bit, and I held her to me, thrusting hard once more, coming like a fucking volcano erupting inside her, not caring that she didn't come, not even pulling out, emptying, emptying, my arms tight around her until finally, spent, my cock slid out, semen slippery between us.

I stumbled backward and pulled my jeans up. Gia straightened, turning to me, my pistol in her hand. I watched her and she me, and I knew what she wanted. I saw her hate; saw her need, her desire.

"Were you there? When they killed my brother?" she asked, cocking the gun. "They wore masks. They all wore masks."

"No."

"Were you there when Victor had me branded?"

I shook my head and dropped to my knees before her and gripped her hips, tilting them toward me, taking her clit into my mouth and sucking, my scent on her, my taste on her. Her free hand gripped the table at her back, and I spread her open, her pussy dripping, a mixture from both of us. I smeared it up along her opening with my fingers, sucking her clit harder, feeling her knees give away as she cried out, coming, the hand still holding the cocked pistol on my shoulder to keep herself upright, her body shuddering, her breath hitching.

I loosened my hold on her and looked at her face, her beautiful, soft, sad face. She slid to her knees, and we stayed like that, watching each other, enemies, lovers, pawns in a game.

"Kill me, Gia," I whispered, my voice failing as I took her hand, the one that held my gun, and set the barrel at my chest. "Kill me after I kill my uncle. After I kill Victor."

She watched me, and for a long moment, I wasn't sure what she'd do. All it would take was the quick pull of her finger, and I'd be dead. Out of my fucking misery.

I wasn't even scared.

But she shook her head and set the weapon down beside us and held onto my bloodied cheeks. She ran her tongue up along my face, then brought crimson-stained lips to mine and slid her tongue between my lips before kissing me, the taste of her mixed with that of my own blood.

"I want to pull the trigger on Victor. *I* kill him. Not you."

She barely took her lips from mine as she muttered the words.

I nodded and kissed her and remembered how I'd called Isabella my vengeful little bitch once. I grinned behind the kiss, holding onto Gia like she held me. Knowing we knelt on the very spot I'd nearly killed Salvatore, knowing I'd fucked Gia standing on the stain of his blood. Knowing I was truly a monster because I didn't find it wrong. I didn't feel guilt. Not anymore. And as I stripped Gia's clothes off her and spread her legs open to feast again, I felt good. I felt hungry. Hungry for vengeance. Hungry for her.

Gia was my match. My perfect match.

I was right when I'd told her she was like me. She hated like me.

And I trusted she'd do what she promised.

She'd end me once this was finished.

I'd help her get her revenge.

And then I'd be finished.

And I'd take all that was left of the Benedetti family down with me once and for all.

16

GIA

I kept Dominic's gun. I laid it beneath the pillow beside me and slept.

I wasn't sure if Dominic slept that night. I don't even remember getting upstairs and into bed after what happened in the dining room.

The scent of sex permeated my room. It was the first thing I smelled, his smell, my own, when I opened my eyes. I sat up in bed, rubbed my face, and picked up the loaded weapon.

I'd kill Victor Scava with this gun.

Then I'd kill Dominic with it.

He wanted me to. He'd asked me to. I finally understood him last night. I finally saw him. Really saw him. He'd been at odds all along, at once my cruel captor, then ally, then lover. I knew why now.

I got out of bed and walked through the door that connected our bedrooms. I didn't care what I looked like, that I was naked, unwashed. That his cum had dried and crusted between my legs. I didn't care.

I only cared about the gun in my hand.

Dominic walked out of the bathroom, a towel wrapped low around his waist, another in his hands, drying his hair.

"How long have you been hiding?" I asked.

He stopped and looked at me.

"You need a shower, Gia."

He resumed walking, tossing the towel he used to dry his hair on the bed.

"How long?"

He stopped and turned to me, paused, then walked right up to me and cocked his head to the side.

"Get your facts straight before you walk around demanding answers with a gun in your hand."

He easily wrapped his hand around the wrist that held the gun.

"You need a shower," he said again.

"Can't stand your own smell?"

His eyes narrowed, and he forced the weapon out of my hand.

"It's mine!" I followed him to the dresser, trying to reach around him to get it when he opened a drawer and set it inside.

He caught my wrists and walked me backward a few steps.

"You need to keep your shit together, and you need to have a fucking shower."

"It's mine," I said again, looking up into his eyes, blue-gray pools so deep, I could lose myself inside them if I wasn't careful.

"I'm not taking it away. It's yours. Come on."

His voice was quiet, as if talking down a child throwing a tantrum.

He walked me into the bathroom and ran water into the tub. The first time he'd bathed me came rushing back, and I pulled away. But he kept hold of my wrist and held me there.

"Relax. Do you want me to give you something to relax?"

"Your little pills? No, thank you."

"Then be a good girl and get in the tub."

I glanced at the tub filling up with water, saw him check the temperature and adjust it.

"In."

"I want this off too." I pointed to the collar.

"And I told you once before, it will come off when I'm ready to take it off."

"Why are you doing this?"

"Because I need you to keep your shit together if we're going to get the bastards who killed Mateo and branded you."

I took in his words, studying him, his face, his eyes. He gestured once more to the tub and released my wrist when I climbed in. And I remembered something.

"You have a daughter."

He stopped, as if that were the last thing he expected me to say. Then he nodded once and brought over a bottle of body wash and a washcloth. He sat on the edge of the tub, dipped the cloth inside, and rung it out before squeezing body wash onto it. He began to lather my neck and back.

"Effie. She's eleven now."

His face looked so sad right then. It was like the man I'd glimpsed last night, the one who hurt. The broken one.

"I haven't seen her in a long time. Almost seven years."

"Why?"

He looked at me, and for a moment, I thought he was going to say something other than what he said, but then, as if he'd just given himself over to it, the truth came out.

"Because I'm a coward."

He dropped my gaze, dipped the washcloth into the water, and brought it back to me.

"She's better off anyway."

"What happened that night?"

He knew the night I meant. There was no other night.

"I shot my brother," he said flatly. "I almost killed him."

He refused to look at me. I reached for his hand the next time he dipped the cloth into the water and held it, then reached up to cup his face, seeing the scratches I'd left yesterday, thinking I should have bandaged them for him.

Dominic met my gaze, the look in his eyes strange, dark...empty. As if he'd used the last seven years to create a gap so wide, a hole so big, he'd never be able to cross the chasm.

He shook my hand off and resumed washing me, his attention wholly on that as he spoke.

"Don't misunderstand, Gia. I'm not good. Being a father doesn't make me good. Missing my daughter doesn't make me good. When I say she's better off, I mean it. I know myself. I know what I've done, what I am. I know what I'm capable of."

He hated himself. I'd accused him of that very thing in the beginning, and it was more true than I'd realized then. And some part of me, hell, not some part, not any part. *My heart*...it broke for him.

"Tell me about that night," I said after a while, once he'd started shampooing my hair.

"Salvatore finally figured out what was going on. Roman—hell, Roman had been looking for shit all along, I have no doubt of that. Anything to discredit me. Although, it's not like I needed much help with that."

"From the beginning. Please."

"Salvatore and Roman figured out I was the

father of Isabella DeMarco's little girl, Effie. The DeMarcos were our biggest rival then."

He paused, giving me a minute to absorb.

"We'd met when we were both young—well, she was young, and I was stupid. Didn't know who she was at first, and she didn't know who I was. She got pregnant, and the night we'd agreed to tell our families, I chickened out. She didn't. She told. And then, she disappeared. It was either that or old man DeMarco wanted her to get rid of the baby."

"I remember the war between your families." It came back vaguely. I'd been too young to really pay attention all those years ago. "Lucia was given to Salvatore like she was restitution or something."

"Yeah, something like that."

"It would have been her older sister if you hadn't gotten her pregnant?"

He nodded.

"Well, they figured it out," he continued. "Luke, her cousin, an imbecile if you ask me, managed to get himself shot by another imbecile. It's what triggered everything. Roman, my fucking uncle," he spat the words, "tried to pin it on me, but Salvatore, my brother who can do no wrong, just wanted peace. Well, fuck peace. This is the fucking mob. You don't get to choose peace."

He stopped shampooing for a minute and looked off into the distance. I was glad for it. In his growing anger at his family, the massage had turned a little rough.

"You know what you get if you're the last-born son in a mafia family, Gia?"

I waited, eyes on his when he turned back to me.

"Nothing. You get nothing."

He picked up shampooing again, and I bit my tongue to keep quiet and let him tell his story.

"And if you're a bastard—"

"Bastard?"

"I was pissed that night. Salvatore, he could never be boss. Never. Hell, he didn't even want it. But he was getting it. He called a meeting at his house, and my uncle dragged me to it. I admit, I was half drunk when I walked into the dining room with a loaded gun." He shook his head. "Then my father called Isabella a whore. Called my mother a whore. I couldn't take it."

He swallowed. I watched his throat work.

"It was always about Sergio. About Sergio's kid. Well, he had another grandchild. It was time he acknowledged that." He shook his head. "But he had another card up his sleeve."

Dominic grimaced, his eyes distant as if he saw it all again.

"Always did have the last word, Franco Benedetti."

"What—"

"Turned out I wasn't his." He met my gaze. "I was

the bastard son of a foot soldier and Franco Benedetti's wife."

Oh. My. God.

My mouth fell open. Nobody knew this. They only knew Dominic had tried to kill his brother.

He shifted his gaze to mine. "You see, I wasn't actually trying to kill Salvatore."

Dominic shook his head again, eyes glistening, at least for a moment.

"He just got between me and Franco and almost died for it."

Dominic dropped the washcloth he'd picked up into the bathtub. Water splashed, and he stood. He turned his back to me and ran a hand through his hair.

"Dominic," I started, climbing out, dripping wet, soap suds and shampoo clinging to me. I went to him, laid a hand on his shoulder, and forced him to turn around.

"I almost killed the only person in that family who is worthy of living, Gia."

He had a crazed smile, one I knew kept a surge of emotion at bay.

"You didn't, though. You didn't."

He pushed me away when I put my hands on his shoulders, but I refused to budge. I took his face in my hands and made him look at me, made him see me. See the present moment. See what was right there in front of his eyes.

"He was wrong to tell you like that."

"Leave it alone, Gia. Leave me alone."

"No." I kissed him even as he tried to walk past me. I just kissed him, trying to hold on to him.

His hands came to my waist, still trying to push me away, trying to make his way out of the bathroom.

"Gia—"

"You need to keep your shit together if you're going to get the bastards," I said, kissing him harder when he stopped, when he heard the words he'd used on me just a little bit ago. "Kiss me, Dominic."

He looked down at me, then turned his face to the side, his hands still on my waist, but no longer pushing me away.

"I said fucking kiss me."

This time, he didn't turn away and he didn't pull back. He kissed me, walking me backward out of the bathroom, his arms wrapping around me as his kiss became hungry, ravenous even. When the backs of my knees hit the bed, he pushed me onto it and stood back to drop his towel, his erection hard against his belly, eyes hungry as I lay back and spread my legs for him.

"Dominic," I managed as he knelt between them, then lowered himself onto me.

"I came inside you yesterday," he said between kisses.

"I'm protected." I kissed him back, our hunger matched. "And clean."

"Me too."

He thrust inside me then, and for the first time since we'd been together, we didn't fuck. We made love. Dominic moved slowly deep inside me and held me so close, there was never an inch between us. Our eyes were open the entire time, locked on each other. And when it was over and we lay spent, we still clung to each other, unable to let go, knowing, in a way, that we would be each other's savior. Knowing that as our enemies collected outside of this sanctuary, we had each other, only each other.

I wondered if we would die together, knowing I couldn't do what I'd said yesterday, not now, not anymore after knowing what I knew. I understood his self-loathing. His hate. His loss. I felt it from him. I felt it *for* him. It didn't make him good. It didn't clean the slate; didn't wash his hands of the blood he'd spilled. Nothing could ever do that. But it made him different. It made him human.

Ever since that night, he'd been trying to kill himself. And now, he had an end in sight. And after that end, he wanted me to kill him.

Well, I knew I wouldn't.

I couldn't.

I sat in my study, listening to Leo's cell phone ring. It was the day before the auction, and I needed to check in. It was procedure. A day or two before the auction, I'd get the address for delivery. The auctions were held in different locations every time. Some at private homes, some in the woods. You just never knew.

"Leo"

He always answered the same way.

"She's ready to go," I said.

"Good. I'm sending you the address now."

"How many do you have?" I always asked this question, so it wouldn't seem out of the ordinary.

"Eleven."

"What about buyers?"

"Two dozen."

"Any names I should know?"

Leo paused. This wasn't on my usual list of questions.

"No," he said after a moment. "No names you need to know. The restrictions didn't cause a problem, I hope?"

He'd made a point of going over the "no fucking" rule when he'd delivered Gia to the cabin. Now it made sense.

"No. I am curious about it, though. It makes my job harder," I said.

"Buyer's request."

"She has a buyer? Why the auction, then?"

"It's a humbling experience, isn't it?"

I fisted my hand, fingernails biting into my palm. "Very." My phone dinged with a text. I glanced at it quickly. "I have the address." I already started to type it into google maps.

"See you tomorrow."

We hung up, and I zoomed in on the location.

"I want to go to the auction," Gia said.

My gaze shot up to find Gia standing in the open doorway. I hadn't heard her come down the stairs. She wore a dark gray knitted dress, the tight fit accentuating every curve, every soft swell, every sharp edge.

I cleared my throat and adjusted the crotch of my pants, forcing my gaze back to her eyes. The slight rising of one corner of her mouth told me she knew how she affected me. Told me she knew how beautiful she was. I knew too. Had seen it on day one, when she'd been huddled in a corner, beaten and filthy and stinking. But today, it was different. Today, she stunned; every part of her alive, charged. Her hair hung loose down her back, the thick fringe of bangs a stark contrast to her pale, creamy skin, intensifying the emerald eyes that seemed to shine brighter. Perhaps for her newfound mission, her renewed hate.

"No." I leaned back, folding my arms across my chest.

She leaned against the door frame and did the same. "Why not?"

"Because it's dangerous."

"Really? I hadn't realized that."

"Don't be a smart-ass, Gia."

"Why shouldn't I go? Victor will be there, right?"

"I don't know."

"He will. He's expecting me on the auction block, isn't he? Won't he want to see me humiliated? He told me when they branded me he'd see me on my knees. He swore it. I just didn't realize he meant it so literally."

I studied her. She was right. He'd likely be there to watch exactly that.

She walked into the study, casually scanning the books along the wall before sitting down on the couch. "Who was that on the phone?"

"Leo"

"Who's Leo?"

"The man who fed you while I was...away."

"Charming man."

"Dangerous man."

"What did he say?"

"He confirmed what you think, that Victor is planning on buying you back. He'll still take bids, but he's not planning on selling you. He wants to see you humbled, in Leo's words."

Her eyes narrowed infinitesimally, and inside them I saw her rage, raw and unrestrained. I'd need to make sure I had full control of her before letting her out of my sight. We needed to be smart about this. What I was planning would put a target on my back with too many men shooting to kill.

"I don't want to hide anymore, not from Victor, not from anyone."

"I understand," I said, scratching my head. I glanced again at the image of the large stable in the middle of fucking nowhere. It'd stink. I knew that already. This wasn't the first auction held in a barn, and old piss was the worst.

"What are you looking at?" she asked, coming around the desk.

I let her see. "Auction house."

She zoomed in but didn't say anything. I watched her face, saw her unease, the fear she felt that she tried hard to hide.

"You don't have to hide from me," I said.

"Hide what?" Her face closed down.

"Fear."

"I'm not afraid."

But she didn't quite meet my gaze when she said it.

"Of course you're not." I stood. "Do you know how to shoot the gun I gave you?"

She shook her head.

I smiled and pulled the weapon out of the drawer I'd put it in. "Figures."

"I guess you've had a lot of experience," she said.

I glanced at her. "More than you want to know," I answered, my tone deadly serious.

Her eyes searched mine as if she were deciding whether or not to ask the next question. She dropped her gaze.

No, she wouldn't want to know just how bloody my hands were.

"Bring the ammunition."

She looked inside the drawer at the two boxes, obviously not knowing which. I picked up the box and shook my head, leading the way out back. Gia followed.

I realized I'd left my cell phone back in the study when I heard it ring just as we reached the doors.

"I'll be right back," I said to Gia. "See if you can manage getting the gun loaded without hurting yourself."

She took the box and the pistol and gave me a smirk.

"I'll see if I can do that. I'm just a stupid girl, you know."

"Nah, not stupid. But definitely a girl," I said, taking her chin in my hand and tilting her face upward to kiss her mouth. Being around her, it made me want. It was like all I could think of was fucking her, how I wanted to fuck her. The many ways I still needed to fuck her. It was like I couldn't get close enough. Like being inside her was the only way.

The call went to voice mail, but whoever it was must have bypassed that to call back because it started to ring again.

"Persistent." I watched Gia swallow, her eyes wide on mine when I released her.

I went into the study and checked the display, swiping the screen to answer the call.

"Salvatore?" I hadn't expected him to be so quick with the information.

"I have some bad news."

His voice was so low and grave, my heart fell to my stomach.

"What is it?" I sounded normal, like myself, but it was like I stood outside myself, watching. Like it wasn't me at all who held the phone and listened to him tell his news.

"It's our...it's Franco."

I sank onto the couch, a sudden chill raising goose bumps all over my body.

"What?" It came out tight.

"He passed away, Dominic. Roman found him."

"Just a girl…"

I turned to find Gia coming inside, watched her smile vanish when she saw my face.

What? she mouthed.

"They think it was another heart attack," Salvatore continued.

I didn't care. I didn't care. I didn't fucking care.

"You should come to the house," he said finally.

"When did it happen?"

"More than a day ago. He'd sent his staff home. Stupid old fool. He'd sent them all away."

"He was in the house dead for more than a day?"

"Yes."

Silence. Gia knelt at my feet, her curious, worried face turned up to mine as if she'd draw information from my mind.

"Will you come to the house, Dominic?" Salvatore asked. "I'm on my way. My flight boards in a few minutes."

"What is it?" Gia whispered.

"I have to go," I said.

"Dominic," Salvatore started again, then sighed.

"I have to go," I barely managed before hanging up, shock having made a mute out of me.

"What?" Gia persisted.

I looked down at her eager face. "Franco Benedetti is dead. My uncle found him this morning."

No emotion crossed her face. She watched mine instead, waiting.

"I should be dancing, right?" I said wildly, standing swiftly, rubbing the back of my neck, walking a circle, not seeing her rise, not seeing anything. "I should celebrate."

"Dominic."

She touched my shoulder. I flinched, shrugging her off.

"Dominic."

She was more persistent this time, her touch more firm. "He was the only father you knew. It's natural—"

I looked at her, unable to speak. Not wanting her to see me, not now, not like this. Too much fucking emotion I should not be feeling. Too many memories flooding back, too much anger, too much rage, too much fucking goddamned regret.

"Go away, Gia."

"No."

"Leave me alone."

She shook her head.

Franco Benedetti was dead. And his last words to me had been to deny me. To humiliate me. His last fucking words disowned me.

"Dominic."

"Fucking let me go, Gia," I snapped.

What she saw in my eyes frightened her. I knew it. I saw it. Hell, I felt it. She stepped backward, like she'd done in that room in the cabin. She kept her eyes on me, watching, as if she waited for her enemy to strike. To be prepared for when he did.

I ran a hand through my hair. I almost said something, but then I didn't. I walked out the door instead, fished the keys out of my pocket, made sure she was locked in the house behind me, and I drove off the property. I needed to think. To get these fucking emotions under control. He had made me weak in life; he would not do so in death. I wouldn't give him that power over me, not ever again.

I hated him.

I needed to remember that I hated Franco Benedetti.

Dominic's cell phone rang again. He'd left it in the study. I rushed back into the room and picked it up, reading the display before swiping to answer the call.

"Hello?"

Hesitation on the other end.

"Salvatore?" I asked.

"Who's this?"

"Gia. Gia Castellano."

Silence.

"Are you still there?"

"Where's my brother, Gia?"

"He just left. He wouldn't talk to me. I think he needs space to process what you just told him."

"Yeah, I can see that. Where are you? No, don't tell me."

I heard a final boarding announcement in the background.

"Look, I don't know you. I heard about your brother, though, and I'm sorry for your loss."

I snorted. Didn't people know it didn't help to hear that?

"But *my* brother needs someone right now. He probably shouldn't be alone, Gia. I don't know your relationship—"

"He'll be back."

"You sound confident of that."

"I am. And I'll be here when he is."

"If you can, try to get him to come to the house. The funeral will be tomorrow afternoon. It's probably good for him to say good-bye."

"I don't know that he's ready for that. I don't know the whole story, but from what I've seen, he's been running from this for seven years."

"I know. That's Dominic. Predictable. He'll always take the most extreme route."

It irritated me that he called Dominic predictable, but then, in the way Salvatore said it, I had to agree. My mind moved to something else. "Will the Scava's be at the funeral?"

There was a pause. "I assume Angus Scava will be."

A woman's voice came through, telling him they would be closing the doors if he didn't board immediately.

"Why?" he asked.

"You have to go. I'll talk to him. I'll make him come."

I disconnected before he could ask again. I had a feeling he knew at least a little bit about me. I paced the study, thinking, planning. The auction would take place tomorrow. But now, with the funeral on the same day, it changed things. I didn't know Dominic's plan about the auction, but the funeral opened up another door, another way in. Maybe a smarter way.

I went upstairs to Lucia's closet and found an overnight bag and began to pack. I found a black dress. I'd look stunning in it. It would be perfect for the funeral. And for showing Victor Scava he'd failed. That he'd now pay. Tomorrow may be Franco Benedetti's funeral, but it was my coming-out party. I didn't care about Benedetti. No, check that. I cared that the news held so much power over Dominic, considering their history. I knew now he'd truly done nothing but run, nothing but dig himself deeper into this black hole over the last seven years. A hole he would not be able to climb out of, not on his own. I saw it in his eyes, read it in his reaction. It was the same thing that I'd seen while he'd held me at the cabin. That hint of the humanity, the vulnerability behind all the hate and rage. Dominic Benedetti may be a monster, but he was a monster with a bleeding heart. That heart was in no way made of gold. It was more barbed wire and steel and sharp, deadly edges.

And those were the things that drew me.

Maybe it was because he wasn't the only monster in this strange thing happening between us. Maybe we had both truly met our match.

Love wasn't always beautiful. It wasn't always kind or sweet. Love could be a twisted, ugly bitch. I'd always known this was the kind of love I'd find. The only kind that could touch me. Because some of us, we belonged in the dark, and Dominic and I belonged in the dark.

After I finished packing my bag, I went into Dominic's room and found his duffel. He hadn't unpacked it since arriving. I emptied it to see its contents. Two pair of jeans, a couple of shirts, that was it. That and a small, worn-out envelope that fell out from the pocket of one of the jeans. I picked it up off the floor and opened it. I pulled out a worn photo of a little girl wearing a hot-pink cast on her arm and beaming into the camera. Dirt smeared on her face and wisps of hair stood wild, defiant, unwilling to be contained by her ponytail. She looked to be about nine years old.

I had to smile back at the little girl with creases across her face from the much handled photograph. Effie. I would have recognized her to be related to Dominic even if I didn't know about her. It was her dimple in exactly the same place as Dominic's. But more so, her eyes betrayed her heritage. The color, the shape, the shrewd cockiness inside them. It was all Dominic.

How could he stay away from her? If I had a child, could I stay away from her? Walk out of her life? He loved her. I knew it from the way he talked about her. But it was his punishment, his self-flagellation. And it made perfect sense. Dominic hated himself for what he'd done. Hated himself for *who* he was, and more importantly, who he was not.

I tucked the photograph back into its envelope and went into the closet to find him a suit. I figured Salvatore's clothes were likely still there like Lucia's had been, and I was right. I wondered why he'd left in such a hurry. I'd have to ask him.

I realized he'd asked me where we were. He didn't know we were at his house? Well, Dominic had said it was his house now. I wanted to meet Salvatore, wanted to see the dynamic within the family. I wondered if Salvatore would recognize the suit I chose for Dominic. I grabbed Dominic's toiletries, finished packing his bag, and went downstairs to wait for him to return, knowing what I'd do while he was gone.

He'd left his laptop in the study, and the little flash drive I recognized as the one he'd used to copy Mateo's file stuck out of one of the ports. I sat behind the desk and listened, steeling myself, telling myself it would be over soon. That I'd have my revenge soon.

————

Darkness had fallen when a car door slamming shut startled me awake. I lifted my head up off the desk and looked around, confused for a moment before remembering. I looked at the time on Dominic's phone. A little after two in the morning.

I ejected the flash drive from the computer and tucked it into my pocket then walked out into the foyer. Dominic stood just inside the door, his eyes looking as though he were a million miles away.

"Hey. You okay?" I asked.

"Why are you still up?"

"I was waiting for you. Thought you might need someone."

He seemed confused by my answer.

Shadows darkened his eyes, and his hair looked as though he'd been running his hands through it for the last few hours. "You don't look so good."

"What are those?"

His gaze fell on the bags I'd packed and set at the bottom of the stairs.

"I figured we'd need clothes for the funeral." I stood anxiously awaiting his response.

He studied me. "You can't go."

"You can't stop me."

"Scava will be there. Not to mention others who may be involved."

"I'm not hiding. I already told you that. I'm going to use this as my debut."

"A funeral for a debut." He chuckled, shaking his head. "You are one twisted girl."

"What difference does it make anyway? He's going to find out day after tomorrow we're MIA when I don't turn up at the auction. What better place to confront him than publicly within his own community?"

"There's more, Gia. More players. These are very dangerous men you're talking about."

"Ever hear of David and Goliath?"

"What are you going to do, take Victor Scava out with a slingshot?"

"Don't laugh at me. It's not always the biggest and the baddest who wins. *I'm* going to win this round, and I'm going to win this war."

"I said no." He turned to walk toward the kitchen.

I chased after him. "You don't get to decide for me. Not anymore."

"No, Gia. N. O."

We walked into the kitchen, and I tugged his arm back, forcing him to stop. "You don't get to tell me no. Not this time." Anger fueled me. I would not stay back. No fucking way. "You know you owe me this. I have a right, Dominic."

"You have every fucking right, but you're going to get yourself killed. Let me go. I'm tired, and I'm hungry."

"Well, there's no food in this house that isn't seven years old! Turn around and talk to me." He freed his arm and opened the pantry door. "Look at me, damn it!"

"You don't understand how these men work. The ruthlessness with which they kill."

He kept his back to me, like he couldn't care less.

Well, I'd make him care. "Like you, you mean?" I said, stepping backward as his body tensed before my eyes.

Dominic turned then, closing the space between us. He stood facing me, all his fury focused on me.

I forced myself to hold my ground even as my mind worked frantically, wishing to somehow call the words back the instant they'd spilled from my mouth.

He gripped me by the arms and walked me as far back as the counter. My heart raced, sending adrenaline-charged blood pounding in my ears.

This was scary Dominic. This was loose cannon, wild Dominic.

This was the Dominic that made me wet.

And he knew it.

I saw the change instantly, saw how one side of his mouth lifted into the smirk that said he knew his power, he read it on my face, he was used to it. Used to having women doing as he said. Used to them dropping to their knees before him.

Fuck him. I wouldn't kneel for him. Not for any man. Not again.

Wrapping one hand around the back of my neck, he thrust his other one under my dress and roughly up between my legs to grip my sex.

"You talk like you have a dick," he whispered. "But all I feel here is a dripping wet pussy."

"You're a sexist pig," I said, swallowing hard.

"I think you like this. You like fighting with me. It makes you hot, doesn't it, Gia?"

His grin grew wider, his cock hard at my belly while his hand began to work, fingers sliding inside my panties and finding my clit.

"Stop," I managed.

"Were you like this with your boyfriends?"

His eyes darkened when he said it as his finger thrust painfully inside me.

"No. Never."

"But you like it with me?"

I failed to contain the tremor that ran through me, but I forced myself not to look away. Not to let him win.

"You like it rough with me?"

He kneaded my clit, and I sucked in air. Fuck. I gripped his forearm, trying to pull his hand away.

"Stop."

"Make me."

He curled the hand at my neck into my hair and tugged my head backward.

"Make me stop, Gia."

His voice came dangerously low, a warning.

A challenge.

I watched him, hating the weakening in my legs as he slid his now slippery fingers inside me.

"Look at you. You're one woman. You're no match for me, and I don't have some twisted vendetta against you. How do you plan on fighting Scava's army off?"

"I'm going," I hissed through gritted teeth.

"I like your fight, Gia. I do. But you need to learn to listen."

"What are you going to do, whip my ass again to make me?"

He rubbed the length of his cock against me, and I felt every inch of his hardness even through the barrier of clothes.

"Maybe."

He kissed me hard before twisting my head so his mouth was at my ear.

"But I don't think I need to."

Fingers slid into my pussy, then traveled back toward my ass, smearing my arousal over it. I sucked in a ragged breath.

"I think, in fact, fucking your ass will be much more effective than whipping it, and I might like it even more."

He turned my face to his again.

"Why are you doing this?" I asked.

I had to close my eyes when he began to play with my clit again.

"You wanted my attention. You've got it."

He released my neck and tugged the dress up and over my head, tearing it a little as he forced it off me.

"You're playing with fire, little girl."

He threw the dress aside and looked down at me standing before him in borrowed bra and panties. He tore the bra away then met my gaze again.

"And if you're not very careful, you're going to get burned."

He reached down and took my nipple into his mouth while working my panties off.

"Stop," my voice came out weak. "I don't want this."

"I think you do."

He rose up again to look at me.

"You want me, Gia. As fucked up as it is, you want me."

"I don't." It didn't even sound convincing to me.

He grinned. "It's okay, though."

He leaned his face toward mine, licking away a tear I hadn't realized had fallen.

"I want you too. I want you to fight me. I want to make you. I want to hold you down and fuck you until you scream my name. I want to come all over you, so you know who you belong to. So you know who owns you."

He released me to tear his shirt over his head, baring his chest. He stood with his arms on either side of me, caging me in but not touching me.

"Touch me, Gia."

His low, deep whisper made me shudder.

I stared up at him. His pupils had dilated so that thin rings of blue-gray circled black. My breathing grew shallow, every hair on my body standing on end.

I moved slowly, tentatively, dropping my gaze to his muscled chest, the tattoo there, and down to his belly, to the trail of hair disappearing into his jeans. Hands shaking and with the lightest touch of my fingertips, I did as he said. I touched him, the tops of our heads coming together as we both watched my fingers move over hard muscle wrapped in soft flesh.

"You make me fucking crazy."

His chest rumbled with the rawness of his words. He gripped my wrist hard and laid my hand flat against his chest, over his heart. His other hand circled my hip.

"Feel this."

His heart beat a frantic staccato beneath my hand, and I found myself biting my lip when I turned my gaze to his, both our heads still bowed. He slid his hand over my belly and brought it to rest at my heart. He didn't speak the obvious, that my heart beat as loudly and as frantically as his. I didn't know what this meant. What he wanted. All I knew was that I wanted him. I wanted all of him.

"Take my cock out," he ordered.

I let my fingertips slide down over his belly, obeying, both hands working clumsily to undo his jeans and push them and his briefs down far enough to grip his cock in both hands. I held the hardness, wrapped my hands around it, and smeared the wetness at the tip.

"Get on your knees," he commanded.

I wouldn't do that. Didn't I say I wouldn't kneel for him? For any man?

Dominic's hand nudged my shoulder, and, weak willed, I slid down, the floor cold and hard against my bare knees.

He waited until I looked up at him.

"Suck my cock, Gia. Keep your eyes on me, so I can watch you take me. So I can watch you choke and cry when I fuck your mouth."

He gripped my hair, and I felt a drop of my own arousal slide down one thigh as I opened my mouth to take him, liking the salty taste of him, wanting him to make me, to do it hard, to hurt me a little maybe. He was right. I was fucked up. And as I took him deeper and watched his eyes, I knew he was too. We were both fucked up, and somehow, we'd found each other, and together, we became something else, something twisted but not ugly. Dark but deep and full, and I knew without a single doubt that when the time came to walk away, I would be leaving a piece of myself behind. A piece that no longer belonged to me.

I choked, and he thrust. He did this three times, until tears blurred my vision before he drew me to stand and kissed me, his mouth devouring mine as he lifted me only to impale me on himself, his thick cock calling a cry from me as I slid down over it, every inch stretching me wide, the touch of my clit against him making me cling tighter, wanting to be closer, to feel him, to feel.

"Fuck, Gia."

He kissed me, trapping me between him and the counter, fucking me. When he dropped to the floor, I wondered if his knees hurt with the impact of both our bodies, but he only pulled back to look at me, to untangle my limbs and turn me and push me down on all fours. He shoved my legs apart, and I arched my back. When he drew me apart and thrust into me again, I cried out. He thrust harder, his breath coming in short gasps and grunts. When he stilled inside me, his cock throbbing, releasing the first rush of semen, I came. I came hard, my pussy squeezing him as if it too needed to cling to him, needed to be possessed by him, needed to be close to him.

I would have collapsed, but he slid out of me and drew me backward to sit between his legs, my back to his chest, his back to the wall. The cold tiles felt good against my sweaty, hot skin. Dominic held me to him. His breath warmed my ear. Neither of us spoke for a long time. I wondered what he was thinking. If he was trying to figure out a way to keep me from going. He could leave me behind and go himself. He could make me do anything he wanted me to do. For all my talk, I knew he would decide. It came down to basics. He was bigger than me. He was stronger than me. He could make me do whatever he wanted.

"I want to go with you. Please, Dominic," I said.

"It's not safe."

"You'll keep me safe," I said, wondering who was more surprised by the words, Dominic or myself.

I'd lost my mind, surely.

I glanced at Gia sitting beside me, her face closed off, both of us silent. A thick air of anxiety hung between and all around us, both of us tense for what would come. How would I be treated? How much did people know? And why in hell did I give a fuck? Why in hell was I going anyway?

The knowledge of Franco's death settled like a heavy black cloak around me, inside me, swallowing me up. I didn't know what I should feel. Hatred? Anger? But all I felt was regret. And a sense of loss like I'd never experienced before.

It was over.

He was dead.

There was no going back. No making amends. No saying sorry.

Salvatore told me he'd asked about me. Had he

truly regretted what had happened? Had he regretted telling me like that? All those years, I'd thought he'd loved me. I had. It was maybe stupid, but I had believed it. Losing that love, I realized now, it had broken a part of me.

And through that break seeped a darkness that had oozed into my soul. Made me into a man I no longer recognized. But then I found Gia, bruised and afraid, huddled in a corner of that decrepit room. The moment she set her burning gaze on me, she saw me. She saw right through me. All the broken pieces of me. And now that she knew, now that I'd told her my story—the first time I'd ever done that—it was like those pieces slowly fused together again, even if it was inside out and backward, scar tissue barely covering too many razor-sharp edges.

I was no longer the man I had once been.

But I was stronger. I may be harder. I may be darker, but I was stronger. And I would never be fooled again. I would never be weak again.

Nerves twisted my gut as we neared the house in the Adirondacks. His favorite place. The last time I was here had been to celebrate his birthday.

I turned to Gia. "You do as I say. Every word, understand? You do not leave my side, and you do exactly as I say."

"You told me that already, and I promised I would."

Gia's gaze bounced from me to the road and

back. And even as she acted tough as nails, the shadows beneath her eyes and the fact she'd refused to eat told of her anxiety.

"What about the auction?" she asked.

I grinned. That piece did truly give me joy. "I took care of it."

She tilted her head to the side, waiting for more.

"Watch them all at the funeral tomorrow. We'll see just who is involved."

I wouldn't say more yet.

We drove the last fifteen minutes in silence. As we neared the gates of the house, I saw several cars already lined the driveway. I parked behind the last one, recognizing several of the vehicles. I switched off the engine and took a deep breath. Gia's hand touched mine, startling me. She didn't say anything but looked at me with those eyes that seemed to know much more than spoken words.

I broke the gaze. "Ready?"

"Ready."

We stepped out of the SUV at the same time. I tucked a pistol into the back of my jeans, making sure my jacket shielded it. Gia had hers in her purse, although we'd run out of time for those lessons. Leaving our bags in the trunk, I went to Gia's side and took her hand. It felt cold and a little clammy. Strange enough, it made me stand taller, giving me strength enough for both of us.

"Whatever you do, do not show fear," I whispered.

She didn't deny she felt it this time. She simply nodded as we approached the foreboding double doors.

Without hesitation, I pushed on the doorbell. Last time I was here, I'd walked in, using my own key to enter. That key sat in my pocket today.

To my surprise, Salvatore opened the door, as if he'd been there waiting for me to arrive. We both stopped. His eyes scanned me from head to toe, and he gave me a small smile and a nod, holding out his hand.

I took it, meeting my brother's firm grip with my own as he pulled me in for a hug, patting my back.

"Good. You did good to come."

He released me. I looked at him, saw how much more gray was now mixed with the black of his close-cut beard, saw more lines around his eyes and mouth, not lines of worry or of a hard life. No. Lines of happiness. His skin glowed bronze, a byproduct of living happily under the sun.

Lucia turned the corner, looking tanned but otherwise just the same apart from her rounded belly protruding from the close-fitting dress she wore. She came to stand beside her husband, and I saw how his face changed, how his smile grew, how his gaze had brightened as he'd followed her path across the room.

How I felt, though—it was different this time.

It wasn't with envy that I looked at them. Jealousy had given way to something else. I didn't know when that had happened, but I was conscious of how my hand wrapped tighter around Gia's waist as I pulled her closer to me.

Salvatore's gaze moved to Gia while Lucia's found mine.

"Lucia," I said, giving her a short nod. "You look beautiful. Pregnancy becomes you."

"Dominic," she said, squeezing a little closer to Salvatore. "I'm glad you came. For Salvatore." There was no missing the meaning of her words. She hadn't forgiven me for what I'd done. For any of it. Not for abandoning her sister, her niece. Not for almost killing the man she loved.

I understood that and accepted my responsibility. It would take more than me showing up to win Lucia's favor.

"You must be Gianna," Salvatore said, studying Gia.

"Just Gia," she replied, taking his hand.

Lucia's gaze moved to Gia's clothes, a pair of jeans and a sweater. Gia stepped out of my grasp and did a little twirl.

"They're yours," she said to Lucia. "I was in a bit of a bind. I hope you don't mind."

"They look great on you," Lucia said. "I'm Lucia. It's nice to meet you. I'm sorry about your bro—"

Gia shook her head. Lucia stopped.

Salvatore's gaze returned to mine. "You came from Saddle River?"

I nodded.

"Was it you who bought the house outright?"

Again, I nodded, feeling embarrassed for the first time in a very long time.

He studied me but didn't say anything more about it. "Come in. I think Roman has you staying in your old room. He didn't mention a guest."

"Gia stays with me." Even I heard the possessive tone of that.

Lucia and Salvatore exchanged a quick glance but stepped back to let us in.

"How are Effie and your sister?" I asked Lucia, feeling like an asshole actually. A real asshole. A father who is a no-show.

"Great. Luke has been great for both of them." Her delivery put me in my place.

"Lucia," Salvatore cut in brusquely, giving her hand a squeeze.

Lucia cleared her throat. "When Effie heard we'd see you, she wanted to make sure to send you some of your favorite cookies. I have a tin for you upstairs. Not that you deserve it."

"Enough," Salvatore said, wrapping his hand around the back of her neck in warning.

She turned her stubborn face to his, and their gazes locked. Salvatore must have squeezed a little because Lucia narrowed her eyes but bit her lip. Probably to stop herself from talking.

"She's right," I said. "I'm a shit of a dad. Lucia's just speaking the truth."

"We're not here to fight. We're here for a funeral. Our father's funeral."

"Not—"

"He raised you as his own. And he regretted that night. Put your anger aside, at least for now. The man is dead, for Christ's sake."

Salvatore and I locked gazes. Our hands fisted.

Gia cleared her throat as Roman walked out of the study. What Roman felt at seeing me, I didn't know. He'd long ago learned to conceal any emotion from his face. But when his gaze fell on Gia, I saw the infinitesimal change in his eyes, that spark of surprise.

No. Of shock.

"Dominic," he said, extending his hand to mine, drawing me in for a brief, cool hug. "I know Franco would be glad you came."

"You're looking well, Uncle." He did. His suit was more expensive than any he used to wear when he wasn't head of the family, and I didn't miss the Benedetti family ring on his finger. As if he had any right.

"I didn't realize you'd be bringing a guest."

He turned to Gia. He studied her closely but revealed nothing of how he felt.

"Gianna Castellano," Roman said, addressing her.

His mouth moved into a smile. It almost touched his eyes.

"I think you were this big when I last saw you." He gestured to his waist. "Franco would be pleased to have you here."

Gia shook his hand, betraying nothing even as I felt her tense beside me.

"You know my uncle Roman?" I asked her.

Her gaze flickered to mine, perhaps remembering what I'd said I'd do to him the night I made her promise to pull the trigger on me when it was over. When she had her revenge.

She cleared her throat and returned her gaze to his. "I vaguely recall the name, but I'm sorry, I—"

"I'd be surprised if you remembered me. You were a child," Roman filled in.

"Did you know my father?" she asked.

"I did."

I could see from Roman's face he did not expect or welcome Gia's questions.

"And my brother, Mateo?" she pressed.

I released Gia's waist to take her hand, squeezing a warning.

"Yes. I'm sorry for your loss."

"And I'm sorry for yours," she managed.

Roman nodded. "I'll have a room made up—"

"She'll stay with me. Have the maid send up extra towels," I ordered.

For the briefest moment, Roman's eyes went flat and dark, and for the first time, I thought I glimpsed the real Roman. But I'd always spoken this way to him. I'd always felt superior and never hid the fact.

"Of course," he said. A couple walked up the front steps just then, and he excused himself. The four of us stepped to the side, each of us watching every move anyone made.

"Did you bring your brood?" I asked Salvatore, not hearing any children running around.

"No. They're staying with Isabella and Luke."

"I don't like this," Lucia whispered loud enough in Salvatore's direction for Gia and I to hear.

"We'll be fine. Nothing's going to happen. We'll fly home tomorrow as soon as the will has been read," Salvatore said.

A maid came then, and Roman instructed her to take Gia and me up to our room.

"Why don't you go ahead? I need to talk to my brother."

"Lucia, maybe you can go help Gia," Salvatore started.

"I know when I'm being excused," Lucia said. "Come on. You look like you like this about as much as I do," she said to Gia. The two of them turned and followed the maid up the stairs.

Salvatore and I walked toward the dining room.

"A man named Henderson who claims he was a friend of father has requested a secret meeting with us," he said in a quiet voice. "He said it's urgent. He wants to meet before the funeral if we can. Definitely prior to the reading of the will."

"Why?"

"Another body turned up. I'm not sure if Roman is aware just yet."

"Body?"

"Same brand. Ours." He paused. "He was a federal agent. Henderson believes he was Mateo Castellano's source."

"A fucking federal agent? Branded with the Benedetti name?"

Salvatore nodded.

"Who is this guy, Henderson?"

"I'm not sure. He did some work for father over the last few months. Roman doesn't know about him apparently."

"Urgent meeting?"

Salvatore nodded. "I think we should go before the funeral. We'll leave together, the four of us, and meet at Henderson's home office. He was adamant no one would know. He seemed...nervous. Rumors are circulating, Dominic. The family has weakened, and with father's death, our enemies are becoming less and less subtle. The method of Mateo Castellano's death has brought unwanted attention to the family. And now, with a federal agent's dead body turning up, there will be more."

"I heard the recording Mateo made. At least what he got out before he was killed."

"And?"

"Scava names Roman. They were in this thing together. Roman is part of the human trafficking ring."

"How? Father would never have approved that."

"Maybe he was working alone. I know that was one thing the family did not dip their toes into. That's a whole other ballgame."

Salvatore nodded. Franco had always been adamant about that. I didn't know the reasons behind it but hadn't ever given it much thought.

"From what I could make out, Scava wants people to believe it was Roman who put the hit on Mateo. And now, I assume the federal agent as well. Why? If they were in on this thing together, why? Unless he wanted Roman out."

We looked over at Roman, who appeared out of another room just then, talking to an older woman with a bereaved expression on his face.

"Snake."

"Be careful, Dominic. Don't let on that you know. Although bringing Mateo's sister may have clued him in. Why did you do that? Not really your smartest move."

"No. But I wasn't going to leave her alone either. Victor Scava wants her. He's apparently already bought her. The auction is just a formality. A humbling."

Salvatore flinched, his mouth curling in distaste.

"She stays by my side," I added.

"If I didn't know any better—"

"She has my protection, that's all."

"What's going on with the auction?"

I grinned. "I'm guessing phones will start lighting up tomorrow around the time of the church service."

"You called it in?"

I nodded.

"Anyone know where the information came from?"

"No." I paused, and we both turned to watch our uncle. "Roman's involvement will be confirmed tomorrow."

"Let's go upstairs. I know Lucia doesn't want to be alone." He paused. "Memories of the last time," he said, his gaze sliding toward the dining-room.

I recalled and didn't miss the note of shame in my brother's words, in his face, or in his behavior.

"I just need to get our bags," I said.

"I'll help you."

Salvatore and I carried the two overnight bags upstairs and parted ways at my door. I watched Salvatore disappear down the hallway and into his room. After a brief knock, I opened my old bedroom door to find Gia standing by the window, biting her fingernail.

"Lots of people coming," she said.

"It'll just be family tonight. You don't need to look for Scava."

She picked up the tin of cookies that I assumed Lucia had given her.

"Here. These are for you. And there's a note."

I took the envelope and the tin out of her hand and sat on the edge of the bed, just looking down at the things on my lap. I touched the lid, tracing the brightly-colored pattern there. Then I opened it to find a pile of chocolate-chip cookies. I offered Gia one. She shook her head and watched me, one hand at her neck, her fingers rubbing her chin. I chose a cookie and bit into it. My throat closed up, seven years' worth of emotion I'd kept bottled up coming up now, threatening to choke me.

It took all I had to swallow the bite before I set the rest of the cookie back in the tin, not tasting a thing.

"I'll give you a minute," Gia said, disappearing into the bathroom.

I set the tin aside and took the letter out of the envelope. Her handwriting was pretty, very different to that of the small child who'd written in huge block letters way back when. Now, she wrote in a neat script.

Dear Uncle Dominic,

Thank you for all the toys and clothes and things you send me every month. When I heard Lucia would see you, I wanted her to give this to you.

Mom told me why you had to go away like you did. She told me the real story of what happened that night. I want you to know that I don't think Salvatore is still mad at you. I know because sometimes I get up for a drink of water and overhear things. Not that I'm eavesdropping or something. I just overhear by accident. Besides, I think Uncle Salvatore just misses you, and you should know that. No one is mad at you. We all miss you, especially me. Well, maybe Aunt Lucia is a little mad, but she just needs to get to know you like I know you, and the only way she can do that is if you come for visits. You can even stay with us. And maybe I am a little mad too, since you just up and left without saying bye to me. But I'll forgive you if you come. Promise. Okay?

I love you, Uncle Dominic.
Effie

PS: I hope you like the cookies.
PPS: I got a phone for my 11th birthday. This is my number if you want to call me.

I read the letter twice, memorizing the phone

number, the surge of emotion as I heard her little voice through her words breaking my heart but also filling me with hope. How did she not hate me for having up and left? How could she forgive me?

How had I created something so good?

I had to smile at the eavesdropping piece. She was my daughter through and through. And I wondered at the gifts. I sent money monthly. I never sent things, though. Did Isabella buy them and say they were from me? She'd do anything for her daughter. She loved her fiercely. Would she even cover for my lack?

Gia returned from the bathroom and sat down beside me on the bed. I didn't pull the letter away when her gaze fell on it.

"Will you ever tell her the truth?"

"I don't know."

"She loves you. And she has a right to know."

I folded up the letter and tucked it into my pocket, rising to stand. "She's safer if my enemies don't know about her." I walked over to look out the window at the growing number of cars. "And after tomorrow, I will have enemies."

Gia came to stand by my side.

"This is only just beginning, Gia."

THE FOUR OF US LEFT EARLY THE FOLLOWING MORNING, filling Lucia and Gia in on the way there.

"The agent, do you know his name?" Gia asked.

"David Lazaro. Ring a bell?"

"He was Mateo's contact."

"Roman will have found out by now," I said.

"No doubt. Henderson's house is here to the left." We parked around the corner of a beautiful, not too large house and climbed out, the early morning damp and chilly. We walked to the house in silence. The old man, Mr. Henderson, greeted us, obviously surprised by the presence of the women.

"Ladies, you'll stay here while we meet?" Salvatore said as if he were asking the question.

"My housekeeper will make coffee," Mr. Henderson said.

With that, we went into his office and closed the door.

"Thank you for coming. I know we don't have much time, so I'll get right to business. First, I'm sorry for your loss."

"Thank you."

Salvatore answered while I tried to keep my face hard and unexpressive as stone.

"I realize you don't know me, but I used to work for an agency where I had access to certain...things."

"What sort of things?"

"Surveillance. Video, audio, a few other things."

We both sat there, confused. "I'm sorry—" Salvatore began, but Henderson cut him off.

"We'll get to it. But first, the will. What will be read this afternoon will come as a surprise to your uncle. I know for a fact he is unaware of this last change made just days before your father's death."

"What change?" I asked. "And how do you know about it?"

"I stood witness. Your father trusted me."

"Mr. Henderson, I'm sorry, but I don't understand," Salvatore said.

"You will." Henderson turned to me. "Dominic, your father is naming you as his successor."

The words slammed into me. "What?"

"It was his wish that you become head of the Benedetti family."

"But—"

Salvatore put a hand on my forearm. "Everything has been decided already. I signed over power to Roman," he told Henderson.

He shook his head. "Your father was living when you did that. He has the final say. And he has spoken."

"You're going to take everything away from Roman?" Salvatore asked.

"Not me. Your father."

"Why me? I'm not even—" I started.

Henderson turned to me. "Franco Benedetti is named as your father on your birth certificate. You are his son, raised as a Benedetti. And you are named as head of the family."

"What happens to Roman?"

"He's cut off. He won't inherit a cent."

"Why?" Salvatore asked. "Why this sudden change?"

Henderson cleared his throat. "Because of me." He looked at each of us, his face grave. "I came across something some time ago, something I had to keep quiet for too long. Time came for me to go to your father with what I'd learned."

"Spit it out," I said. "What are you talking about?"

Salvatore didn't speak.

"The man who ordered the assassination of your brother was closer to home than you know."

No.

"Your uncle ordered the hit." He paused as if for effect. "And had you been there, Salvatore, as was planned, you would have died too."

"What?" I had to clear my throat. "What kind of proof do you have?"

"A phone conversation with a man named Jake Sapienti."

Time stopped. Apart from the pounding of blood in my ears, the room went completely silent. Henderson's eyes locked on mine as if giving me the time to see. Willing me to understand.

It felt like I'd taken a fist to my gut when I did see.

Salvatore glanced at me, and I knew he too knew the name of my father.

"Recording?" he asked.

Speech escaped me. I sat wordless.

"Sapienti's phone was tapped. Feds had been looking for information on his employers for a long time. Back then, they had bigger fish to fry than your uncle. And then evidence got old. Lost or forgotten."

"Lost or forgotten?" Salvatore asked. "How does something like that get 'lost or forgotten?'"

"We're human, and there are a lot of bad people out there, son. Your uncle wasn't the worst of them, not then."

"I want to hear it," I said.

Henderson glanced at me, and I wondered if all color had drained from my face.

"Are you sure?"

Salvatore's hand fell on my arm. I didn't look at him, though. I only nodded once. Henderson got up and fiddled with some ancient-looking equipment.

As soon as the phone connected, Roman's voice —laced with disgust—came through, the line clear.

"You're one short," he hissed.

Salvatore stiffened beside me. We both knew what he meant.

"Keep your money. You didn't tell me who he was. Find someone else to do your dirty work, rat. When

Benedetti learns who ordered the hit on his son, you'll get what you have coming," Jake hissed.

"And you won't? He'd never believe you, and he'll kill you."

"If I had known who he was..."

Sapienti trailed off, his tone quieter.

I'd never heard Jake Sapienti's voice, but I had to first process the fact that the man who had fathered me, the man whom my mother supposedly loved, had killed my brother. Had shot down her beloved son.

"Mr. Sapienti's body turned up shortly after Sergio's assassination."

"How did you come by this recording?" I asked.

"The federal government hired the services of the agency I worked for. That's all I am at liberty to say on that," Henderson replied.

"Why now? Why go to my father after all this time?" Salvatore asked.

"And how do we know you're not fabricating this? Why do you give a shit what happens to the Benedetti family?" I asked, on my feet now, pacing to stand behind my chair and glare at the old man.

"Dominic—" Salvatore started.

"People don't do shit like this out of the goodness of their hearts, Salvatore. Get a fucking clue."

I turned and walked the length of the room, running both hands through my hair, trying to make sense of what I'd just learned.

That my uncle had hired the man who had fathered me to kill my half-brother.

"Mr. Henderson, perhaps—"

"My son was the bystander who died that day along with your brother. He was a young man, engaged to be married in a few weeks' time. So you see, your uncle was ultimately responsible for his death as well."

"Why now?" I asked. "Why didn't you go to my father then?"

Henderson sat back in his seat and turned his palms up on the desk. "Because I'm alone now. My wife passed a few months ago. There's no one left who can be hurt or killed because of what I do now."

"And Roman doesn't know about the change in the will?" Salvatore asked.

"No."

He checked his watch and stood. "We need to go, Mr. Henderson. We'll be late for my father's funeral."

Henderson rose to his feet. I looked at the old man, tall but bent and tired.

"Why would he name me as successor, when it was my father who killed his most beloved son?" I wasn't sure who I was asking.

"It was his final act perhaps to do right by you. He did love you like his own, and he regretted that final night very much. In the short time I knew him, he talked about it often. About you often."

Henderson walked around the desk. "Old age makes us see things differently, son."

He put a hand on my shoulder. I looked at that hand, unable to speak, unwilling to feel. I shrugged it off. Salvatore and I walked toward the door.

"One more thing, gentlemen," Henderson started. We stopped and turned to him. He straightened something on his desk before looking at us. "The guards who will be at the reading of the will are loyal to your father."

I watched the old man's eyes. Heard his message.

Salvatore thanked him and said good-bye. We walked out of the room.

Lucia and Gia stood. Gia's eyes when she met mine turned angry, fierce even, and she shifted that anger to Henderson. Salvatore must have seen it too, because just as she took a step toward the old man, he intervened, taking her by the arm.

"Let's go. We're leaving."

She glanced from him to me and back.

"I said we're leaving," Salvatore said.

Lucia took Gia's other hand. "Come on. We'll talk in the car."

L
ucia told me this morning that she'd worn the dress I wore now to her father's funeral so many years ago. That she'd only worn it that one time. We dubbed it the funeral dress. I decided I would burn it once I finished with it today.

While we waited for the men to return, she asked me about Dominic. Asked if we were a couple. I hadn't known how to answer that, so I shifted the conversation to her and her family. The way she spoke about Salvatore, I knew she loved him. And the way he looked at her, hell, he worshipped the ground she walked on.

I admit, I grew envious. I'd never had anything like that before. Not even close, not even with James.

Now as the men sat silent in the front seat of the SUV as we drove toward the church, I watched them, studying the physical differences, the light to the dark in physical appearance. But the thing that impressed me more was the similarity of the darkness inside each of the brothers. I knew the life they came from. Shrouded in shadow, they had seen and done terrible things. Things neither would forget. Things perhaps neither should be forgiven.

I was a part of this world too. Their world. The day I'd seen Mateo tortured and killed had plunged me into its murky depths. We sat there now, all of us. The difference between Dominic and I, and Salvatore and Lucia, was that Salvatore and Lucia lived in the light. They could walk away. They had once and would again. In a matter of hours, they would shrug off the darkness and leave it behind, scrub it from their bodies before touching their children. But Dominic and I—I knew in every cell of my body there would be no walking away. He and I were embedded in dark. We would die in it.

"I don't want to stay for the reading of the will," Lucia said. "I don't want you in there either, Salvatore."

Her face had lost its shine and gone pale. Neither man had spoken since we'd gotten into the car, but she must have picked up on the thing vibrating off them just as I had.

Salvatore climbed out of the SUV and opened Lucia's door. They stood there then, just outside the vehicle, heads bowed together, talking in whispers, having such a private moment I felt like an intruder to watch but found myself unable to drag my gaze away.

Salvatore wiped her tears with his hands. They stood so close. It was as though they were one person. He then kissed her forehead and lay a hand on her belly. Lucia nodded, and Salvatore met Dominic's eyes, a signal passing between them.

"Let's go in," Dominic said.

My heart raced; my belly was in knots. Black sedans lined the street, the hearse already emptied, Franco Benedetti's body likely already waiting at the top of the aisle.

"Is Victor here?" I asked, clutching the bag that held the pistol.

"I don't know."

"Why didn't Lucia want Salvatore to go to the reading of the will?"

He shook his head, his mind obviously a million miles away.

"What is it? What did that man tell you?"

Dominic turned to me, but if he was about to tell me, he changed his mind.

"Let's get this over with."

He shifted his gaze to a point ahead, disappearing into thought, moving through the motions.

The organ began to play just as we entered the church. Everyone stood and turned. and I felt my face burn as every eye in the place landed on us.

The service was about to begin, but we'd interrupted. And now, we were the center of attention.

"So much for a subtle entrance," Dominic whispered in my ear, straightening, his body seeming to grow taller.

I looked up at him, seeing how he'd schooled his features to reveal nothing, seeing his strength, the cruelty in his gaze as he scanned each and every person in the place with cold, shuttered eyes.

I shuddered beside him, grateful that gaze did not fall on me.

He placed his hand around the back of my neck, pressing the cool collar into my skin; a symbol of protection. One of possession. He would have me and everyone know it.

Dominic Benedetti owned me.

And in some strange, sick way, I wanted to be his.

I told myself it was for now. A game, a role I would play. A necessary thing. But if I scratched lightly at the surface of that thought, I'd see the lie.

We walked up the aisle slowly, purposefully. Dominic cast his gaze down every row we passed, as if he were boss. As if he owned each and every one of the people here.

The first telephone rang, and Dominic checked his watch. I looked up at him and saw the ruthless set of his eyes as he turned to the man who answered. Someone I did not know. Someone I felt sure he made a mental note of.

But then, in my periphery, I saw Angus Scava, James' father. My would be father-in-law and Victor's uncle.

I swallowed, unable to take my eyes from his. He cocked his head to the side, one corner of his mouth rising infinitesimally as he nodded as if to say, "well done."

Another phone rang somewhere behind us, but we walked on. And there, just two rows ahead of Angus Scava and directly behind the near-empty pew that awaited us, stood Victor, his face red with rage, his gaze burning into mine.

My first instinct wasn't fear. It was to laugh. He looked like he would explode.

Dominic's hand around my neck tightened, and I clutched my bag closer, feeling the hardness of the pistol.

I returned Victor's glare. Then, just like his father had done to me, I cocked my head to the side and narrowed my eyes, conveying to him my warning. War had come to his doorstep. An eye for an eye. A life for a life. He had killed my brother. I would kill him. Dominic would make certain of it.

Victor's phone rang. He broke our gaze to dig it out of his pocket, and when he did, we stopped walking. We'd reached the open casket.

One more phone was answered then. Dominic's uncle, Roman, quietly put his to his ear. Dominic glanced at Salvatore, whose eyes had narrowed. A silent understanding passed between them.

Dominic shifted his attention to me, turning my face to his, his blue-gray eyes looking for a moment like they had behind the death mask he'd worn those first days. But then, they changed, not quite softening, no, not that. Dominic burned too hot for that. They smoldered and burned instead, and in front of all those people and God and Franco Benedetti's open casket, he kissed me full on the mouth.

Women gasped, and when he abruptly released me, the entire church seemed to hold its breath.

I stood shocked. His gaze challenged me, dared me to make a move while warning me to be still. He glanced at the priest who watched this arrogance, this effrontery, this sin against God and man. Dominic didn't flinch. Instead, he looked once more over the assembly, satisfied with what he saw, before turning his gaze to the casket. His face betrayed no emotion, nothing, as if he were unaffected. I knew he was not. I knew Dominic felt. He felt deeply. He behaved as though he didn't give a shit, but inside, he was like a bubbling volcano of emotion, hyper-sensitive, and so, so well-schooled in hiding it all.

I waited with him, standing beside him until he was ready. I glanced at the old man in the box, feeling nothing myself.

Dominic turned back to me, eyes flat, and

ushered me into the aisle so that I stood between him and his uncle. Roman's face had gone white. He tucked the phone into his pocket. Dominic leaned toward him.

"Urgent call, Uncle?"

Roman stood a few inches shorter than Dominic. His hands fisted as his throat worked, and he swallowed. He didn't have a chance to reply, though, because the sound of the priest clearing his throat rang out over the loudspeakers, and he began the service. All went silent apart from the man's booming voice, but I wondered how many in the room actually heard the service at all.

I FULLY EXPECTED TO SEE VICTOR AFTER THE ceremony. Or at the very least, at the cemetery. But he'd left before the service ended. Disappointment mingled with relief as I stood at Dominic's side while he greeted the mourners, shaking hands, making subtle comments about being back now. Nodding when anyone said anything about Franco Benedetti.

Behind us, calla lilies covered Dominic's mother's and Sergio's graves. I didn't miss the look either brother gave those two headstones.

Salvatore and Lucia stood in the same line and beside them, Roman, looking more anxious than grieved. My gaze traveled over the soldiers circling the gathered mourners, but when I heard the familiar sound of Angus Scava clearing his throat, I turned to look up at the older man.

"Gianna."

He took both of my hands in his, making a point of turning them over.

"Mr. Scava," I said. He'd always called me by my full name.

"You look well."

His gaze momentarily landed on Dominic before he touched my ring finger.

Did he think we were engaged?

"So soon after James' death," he added.

"James died two years ago, Mr. Scava."

"Scava," Dominic said from beside me, his arm circling my waist. "Where's your nephew?"

Angus Scava's face hardened. "He had to take care of some business."

"He took care of some business close to home, and I don't appreciate it," Dominic said, tugging on the cuff of his shirt.

"No. Nor do I. He will be dealt with."

"He kil—" I started, anger rising.

"I'll do the dealing," Dominic said, cutting me off.

They were talking about Mateo's death, about my kidnapping, like it was nothing.

Scava looked at Dominic. They stood the same height, eye to eye, two powerful men unafraid of battle. Beside them, Salvatore watched, dark and dangerous.

"Gentlemen," Roman began, placing a hand on each of their shoulders. "Now is neither the time nor the place."

Dominic's jaw tightened as he turned his face to his uncle. He no longer tried to hide his resentment of the older man.

Mr. Scava watched the confrontation, a small smile playing along his lips.

"What time is the reading of the will, Uncle?" Dominic asked through gritted teeth.

Roman checked his watch. "Within the hour. We should go."

Dominic nodded then turned to Scava. "This conversation isn't over."

"Certainly not," the older man said. "Gianna, pleasure to see you looking so...recovered."

Dominic's fingers dug into the skin of my arm.

"Let's go," he said.

Mr. Scava watched Dominic lead me away, the look in his eyes so different to how he'd looked at me before.

"Was James like his father?" Dominic asked as we climbed into the SUV, Salvatore and Lucia taking the backseat.

Why did it feel like a taunt? "James was nothing like him."

Dominic turned to face me. "He would have been boss of the family had he survived."

I shook my head, perhaps being naive. I didn't care. "He wasn't like his father."

"I'm like him," Dominic said. "Ruthless. Cold. Merciless."

I held his gaze, knowing he used his words as a warning. Knowing I would be smart to heed him.

"Not to me," I said instead. "Not anymore."

Dominic's surprise at my words showed up on his face. It was the slightest change, but I didn't miss it.

"Are you ready, brother? Roman is not going to be pleased," Salvatore said.

"He knows how to behave. I think he's very good at it in fact." With that, Dominic turned the SUV around and drove out of the cemetery and back to the house. We sat silent. Except for Lucia, who spoke with her sister on the phone, asking about the kids. When we arrived back at the house, I was surprised to see so many vehicles there. Had so many family members been requested to attend the reading of the will? It seemed strange to me. But then again, I'd never been to something like this. Funerals, yes. There was no getting around that in the line of work my father had chosen. But those who died around us didn't have the money to require a will.

Dominic parked the SUV and drew in a long breath, steeling himself, then nodded to Salvatore.

"Let's go."

"What's going to happen?" I asked, clutching his arm. "You know something."

"I'm going to be named head of the family," he said flatly.

My hand slid off his arm, and he and Salvatore walked away from Lucia and I and into the library, where about a dozen men had gathered. Two men stood outside. One of them reached to close the door, his jacket falling open, light bouncing off the pistol hidden in its holster.

The attorney executing the will, Mr. Abraham Marino, a man who had worked for the Benedetti family for more than two decades, stood behind the desk. He addressed the collected family members requested to be in attendance, going over preliminaries. Roman stood beside him as if he owned the fucking place. Salvatore sat to my right. Two guards stood just outside the doors and two more at the back of the room. I wondered how they would all react once the will had been read, and I was named as head of the family.

I recognized all the people in the room. They ruled their own smaller families within the larger Benedetti umbrella. Some I hadn't seen since my youth, and some attended every event.

Realistically, Roman could attempt a coup. Hell,

depending on how many men chose loyalty to him, he could win. My father was dead. He could force his way in. Although, without money and the accounts held in the Benedetti name, he'd struggle to pay them. In all my years both in and out of life within a crime family, I'd learned one thing: in most cases, loyalty was a flimsy thing. Money ruled. Loyalty generally leaned toward the side of cold, hard cash. And after the reading of the will, it'd be my cash. This house would be my house. The car my uncle drove would be my fucking car.

He'd hired my birth father to kill Sergio and attempt to kill Salvatore.

He'd betrayed my mother, his sister. He'd betrayed his nephew. He'd betrayed Franco. He'd betrayed the entire Benedetti family.

How in hell did Salvatore sit beside me now, revealing no emotion at all, not confusion, not even hate?

I'd been in my twenties when Sergio had died. For a moment, I wondered why Roman hadn't ordered my assassination too, but then I realized. He'd been playing my father all along. I was a bastard. My father already knew it. Roman banked on the fact that when Franco learned it was the man whose blood ran in my veins who had taken his sons' lives, he'd disown me, at the very least. Hell, maybe he even counted on Franco killing me.

I thought of Henderson's words: *"Old age makes us

see things differently, son." He'd said it didn't matter who my blood father was. I was a Benedetti according to my birth certificate. I was raised a Benedetti. There was some small part of me, something deep beneath the wretchedness, that smiled at that. That felt more happiness at that than I probably should.

Did Franco really regret that night? Did he feel sorry about what had happened? About telling me like that? Had he tried to find me? Roman had known where I was some of that time. At least in the beginning. Had he kept that information from Franco, knowing the old man wanted to reconcile? Had he wanted to reconcile?

I covered my face with my hands and rubbed my eyes.

I'd never know. That was all there was to it. I had to take it at face value. Franco Benedetti named me as his successor. He accepted me as his own in his final act. He was about to give me what I had wanted for so long—the rule of the Benedetti family.

And I felt heady with power.

Salvatore cleared his throat beside me, his gaze falling on me.

I straightened.

"Mr. Benedetti made a few changes to his will in the last days of his life."

Mr. Marino glanced at me.

I kept my face expressionless, but noticed Roman's eyes narrowed.

"This is his final will and testament, and it was his wish that no one should contest those changes but that they would be honored."

A murmur fell among the crowd. The attorney cleared his throat. Roman took a seat as the reading began. Mr. Marino went through mundane things first, small inheritances, moneys changing hands, debts being forgiven or passed on, mentions of family members, of children remembered. Then came the rewards of past and future loyalty.

"It was Mr. Benedetti's wish that I read this next piece as he wrote it, as if he were speaking to you now."

Salvatore and I exchanged a look.

"I realize in a family such as ours, there will be differences. There have been differences. But family is family, and for the Benedetti, family is first. It is our motto. It is our path. In life, I did my best for my family, for all of you. I know it didn't always seem that way, but I did. In death, I hope to amend mistakes I could not be forgiven in life."

It took all I had to keep my face a dull mask.

"Each family has been given a sum of money, which you will receive privately upon the end of this reading. Each envelope also contains a contract. If you accept the funds being offered to you, then your loyalty to the Benedetti family is renewed, the bond welded like steel and unbreakable. If you choose not to sign the contract,...well—"

He stopped abruptly to meet every eye in the room. I wondered if my father had given him that instruction too. It would be like him.

"I hope you do not choose that path."

My father. Franco Benedetti. He was my true father, not Jake Sapienti. Salvatore was right. Henderson was right. I was a Benedetti.

I sat up straighter in my chair.

"My son Salvatore has chosen to leave this life. He chose a different happiness, and I no longer hold that against him. He chose a path I did not. I could and would not. But I respect his decision and his family. My grandchildren shall receive trust funds..."

The attorney named the amount of the funds.

"Salvatore and his wife, Lucia, shall always have the protection of the family."

But no money.

I glanced at Salvatore, whose own mask stood firmly in place.

"To Roman, my once constant friend. Ah, Roman, my beloved wife's brother..."

I could almost see Franco shaking his head.

"You know the saying, 'keep your friends close, keep your enemies closer?'"

All eyes turned to Roman, who looked straight ahead.

"Well, friend, you kept me in your pocket, didn't you?"

Murmurs broke out, but the attorney held out his hand for silence and shifted his gaze to me.

"To my youngest, Dominic. I leave you what you have always wanted. I leave the Benedetti family, your family, in your hands, son. Despite everything, out of all my sons, you are the most like me, aren't you?"

Roman stood. "This is..."

"Please sit down, Mr. Russo."

One of my father's personal bodyguards, a man I'd known to be around since I was a kid, walked behind Roman's chair and placed a hand on his shoulder. Roman sat. Two more soldiers loyal to my father approached the desk and stood behind it, their gazes on no one and on everyone.

"Now, on to those contracts. I have each of the envelopes here. When your name is called, please approach the desk. Mr. Benedetti?"

It took me a moment to realize he was addressing me. Once I met his gaze, he continued.

"Your signature is also required."

He gestured toward the chair behind the desk. Franco Benedetti's chair. My father's chair.

I stood, feeling all eyes on me as I made my way forward. I glanced once at Roman and then sat. Salvatore moved toward the door and took up a place where he could see each family as they were called up, their envelopes opened, and contracts placed before them.

I didn't know if this was custom. If after the passing of the father, old agreements were reinforced, renewed, reminded. I didn't know if he did it for me, to safeguard my position should anyone ever learn the truth behind my parentage. Should anyone contest my right to this seat.

The first man, Antonio Santa Maria, signed the contract. Antonio was a cousin, distant but powerful. His allegiance to my father had never been questioned. His sons, Gregorio and Giovanni, both in their late twenties, flanked him.

"Your father was a good friend. My loyalties have not before and will not now waver," Antonio pledged.

"Thank you, Antonio," I said. I turned to each of the sons and shook their hands, met their eyes, and nodded once. I wondered if they would remain allies or become enemies one day.

They walked out of the room.

The next man approached. Then the next. Each of them pledged allegiance. Each man signed. I took note of those who glanced in the direction of my uncle. These men knew to refuse to sign meant their death. I had no doubt Roman had supporters among them. No doubt they planned mutiny. But today, I would send a message. Today, my first day as head of the Benedetti family, I would send a very clear message.

Finally, almost an hour later, all the contracts were signed and only the attorney, four soldiers, Salvatore, Roman, and I remained.

The attorney packed up his papers, each of the contracts placed neatly into his briefcase. He then turned to me.

"I hope we will continue to work together, Mr. Benedetti," he said, extending his hand. "I look forward to being of service to the son of my friend."

Friend. Funny. But he was loyal. I extended my hand and shook his.

"Thank you, Mr. Marino. I'll be in touch soon."

He glanced once at Roman, then, without acknowledgment, moved toward the door, shook hands with Salvatore, and left.

"Make sure the house is cleared of guests," I told one of the men, my gaze falling on Roman.

"Yes, Sir."

"I want Gia in here."

"Do you think that's a good idea?" Salvatore asked.

"Get her for me, brother."

Salvatore's disapproval clear on his face, he walked out the door and returned a few moments later with Gia at his side.

She looked at the assembled men, her face

betraying no emotion to those who did not know her. But I knew her. And I felt it coming off her.

She stood at the wall near the door by Salvatore's side.

I opened my father's top right-hand desk drawer. I'd been through it before, a hundred times, and I knew where he kept his pistol. Taking it out, I stood. I found the silencer deeper in the drawer and attached it to the barrel of the gun. I did this with a strange sense of calm, of peace. Like finally, for the first fucking time in my life, it was right. *I* was right.

Salvatore questioning whether bringing Gia in here was a good idea was a valid one, but she needed to see this. She needed to see justice for her brother, for herself. But she also needed to see me for who I was. I was not good. I would never be good. She needed to have no reservations, no hopes, no illusions. That last part, it was strange, but I knew who I was now. The clarity of it, of all of it, was undeniable. And Gia was part of that clarity. I knew what I wanted, and she was it. But I owed her truth, and what she'd witness today would be an absolute truth.

"Dominic—"

Roman started talking when I moved to the side of the desk and stood leaning against it, facing him.

"Silence, Uncle."

The guard behind him placed his hand back on Roman's shoulder.

Power. Fuck. A surge of it pumped blood through my veins.

"You hired Jake Sapienti to assassinate Sergio."

Roman flinched.

"Did he know who Sergio was? Did he know the mark?"

It took Roman a moment, but the cocking of my gun got his lips moving. "No. He only knew the license plate of the car. He felt...remorse...when he found out who he'd killed."

"But you didn't." My uncle sat silent. "You would have killed Salvatore that same day had he been where he was supposed to be. You wormed your way into the heart of the Benedetti family to take what did not belong to you."

"Dominic, you and I, we're real family—"

I shook my head. "You are a traitor, Uncle." Distaste curled my lip. "You betrayed my father. You took his trust, his confidence, his friendship—he believed you to be his one true friend, but you never were anyone's friend, were you?"

"It's not—"

"You had his beloved son, your own nephew, murdered. Shot down like a fucking dog." A hot rage fired my words, and my chest tightened. "You used Sapienti to assassinate him. Why? Why would you do that? Why hammer another nail into an already sealed coffin? Why?"

"It was a mistake, Dominic. Just a mistake."

"You don't make mistakes. I know that." I paused, checking the chamber of the gun.

"Please, Dominic—"

"Where did your balls go, Uncle?" I looked at everyone assembled in the room. "What the fuck happens to these 'powerful' men when they sit facing the barrel of the gun rather than cocking it in the face of their enemy?"

No one answered.

"You've learned over the last seven years what it's like to exist just outside, Dominic. To not quite belong. To feel an utter impotence while standing beside the hand that rules the world. You now know what it was like for me all those years. You can't deny that you know."

"I have no reason to deny it. You're right. And you know what, it felt like fucking shit. But I didn't betray my family over the shit cards I'd been dealt. You played us. You played my father. For years."

"He's not your real—"

Someone cocked his gun. I turned to find Salvatore stepping forward, his angry gaze on my uncle.

"You listen, old man. You listen now, and show respect. Sergio didn't get to see his baby boy. He never got to say good-bye to his wife. To any of us. You took that away. You killed your own nephew," Salvatore said, rage slicing through the calm. "Now, you listen." The words were forced through gritted teeth.

Roman swallowed hard, his eyes glistening. Did he feel remorse?

Did it fucking matter?

"Before I kill you," I said, drawing his attention back on me, "I want to know your involvement with Victor Scava."

"Let me walk away, leave town, leave the goddamned country. I'll tell you everything, just don't—" His voice broke.

Fucking coward.

"Don't what?" I probed, taunting. Hating him.

"Don't kill me," he begged.

"Get on your knees, and beg me not to kill you."

He looked around the room. He had to know no one would help him. Slowly, and with trembling legs, he dropped to his knees before me. Fucking fool. Fucking bastard, coward, fool. Did he really think I'd let him live?

I noticed the ring he still wore. "Take the Benedetti ring off your finger."

He looked down at his hand and then met my gaze. I think he decided this one he could concede because he wriggled the tight ring off and handed it to me. I set it on the desk.

"Please, Dominic, I'll tell you what you want to know, just let me live. Let my family—"

I pointed the gun at his shoulder and pulled the trigger. Roman fell backward, and Gia screamed.

"She stays," I said to the men at the door, my eyes on Roman.

"I'm not leaving," she said.

I glanced back at her but spoke to the soldier. "Make sure of it."

"Uncle," I said, looking at him again. "Get the fuck up. Back on your knees."

Salvatore remained silent but deadly beside me. He may have left the family, but this was what he came from. This wasn't the first time he'd seen something like this. Not one of us was clean, not a single fucking one. Not even sainted, dead Sergio.

But still. Loyalty ruled, and treason called for death. In this case, a slow and painful one.

"Victor Scava," I said.

Roman held his injured shoulder and glanced beyond me at Gia.

"I want a deal," he said.

"No fucking deal." I cocked the gun, ready to shoot again.

"Wait!" Roman cried out. "I have information for her."

I glanced at Gia, where Roman was also looking.

"About her brother."

"Don't fucking play games—"

"Wait, Dominic," Gia cried out, running to my side and griping my arm, the one that held the pistol.

I thrust it backward, holding her just behind me. My bullet would find its right mark this time.

Roman started to talk. "Angus won't give Victor the rule of the family soon enough. He wants to take it from him."

"Angus Scava is what...is he even sixty? Victor thought he'd just hand over the rule of his family?"

"Victor was gathering supporters."

"You being his number one?"

"No. My loyalty has always been to our family."

I aimed at his other shoulder.

"No!" He held up both hands. "Please!"

"You've always been loyal to you, Uncle."

"What do you know?"

Gia's voice stopped me from pulling the trigger.

"A federal agent turned up dead yesterday," Roman said. "He too was branded with the same brand as your brother. He was Mateo's contact."

"I don't understand," Gia said, her desperate gaze on mine.

"Talk faster," I told Roman.

"A deal," Roman said.

"Dominic, let's hear him out," Salvatore said.

"Deal depends on what you tell us, then," I said. "Start talking. If I even think I smell a lie, I pull the fucking trigger, understand?"

Roman nodded. "I stopped dealing with Victor about a month ago when Angus Scava got wind of what his nephew was up to. Victor wasn't very smart in how he did things. He underestimated Angus. He thought an alliance with me would give him the leverage he needed to take over the Scava family. I… made a mistake."

"Just facts," I said. I had no interest in his lies.

"I promised to help him in exchange for new territory. Then, once," he hesitated, choosing his words. "Once I took over, we would assassinate Angus Scava, who has no shortage of enemies, and Victor would take over as head of the family. I thought it would be easier to manage Victor than Angus. That's why I went along with it."

"How do the stolen girls fit in?"

He hesitated. "I took a percentage."

"You had no qualms about kidnapping and selling human beings?" I asked, disgusted.

He simply lowered his eyes to the floor, perhaps realizing it himself.

"My brother," Gia said.

Roman met her gaze. "Mateo was…uneasy with the girls. Beating up some asshole who doesn't pay what he owes is different than taking young girls—"

"Because he had a conscience," Gia cut in.

"He went to the feds, but he got unlucky. That agent happened to be on Angus Scava's payroll. That's how Angus found out. Needless to say, he was not pleased with his nephew's agenda, but he's family. He couldn't bring himself to kill him outright, I guess. And he smelled money. Angus

Scava took over the operation. He left Victor in charge, at least for the sake of appearances, but he made all the decisions."

His eyes bored into Gia as if he would make sure she understood that part.

"Angus Scava wouldn't have ordered my brother's execution," Gia said quietly.

"He not only did that, but he ordered yours."

She shook her head beside me.

"No. I don't believe you."

"Victor was supposed to kill you."

"Why didn't he?"

"Rebellion against Angus. Lust. Who knows? He's completely unreliable."

"What about the agent? Why kill him?" Salvatore asked.

"All human life is expendable to Angus Scava. And there's more than one corrupt agent employed by the federal government. And now that Angus took over the operation, he wanted me out. He had no use for me, and that presented an opportunity to put the Benedetti family out of commission for good. Franco and/or I would be picked up, and that would be the end of us. Feds don't take the killing of their agents lightly."

"Angus Scava wouldn't have ordered my brother's execution. He wouldn't have ordered for me to be killed."

I glanced at Gia, who had her eyes squeezed

shut, her hands on her face, fingers pressing against her temples.

"He did."

He said it so coldly. I raised my gun and pulled the trigger, putting a bullet into his other shoulder.

Roman cried out in agony.

"Get him up," I ordered the guard behind him, who lifted him back to his knees.

"A deal!"

"So before Angus stepped in, you'd agreed to help Victor overthrow his uncle for support for yourself, for money, for power, so when the time came that Franco Benedetti died, you'd be ready to take over more than the Benedetti share, the mourning *Consigliere*, a man like a brother to the fallen Benedetti whose sons deserted him."

"Mercy, Dominic," Roman begged. "I made mistakes—"

"You ordered Sergio's murder. You betrayed my father. Those things cannot be forgiven, Uncle," I spat.

"Please, Salvatore—" He turned to him, his final plea.

Salvatore remained silent.

"I can drag this out for hours, but because you gave me this, I'm going to show you that mercy," I said.

"Please, Dominic. Please, I—"

"I'm sending a message today, Uncle. I'm letting

everyone know that if you betray me, you die. You die a very slow, a very painful death."

Roman sat on the floor in a bloody heap, crying like a fucking baby, begging for his worthless life.

I turned to Gia and held out the gun. "Do you want to finish him?"

She stared at him, never once looking at me. Tears ran down her now alabaster face, all color having drained from it as she watched the horror before her. She shook her head and turned to me with a look of such utter desperation that I faltered.

"Take her away. I'll finish this," Salvatore said.

"I need to—"

Salvatore turned to me. "No, you don't. Take care of her."

I looked once more at my uncle, who now began to beg Salvatore. Tucking the pistol into the back of my pants, I took Gia and walked her quickly out of the room and up the stairs, lifting her into my arms and carrying her when she shook too badly to walk. I closed the door to my bedroom behind us and set her down in the bathroom, wanting to clean the blood that had splattered onto her bare legs, her shoes, her dress.

She trembled as I stripped her, talking to her, not sure she heard a word I said as tears poured from her eyes.

"He is partially responsible for your brother's death. You shouldn't feel sorry for him."

"I know."

She said it on a sob as I turned on the shower and waited for the water to warm.

"It's not that. I don't—"

"He killed my brother," I said. "He would have killed Salvatore."

"I know," she said again, clinging to me when I tried to move her into the shower.

I took off my jacket and set the pistol on the counter. Her gaze closed in on it. Her tears came faster. Holding onto her, I stepped into the shower with her. I stood fully clothed and forced her beneath the stream as she held me, as if she would fuse us together, as if she were unable to stand on her own.

"You needed to see, Gia."

She nodded, burying her face in my chest.

"You needed to know what I'm capable of."

"You think I didn't know?"

Her voice was full of anguish as she turned her emerald eyes to mine.

"Then...I don't understand. I thought you'd want to see—"

"I do. I owe it to Mateo. I swore it to myself. I just...I don't think I can do it. I don't think I can pull the trigger on Victor. I don't think I can keep my promise to kill him."

Something inside me broke open, and I held her tight to me, cradling her head, rocking her as she wept. Her pain, it had this strange impact on me. It made me feel. For the first time in my life, I *felt* another person's pain.

"You don't have to," I said in a whisper.

"I do. I swore vengeance."

"You'll have it, but you don't have to be the one to do it. You don't have to have blood on your hands."

She shook her head and pushed us out of the stream of water. "No matter what, the blood will belong to me."

"Shh. No."

"I'm weak," she said quietly, looking up at me, her hands on my cheeks now.

"Killing doesn't make you strong, Gia." I wiped the tears from her eyes and held her sweet face.

"I won't be weak."

"Maybe it's time you let someone take the weight. Maybe it's time to let go, and let me carry it. Let me carry you."

She pushed wet hair from my face and looked like she was about to say something, but then stood on tiptoe and covered my mouth with hers, her kiss soft and testing. I liked kissing her like this. Kissing her like we weren't battling as her hands fumbled with the wet buttons of my shirt until she pushed it off my shoulders, halfway down my arms. We kissed like we couldn't stand to separate, as if we needed to be touching while I lifted her and carried her into the bedroom, laying her dripping wet on my bed as I tore off the rest of my clothes and climbed between her thighs, her legs and arms wrapping around me, drawing me down to her, her mouth locking on mine again as I thrust into her, never letting her go, not once, not until we lay spent on the bed.

She knew who I was now. What I was capable of. And she didn't cringe away from me. She didn't fear me. It was the opposite. She clung to me. We clung to each other as if for life. As if for breath. As if without the other, it would no longer be possible to breathe, to live, to be.

The following morning, I woke alone in Dominic's bed. The sight of his uncle kneeling before him, cowering, begging, pleading for his life as Dominic coolly cocked and fired the gun, haunted me. I thought about Mateo. About how he'd died. Dominic wanted me in that room yesterday. He wanted me to see one of the men responsible for Mateo's murder on his knees, being brought to a different kind of justice—mafia justice —paying back what he owed: a life for a life.

I didn't feel sorry for his uncle. He deserved what he got, and not only for Mateo, but for all the rest. Dominic had told me the story, the whole story, after we'd made love last night. He told me what the old man, Henderson, had told him. Told me about the reading of the will, of the provision his father had made to have each of the families renew their pledge of allegiance to Dominic as head of the family. He told me of his uncle's betrayal. Told how his father— and Dominic now called Franco Benedetti father— sealed Roman's fate and had left it for his sons to mete out justice. And he told me why he wanted me in that room. Not only for Mateo, not only for me to see that Mateo's death would be avenged, but to see him. To see Dominic step so naturally, so easily, into this new role as head of a bloody family.

Dominic Benedetti now owned the Benedettis.

I touched the scar on my hip.

I guess it fit. He owned me too. Would he let me go once this was over? What we'd discussed that day in the dining room, that day I'd learned the truth of the brand, the truth of who he was, the day he'd fucked me in that bloodsoaked room when I'd been out of my mind. When he'd been out of his. The day he'd promised me he'd make sure my brother was avenged, and I'd promised him I'd kill him once it was over.

But it all had changed now. His father had left him everything in his final act of contrition. Dominic got what he had always wanted.

I wouldn't have been able to keep my promise and kill him anyway, but now I even wondered if he wanted me to.

Everything was different now.

Throwing the covers back, I got out of bed and went to the bathroom to have a shower.

Ironic, that. *Be careful what you ask for. You just might get it.* James would say that to me way back when I thought the mafia life glamorous. When I hadn't yet witnessed its dark, gruesome side. When I hadn't yet seen death.

Dominic's words came back to me. *"Killing doesn't make you strong."* He was right, I knew that. But to hold the gun that brings your enemies to their knees, it was heady stuff. The thought made my heart pump harder, made my blood run hotter. It made me feel powerful.

But then the image of the bleeding man impressed itself upon my brain, as if branding itself onto the insides of my eyelids, and I bowed my head. He'd looked much like Mateo had when Victor had brought him to his knees. Weakened and powerless and afraid. Mateo was no saint. I knew that. No one in this world could be. Not a single one. I did not have illusions on that note. I wondered if before it was through, once all was said and done, would I have blood on my hands too? Didn't I already, even if it wasn't me who'd pulled the trigger yesterday?

I switched off the water, shuddering at the memory of Dominic standing there so cool, so unaffected as the condemned man knelt before him.

He'd wanted me to see him like that.

I went back into the bedroom to get dressed and heard a car door closing outside. Dominic's room overlooked the front of the property, and I could see

Salvatore loading a suitcase into the back of an SUV. Lucia stood beside him, one hand on her belly, the other on the door. She wanted out. She wanted to be gone. I understood it. But she and I were different. She was the mafia princess who'd been locked away in a tower and had never wanted any of this. Me, I was the daughter of a foot soldier, someone no one gave a shit about, and I was the one who ended up in the bed of the new king.

Question was, where did I want to be?

Who did I want to be?

Salvatore and Dominic spoke, hands clasped together like two powerful men making an alliance. They then hugged briefly, almost awkwardly. Dominic turned his attention to Lucia, who must have said good-bye before Salvatore opened her door, and she climbed in. No hug from her. To say she did not like Dominic would be an under-statement.

Dominic stood on the front steps and watched the car drive off. He remained there until it disap-peared down the thickly wooded road. He then glanced up at the window as if he knew I stood there. Our gazes locked, and my heart momentarily lost a beat. He turned to one of the men flanking him—of which there stood two, bodyguards I real-ized—and I stepped away from the window to dress and then went downstairs.

The door to the study stood open, and I heard

Dominic speaking inside. I forced myself to walk into it, wondering if it would smell like it had yesterday—the metallic scent of blood mixed with fear and hate. But the desk had been moved, and the carpet was gone. Only bare floorboards remained.

Dominic looked up at me and told whoever he spoke with he had to go. After hanging up, he stood.

"Gia."

I looked for evidence along the walls, splatterings of blood, of tissue, but none remained.

"It's been cleaned," Dominic said, coming to my side. "You're probably hungry. Let's go have breakfast."

He spoke so casually. "Does what happened yesterday upset you?" I asked as he led me out of the room.

He paused. "I wouldn't say it upsets me, but it's not like I'm dancing with joy here, Gia. He was my uncle. He played ball with me when I was little. I don't remember him not being in my life."

"I'm sorry."

He didn't respond. We walked into the dining room, where a buffet of warm and cold foods sat waiting on the table. Dominic poured two cups of coffee, and I took one, not feeling hungry enough to eat.

"I thought I'd feel better," I said.

He set his cup down, took a plate, and began to fill it with scrambled eggs and bacon.

"You never do."

He spoke without looking at me.

"You just figure out how to go on." He chose a seat and began to eat. "Eat, Gia."

I picked up a plate and stood there, wondering if I'd ever have an appetite again.

"Tell me something," he asked.

I still hadn't moved to fill my plate.

"What do you want?" He leaned back in his chair and chewed on a strip of bacon.

"What do you mean?"

He studied me as if taking my measure.

"What they did to your brother, to you...What do you want?"

I understood what he was getting at, and I steeled myself, knowing exactly what I wanted, knowing who I was, what I could live with. I turned to the buffet and filled my plate, then sat down beside him to eat. He nodded and picked up his fork again.

"Salvatore and Lucia had to catch their flight home. They asked me to tell you good-bye."

"Did he..." I shook my head. I didn't want to ask. Of course he'd finished the job Dominic started.

"My uncle is dead if that's what you're asking."

"Do you believe what he said? That it was Angus behind it all?"

"Dying men are desperate men." Dominic

looked at me. "But I'm not sure. I wouldn't be surprised and wouldn't put it past Angus."

"I want to meet with him."

"With Angus Scava?" Dominic seemed surprised at that. "What about Victor? We'll go up the ranks, Gia. Deal with them one at a time."

I shook my head. "This is for me. Your uncle, he owed you. But this is for me."

He considered this, narrowing his eyes, studying me closely.

"Are you sure you know what you're doing?"

"I know. I'm very clear, in fact." I picked up my fork and turned my attention to my plate.

I watched Gia all that day and the next. Truth be told, her quiet was a little scary. I had expected her to be more frazzled, more like a woman, I guess.

Like a woman.

I sounded like an asshole. I'd never been attracted to weak women. In fact, only two women stood out for me in the string I'd been with. Isabella and Gia. Two strong women. Two women with an agenda. Two women you did not want to fuck with.

I meant it when I told her I'd do the dirty work of killing. I wasn't sure what she expected out of this meeting with Scava. She had to know she couldn't just walk in there and kill the motherfucker. We'd meet in a relatively public place, but we'd both be armed. And we'd have soldiers around us who were armed. But I didn't ask her what her agenda was.

She was determined and had her own history with Angus Scava. I'd be there with her to protect her, but I'd let her do what she needed to do to make her peace.

"You're watching me."

She sat beside me in the back of the fortified SUV on our way to the restaurant.

"You've been watching me for the last two days."

"I'm curious."

"Are you nervous?"

I shook my head. "No. I do want to be sure you're going to get what you want out of this. If you told me—"

"No, Dominic. This is mine. This has nothing to do with you."

"Fair enough, but if I feel like you're overstepping—"

"It's mine. You told me you'd help me, and I just need you there with me. I need you to carry me a little, or at least let me lean on you. I'm trusting you with that."

We pulled up alongside the curb of the Italian restaurant, a place Scava owned. It was trendy and popular, and the food sucked, in my opinion. Angus Scava would be inside already. I saw two of his men standing beside his sedan parked at the end of the street.

I turned to Gia, taking in how the tight black dress hugged her, how the heels made her legs look longer. She'd let her hair loose tonight, and it hung down her back. Her eyes shown bright, seeming almost to dance tonight. Alive and buzzing as if adrenaline pumped through her even as we sat there.

I touched the flat of my hand to her heart.

"You're nervous."

"Will he know that?"

"No. Not unless he touches you like this, and if he does that, it'll be the last thing he touches."

That made her smile.

"You know how to keep your face impassive."

She nodded.

"I won't leave your side," I said.

"Thank you."

I knocked on the window, and the driver opened the door. I climbed out and saw that my men were already lined up, the number I'd brought matching the number Scava had brought. I didn't expect war, not tonight, but I knew from years of experience to never be caught unprepared.

I helped Gia out and led her toward the entrance, noting every eye on the street that turned her way, liking it. Liking that every man who passed wanted her on his arm. Knowing every woman felt a little pang of jealousy as they pretended not to notice her.

A man opened the doors, and we entered, followed by two of my men. The space was large and modern but completely empty of patrons tonight. Only a few staff I could hear working in the open kitchen, and Scava sitting at the far booth like he was fucking king.

"Why is it empty?" Gia asked.

I had an idea. "Privacy," I said, leaving out anything else I suspected.

Angus Scava smiled. He watched us enter, his gaze sliding over Gia as we approached. Sick prick. He was old enough to be her fucking father. Hell, he would have been if his son had stayed alive long enough to marry her.

I felt a note of possession at that. A hint of jealousy. Which was ridiculous, considering James was dead.

"Gianna." He stood when we neared. "Pleasure to see you." He took her hand and kissed her knuckles, then straightened. "You look enchanting. My son had wonderful taste."

She only looked on coldly.

I cleared my throat. Scava turned to me.

"Dominic."

"Angus."

He gestured toward the booth. "Please. I've taken the liberty of choosing the wine. I hope you don't mind."

"Not at all as long as you take the first sip," Gia said.

Angus chuckled as we sat, and the waiter poured.

He made a point of picking up his glass, swooshing the dark red liquid around and inhaling before drawing a long sip.

"I'm still alive," he said to her.

She still didn't touch hers, but I picked mine up and sipped.

"My condolences, once again, Dominic. I hear your uncle passed not too gently last night."

"He was a liar and a traitor. He got what liars and traitors get."

He cocked his head to the side and raised his eyebrows. "You're as direct as your father."

"You did some business with my uncle?" I asked.

"He and my nephew were involved in some things," he said, his eyes catching Gia's as he sipped.

I felt Gia tense beside me.

"Where is Victor?" she asked.

"I didn't think you'd want me to invite him, considering."

"Can we just cut this bullshit?" she spat out. "You talk like we're all here having a friendly drink, but we're not."

I smiled. "She's direct too."

"You've changed, my dear," he said to her.

"You've opened my eyes," she replied.

Angus snapped his fingers, and we looked up. A door opened, and two men walked in, Victor between them. He wasn't quite standing on his own. Instead, he was hunched over their shoulders and being kept upright, his head lolling from side to side, his face bruised, his feet dragging as they walked forward.

Gia gasped. I held her hand under the table.

"My nephew made some poor choices," Angus said. "Concerning what happened to your brother, Gianna, you have my apology. And you'll have Victor's, well, you would except that he can't really talk at the moment."

"I'm going to be sick," Gia said.

"No, you're not," I told her.

"Not woman's work, this, is it?" Angus remarked. "Gianna, in an effort to make amends for what my nephew did to your brother, I'd like to offer you a gift. Would you like Victor's tongue?"

"You...you're sick!"

"No, only a man who punishes liars and traitors. You see, Victor thought it would be a good idea to try to save his neck by sliding a noose over mine." Angus' face changed, a look of disgust crossing it. "I don't like federal agents on my doorstep. Family business is family business, isn't it, boy?"

Victor's only response was to grunt when one of the men beside him jabbed his elbow into his ribs, which I assumed were broken. At least, considering the bruising on every visible part of him, I imagined they must be.

"I know it was you. I know Victor was no more than your foot soldier," Gia said.

"You know nothing."

"How could you do it?" she asked. "You knew me and Mateo. We've eaten at your table. I've slept in your house. I was engaged to be married to your son. How could you order his death? How could you order *mine*?"

"I never did like seeing you upset, Gianna."

"Are you so heartless? So inhuman?"

"I loved James very much, and had he lived, I would have accepted you as my daughter."

"Why me, then? Why order my execution?"

He didn't answer.

"You're a monster. You're a horrible monster," Gia said.

"I don't leave loose ends. You can't in my business. In cleaning up my nephew's mess, I found he'd left quite a few. James didn't leave them either, by the way. I know you like to fool yourself into thinking he was somehow better than me, better than him—"

Angus pointed to me.

"But truth is, you're surrounded by monsters, Gianna. And you attract them like flies. What does that say about you? What's the expression? Like attracts like?"

"That's enough, Scava," I said, my eyes on Gia, who flinched at his words. I couldn't tell what was going through her head. If she was buying his bullshit. I'd made sure she came unarmed. I wasn't about to take a chance she'd do something as stupid as attempt to kill Angus Scava in the middle of his restaurant. "Get him out of here," I said, gesturing toward Victor.

Scava nodded for the men to take Victor away.

"I want to go," Gia said to me.

"You didn't answer me. Did you want his tongue —" Angus asked again.

She flew at him, knocking the bottle and our full glasses over before I caught her. Two men standing behind Scava drew weapons.

"Put those away for Christ's sake," Scava ordered, picking up his napkin.

Gia struggled against me, but I held her tight. "This isn't the place," I said.

"You're a sick, sick man," she told him. "You want to give me a gift? You know what I want? I want for you to turn the gun you'll use to kill him and put the bullet in your own head instead."

I handed her off to one of my men. "That's enough," I told her. "Take her to the car."

Angus sat there wiping at the bloodred liquid staining his clothes, his face, his hands.

"Let me down," Gia cried. "Let me go."

Once the door closed and Gia was gone, Scava looked up at me.

"I know you were involved, Angus. I know you're the one who ordered Mateo's killing and hers. Your nephew didn't do it, though, not out of the goodness of his heart, of course. He wanted her humiliated. He wanted the woman your son loved degraded." I shook my head. "Gia's right. You are a monster. But you're right too. We all are. You don't go near her again, understand? She's under my protection." I knew my choices. The realistic ones.

"She isn't a threat to me." He nodded and stood. "We go back to the way things were when your father ruled?" He held out his hand.

I looked at it. The thought of touching it meant I betrayed Gia.

I met his eyes, hard and flat, exactly the way I felt. I fisted my hands at my sides.

"No, old man. They don't."

W e didn't talk on the drive back, and when we got to his father's house—his house now—I went to the stairs. Feeling Dominic's gaze burn into my back, I stopped two steps up and turned to face him, although I couldn't quite meet his gaze.

Angus Scava was right. We were all monsters. I'd seen what Dominic was capable of. And I knew James had been the same, no matter what I tried to make myself believe. And me, I wanted vengeance so badly I was willing to do what they'd done to me, to my brother, back to them.

An eye for an eye. A life for a life.

Who was I?

Seeing Victor like that, I thought it was what I'd wanted. I thought I would be satisfied. But it only left me feeling empty and ugly and sick.

"Like attracts like."

I was as much a monster as all of them.

"I want to go home." I'd go back to my mother's house, move back in with her until we could sell it, and move away for good. Far, far away. Although I knew as hard and as far as I ran, I'd never be able to escape myself. My name. My skin.

Dominic nodded once, but I saw how his jaw tightened.

"I'll arrange it."

He took a step toward me, but I shook my head and backed up.

He stopped.

"When?" he asked.

"As soon as possible."

He seemed taken aback. "Tomorrow?"

I shook my head and took the two steps back down. "Now."

He looked surprised. "You need to pack—"

"Pack what? Clothes that don't belong to me?" I felt my lip tremble and my eyes fill with tears, but somehow, I managed to stop the shuddering that wanted to overtake me. Somehow, I held those tears at bay.

"What he said, it's not true, Gia. You're not a monster. You're not—"

"Please...just don't."

Dominic averted his gaze, then took a key out of his pocket. "Turn around."

I looked at it and touched the collar around my neck, which seemed to press heavier against my skin. I'd forgotten it. I'd forgotten all about it.

I turned and lifted my hair up. When his fingers brushed my skin, I shuddered. The sound of the tiny key sliding into the lock sounded as loud as a large iron key turning a Medieval lock, and then I was free. The weight was gone. I was no longer his.

I felt cold, and when I wrapped my arms around myself, Dominic took off his jacket and draped it over my shoulders. I let him and for a moment, we just stood there, watching each other. The draw to slide into his arms, to press against his chest and let him hold me was so strong, but I wouldn't do it. I couldn't.

He turned to one of his men.

"Take her where she wants to go," he said.

The man nodded and walked toward the door.

Dominic took out his wallet and opened it. "You'll need money."

"No. I don't want anything from you." It would only be another moment before the tears fell and drowned me. I needed to get out of there.

"If you ever do—"

"I won't."

"Gia." He started to reach out then changed his mind. "You'll be safe. You and your mom. Scava won't come near you."

I nodded. I couldn't speak.

I shifted my gaze down to my feet and clutched his jacket closer to me. I would keep it. I would keep this one thing of his.

"You'll always have my protection. Anything you need."

I looked at him one last time, memorizing his face, his eyes that studied me so closely, so carefully, eyes that seemed to want to draw words from me I could not say, not now, not ever. Eyes that saw the things I felt, the things I should not feel. That held a tenderness I only saw when their gaze fell upon me.

Without another word, I went to the door. The man opened it, and I walked out of the house. I didn't look back, not when he closed the car door, not when we drove away.

I didn't know if he watched me go but I knew he cared that I had left. I knew he hadn't expected that. But I couldn't think about those things. I couldn't. Not if I wanted to be able to go on.

25

I went immediately into the study and shut the door. The house already felt different. Empty.

I took a seat behind the desk and opened my laptop.

It was better that she left. Better for her. What could I offer her? Life as my—what? Wife? I couldn't condemn her to that. Gia had been born into this world, but she could get out. She needed to get out. For all her talk of vengeance, she couldn't stomach it, couldn't take the reality of it. I knew that. I did. I think it's one of the things that drew me to her. As fierce as she was, inside her, the light of her innocence burned bright.

In a way, I sought absolution.

She was clean.

And I had no business dirtying her, no business staining her with my sins.

I opened the desk drawer and took out the letter Effie had written me, picked up the phone, and dialed. I only checked my watch after it started to ring and realized it might be too late to call her, since it was past ten at night.

But then she answered.

"Hello?" came her little voice.

I smiled, tears warming my eyes as my heart thudded.

"Hi, Effie. It's me, Dominic."

"Uncle Dominic! You called!"

I heard her elation, and it felt so fucking good.

"Well, you made those delicious cookies, how could I not?" I said. There was a pause. She didn't know what to say, how to proceed. "Effie, I'm sorry it's taken me this long to call. I'm very sorry, and you don't have to say you forgive me. I just want you to know I made a mistake, and I hope I can make it up to you now. I'm going to do everything I can to do that."

"Oh, Uncle Dominic."

I heard her sniffle.

"I've already forgiven you, silly. I just really miss you."

"Me too, honey."

"Where are you, Uncle Dominic?"

"I'm in New Jersey, but I am planning a trip to Florida very soon."

"You are?"

"Yep. I just have to talk to your mom to arrange some things. Maybe you can show me around?"

"I'd love that! And I'm a great tour guide. I know everything around here. Hold on!"

I heard Isabella's voice in the background, asking if she was still awake. Effie made up an excuse that she had to get a drink of water, and she would get back to sleep if her mom would stop interrupting. I laughed at that. A few moments later, she came back on the line. This time, she spoke in a whisper.

"Sorry about that. My mom thinks I'm a little kid."

"Well, you are a kid, and I probably called you pretty late. Don't you have school tomorrow?"

"Yeah, but no big deal. I'll be fine."

"I'm not so sure. I'll tell you what. Why don't we say good-bye for now, and you save my phone number and call me tomorrow after school. In the meantime, I'll call your mom and see if I can't arrange a visit."

"That would be great. I will call you at five minutes after three tomorrow when I get off the bus, okay?"

"I am writing it down in my agenda."

"Uncle Dominic?"

"Yes?"

"I'm not supposed to tell anyone, but I'm super excited and can't wait. Since you're so far away, it's okay if I tell you, right?"

"I won't tell a soul."

She giggled. "I'm getting a baby brother or sister soon," she whispered. "Mom told me last week."

Isabella was pregnant. I felt taken aback, left out almost. Like everyone was getting on with the living of their lives, and I was stuck here, in the past, alone.

"That's great, honey. I'm excited for you." I hoped she couldn't hear the effort it took me to say that.

"I'll be able to babysit her too. And I'm not doing it for free!"

I laughed. "Nor should you."

"Effie!" I heard Isabella's voice. "Give me that phone, young lady. You know you're not allowed to be on it after eight."

"Gotta go!"

She hung up. I smiled to myself, wondering when we'd finally tell her the truth. Tell her I was her father.

I held on to the phone, knowing it would ring in the next minute, and right on cue, it did. I answered.

"Why are you calling her at ten o'clock on a school night?" Isabella asked.

"Because I should never have stopped calling her."

WE MADE ARRANGEMENTS FOR ME TO FLY TO FLORIDA the following week. Surprisingly, Isabella wasn't opposed to it. Maybe it was because we were in agreement that we wouldn't tell her until she was an adult that I was her father. It was just safer that way, especially now that I'd taken over the Benedetti family. I had enemies before, and I would have more now. And I wouldn't make her a target for those enemies.

Reuniting with Effie was more wonderful than I could have imagined. I needed her sweet innocence, her clever way of looking at things, and her carefree nature. I spent a week in a hotel nearby and took her to school and picked her up daily. Over the weekend, we drove down to the Keys to visit Salvatore and Lucia and meet my other nieces and brand-new nephew. Lucia tolerated my presence but was too tired to do much of anything but feed little Sergio, who was born weighing over ten pounds and had the exact same eyes of his namesake.

But all the while we were there, I felt like an outsider. Effie loved and accepted me. Salvatore too. But I didn't belong in their world. I felt like I cast a dark shadow on their doorsteps, and the fact disgusted me. I didn't want to be that.

When I returned home, I went to the house in the Adirondacks. To Franco's big, spacious mansion. For the next eight months, I took care of family business, keeping as busy as I could, but walked through the house like a ghost. I kept everything Gia had worn until her scent wore off the clothes, and even then, I packed up the duffel bag and set it in the closet beside my things.

I thought in time I would forget her. Or at least stop missing her. But I didn't. It didn't seem to matter how much time passed.

I kept track of her. She and her mother sold the house she'd grown up in near Philadelphia. Her mother moved back to Italy, where her sister still lived, and Gia rented an apartment in Manhattan. I went into the city often, and each time I did, I got as close as the front door of the building before turning around.

She didn't need me in her life.

I decided I hated the house in the Adirondacks. It only held dark memories of times past, of hatred and jealousy and an old world I wasn't sure I wanted to be a part of anymore. All those years, I'd wanted nothing more than to be boss. All that time, I hadn't realized what it meant to be that. That my father would be dead. That anyone who mattered would be gone. I felt more alone than I ever had in my life, and in a way, as long as I stayed here, I knew I would be stuck in this cold, empty past.

It was on the morning I decided to put the house on the market that I saw the newspaper article. Angus Scava had been indicted on charges of drug trafficking, racketeering, and tax fraud, and was a person of interest in several murders, including that of Mateo Castellano. The key witness? Victor Scava.

I guess he wished he'd cut out his nephew's tongue now.

I closed the paper and stood. Going to the window, I opened it and inhaled a deep breath of fresh, cool autumn air. Summer was at an end.

I decided something else that morning too. I took the keys to my SUV and walked out the door, calling my attorney, Mr. Marino, the executor of my father's will, on the way. I gave him instruction to not only put this house on the market but Salvatore's as well. I also instructed him to find me a place in New York City. One that had never belonged to anyone before me. One that would be mine from the start. It would be the first step in my truly taking over the Benedetti crime family.

I didn't do this in anger. I didn't do it to retaliate. I simply did it because I needed to. I did it because I didn't want this anymore, not alone. I didn't want this empty house. This empty life. I wanted her. I wanted Gia.

A king needed a fucking queen. And I'd been a fool to let her think she could walk away.

I DROVE INTO THE CITY, ARRIVING AT LUNCHTIME. I knew where Gia worked. She waitressed over the weekends while attending law school during the week. I walked into the restaurant, The Grand Café, and looked around the busy place, spotting her instantly.

"I want a table in her section," I told the host.

"Do you have a reservation, Sir?" he asked.

I glanced down at the stocky little man and took out my wallet. "Here's my reservation," I said, handing him some bills.

He cleared his throat, and I followed him to a table. She didn't see me when I was seated, and I opened my menu to wait for her. My heart beat frantically. Although I knew she had no boyfriend and hardly any friends, I wasn't sure how I'd be received. She kept to herself, and I imagined her existence to be as lonely as mine.

She came over, writing something in her tablet as she introduced herself. Then she looked up.

Our gazes locked, and she stopped midsentence. No, midword.

She had her hair pulled back into a messy bun, and she'd let her bangs grow out and had pinned the thick, glossy dark fringe to one side. She wore a white button-down shirt and black pants and the ugliest shoes I'd ever seen, and she couldn't have looked more beautiful to me.

"Wh..." Her voice caught in her throat.

"It's been a long time."

She broke our gaze and glanced around. "I...Dominic..."

"Sit down."

"What are you doing here?"

"I wanted to see you." *I needed to see you.*

She looked around the café. "I...You... I can't do this."

She quickly walked away, untied her apron, and disappeared through a doorway.

I got up to follow her, not caring that I almost knocked a trayful of drinks out of a waitress's hands as the door swung open and I entered the bustling kitchen.

"Sir, you can't be back here," someone said.

I saw the back of Gia's head as she disappeared out another door. I followed, ignoring everyone, and pushed through the door that led into an alley. The stench of the city and the trash containers over-whelmed my senses, and I wondered how the two standing across the way smoking cigarettes could stand it.

Seeing me, they quickly dropped their cigarette butts and put them out before going inside the door I'd just exited.

"Gia!" I called out, looking in one direction, then the other, where I spotted her leaning against a wall. Arms folded across her belly, the sunshine bounced off the natural red tones in her dark hair as she waited there for me, head bowed.

"You shouldn't be here," she said, looking up as I approached.

To be this close to her, to see her, hear her... "I

should be right here," I said, reaching out to touch her, but pulling back, afraid she'd run off, disappear. "In fact, I should never have let you walk away. That was my biggest mistake when it came to you."

She watched me, confusion in her eyes.

"I made a lot of them, but that was the biggest. Letting you believe Scava, that you were somehow some sort of monster—that was another one. Making you watch that night—" I shook my head. "You're too clean for that. I should never have let you see—"

"Stop. I don't want to hear." She put her hands over her ears like a little kid.

"Gia—"

"You have to go," she said, cutting me off.

"Gia?" Someone opened the door and called out.

I took Gia's arms.

"You have customers," the woman said, her cautious gaze on me.

"Just a minute," Gia said, never looking away from me.

"You okay?" the woman asked.

Gia nodded. "I'll be in in a minute."

The woman went back inside.

"I've gone to see Effie," I said. "And I'm selling the houses—"

"You need to go," she said, cutting me off. She straightened and wiped her eyes, attempting to clear all emotion from her face. "You can't be here. You just can't."

The door opened again, and this time, the woman returned with two men.

"Gia," one of the men said, walking out. "Everything okay here?"

"Go, Dominic. I don't want you here."

The man came to stand a few feet from us. "You heard her. You need to leave, Sir."

"Gia." I reached out for her, but she turned her back and disappeared behind the man and back inside the building.

"Sir," the man said.

I glared at him, then saw the woman watching me from the doorway. I turned and walked away. But I didn't leave. Well, I walked out of the alley, but I didn't leave the city.

If she wouldn't have me, then I'd make her keep her promise to me.

I drove to her apartment building and rang random apartments until someone buzzed me in, anger and confusion and rejection circling like a hurricane in my head. It was easy to get into 4A, her shabby little place with its single bedroom, tiny kitchen, and living room barely as big as my bathroom. Light almost penetrated through the window, but not quite, not with the shadow of the building across the street blocking the sun. I looked around the space, opening every drawer, knowing I had no right, but feeling pissed off enough to not care. I'd opened my heart. Fuck, I'd poured it out. And she couldn't be bothered to give me the fucking time of day?

Well, fuck her.

I'd remind her of her promise.

I unscrewed the lightbulb overhead, took my pistol out of the back of my jeans, and set it on her coffee table. Then I sat back on the couch, watched the door, and waited.

I spilled drinks on three customers and dropped two plates of food after Dominic left. I'd never expected to see him again. I'd never thought he'd show up. I didn't bother wondering how he'd found me. He had resources. He'd probably been keeping tabs on me all these months.

It kind of pissed me off, now that the shock had worn off. How dare he walk back into my life, when I was just getting it back together? Scraping pieces of myself into something resembling some sort of normal.

After the day we'd met with Scava, I'd felt cold for a long time. Cold and empty. My mom and I had mourned Mateo together. I was pretty sure neither of us had really stopped grieving, but it had been time to move on. We sold the house, and she moved back to Italy with her sister. I moved to New York City and decided I would get my law degree and put assholes like Angus and Victor Scava away. It was what I could do to honor Mateo's memory.

I'd kept the flash drive with the phone recording. I'd only just turned it over a few weeks ago, in fact. I knew if I did it too soon, Angus would know it was me and retaliate. I'd sent it anonymously, and it had worked. They'd gone after Victor, and Victor was now their star witness against the bigger fish: his uncle.

Seeing Victor like that at the restaurant that night, beaten, his uncle threatening to cut out his tongue, it disgusted me. It made me see without a doubt that this wasn't who I was. Scava calling me a monster? I had believed him. And I guess I would have been one if I'd gone through with what I'd said I wanted.

The bus dropped me off a block from my apartment. It was almost midnight, and my feet and back hurt. I'd worked a double today, but I needed the money. My mom wanted to help me out, but she didn't have any more than I did so I lived in a shitty apartment in a shittier neighborhood and made my own way.

I climbed the apartment stairs and unlocked the outer door, then went up to the fourth floor. The hallway light was out, again, so I used the flashlight in my phone to slide my key into the lock and turn it. When I reached to switch on the lights in the apartment, nothing happened. I wondered if it was a building-wide outage. But then I saw the light coming from beneath the door of my neighbor's unit, and my heartbeat picked up. My eyes widened and I strained to see into the dark apartment just making out a shape in front of the window sitting on the couch.

Was it Scava's men already? Did he know it was me who'd turned over evidence? He wasn't stupid. Maybe I was for having done it.

"Don't fucking try to run."

Relief flooded me when I first heard Dominic's voice. But then, I remembered that afternoon. How I'd sent him away.

"Come inside and close the door, Gia."

I stood there as goose bumps covered my body at the sound of his voice. His command.

"I said come inside and shut the door."

He wouldn't hurt me. I knew that. But his voice sounded strange. Like it had once before on the night I'd found out who he really was.

"I didn't know you broke into apartments," I said, going for casual, walking inside and closing the door.

"There's a lot you don't know about me."

He reached over and turned on the lamp beside

the sofa. That was when I caught sight of the pistol on the coffee table and took a step back.

He stood. "I'm not going to hurt you," he said.

"What do you want, Dominic?"

He stalked toward me, and all I could do was watch him move, remembering how broad his shoulders were, how much space he took up. How being near him made my body feel.

"You owe me something, Gia."

He stopped when the toes of his boots bumped against my shoes. He wrapped a hand around my head and twined his fingers into the hair at the nape of my neck, making me gasp, making my heart pound.

"Domi—" But I never got the word out because he closed his mouth over mine and devoured the sound.

I'd forgotten the feel of him, of his lips. I'd forgotten the way he tasted, the way his body felt so hard and powerful, forgot how he tugged my hair and forced my face up to his. His tongue slipped into my mouth, and I closed my eyes, leaning into his hand as his other one slid up over my hip and waist to cup my breast and squeeze the nipple.

He broke our kiss and turned my head to the side to whisper in my ear.

"You owe me something, and I'm here to collect."

I pressed against his chest, squeezing the muscle beneath it, then moved my hands to his biceps and curled them around before I kissed him back, liking it when he bit my lip a little, liking the feel of his cock hardening at my belly.

Hearing the door lock behind me, I startled. Dominic's blue-gray eyes bore into mine, different than they'd been that afternoon. Harder. Like he used to look at me in the beginning at the cabin. Like he looked at me when he fucked me.

I stood there panting, my mouth open like some puppy, my eyes tearing as he tugged a little harder on my hair.

"Aren't you curious what you owe?"

He walked me through the small apartment and into my bedroom, dropping me on the bed before climbing onto it. It was my old bed from home. I'd had it for more than fifteen years, and it creaked beneath our combined weight.

"Your apartment's a fucking mess."

He pulled his shirt up over his head, the moon-light making the white clock face of the tattoo on his chest appear almost ghostlike.

"Shut up," I said, my hands on his chest, unable to get enough of his heat, his strength. I'd missed him. I'd missed him so much.

He ripped my shirt down the middle and pushed it from my arms. I would have been pissed if I wasn't so turned-on. He looked down at me and pushed the cups of my bra beneath my breasts. Taking one into his mouth, he sucked and then bit a little harder than he had my lip.

I groaned, arching my back.

He laid his full weight on me and looked at me, his face an inch from mine. Watching me, he took my hand and dragged it to himself, to his back, to where I felt the butt of the pistol I hadn't noticed he'd tucked into his jeans.

I gasped and yanked my hand away, or tried to, but he wouldn't let me.

"Take it," he said.

"No."

"Take it, Gia."

I shook my head.

"Fucking take it." He wrapped my hand around it and together, we drew it out so that I held the gun.

I looked at it, then at him.

"Do you remember what you promised me?" he asked, sitting up, trapping me between his thighs.

"Stop. I don't want this."

But he kept his hand wrapped around mine, so I couldn't let it go.

"I don't give a fuck what you want. I did, this afternoon, but you had me fucking dismissed."

"Dominic—"

He brought the gun between us and pressed the mouth of the barrel to his chest.

My heart pounded.

"You promised to kill me. You swore it."

I began to silently weep, heavy tears sliding from my face onto the bed. Dominic wrapped his other hand around my throat and squeezed. The tears stopped, and my eyes went wide as I gasped for breath. He cocked the gun, never taking his eyes off me.

"Pull the trigger, Gia."

I tried to shake my head, but I couldn't move.

"I'm an intruder. It'll be self-defense. Now keep your promise, and fucking pull the trigger."

He released my throat, and I choked and gasped for breath, my hand weak around the gun.

"I don't want to," I said, my voice coming out thin.

He tapped my face, small slaps that didn't hurt but that invaded.

"*I don't want to,*" he mimicked.

Dominic wrapped his hand back around my throat.

"You didn't keep your promise!" I cried out.

He kept his hand there, but his hold remained loose. I thought I saw the faintest hint of a smile play along his lips.

"You didn't fucking keep your promise!" I said again.

He let me pull my hand free from his, and I kept the pistol pointed at him.

"That's it. Get mad," he said.

He took the wrist of the hand that held the gun

and pinned it to the bed and while he kept his gaze locked on mine, his hands worked the buttons of my pants, opening them, reaching inside to cup my sex over my panties.

"Get fucking pissed, Gia."

I closed my eyes, the feel of his hands on me again, of my own need, it fucking overwhelmed everything.

"You let him walk away!"

He slid his hand inside, fingers finding my clit, my slick, ready entrance.

"You let me walk away," I said more quietly.

Fuck. I closed my eyes and thrust up into his hand.

"I couldn't make you stay," he said quietly.

When I opened my eyes, I saw he'd leaned down over me.

"It had to be your choice." His voice came dark and husky. "But that was then and this is now and I changed my mind."

"Fuck me," I managed as he jerked my pants and panties down so I worked them off the rest of the way. "I need to feel you inside me, Dominic."

The pistol lay forgotten beside us as he used both hands to undo his jeans then push them and his briefs off.

"If I fuck you"—

His cock stood ready at my entrance.

"If you say yes"—

I opened my legs as wide as I could.

"You won't be able to walk away. Not again. Not ever again."

He thrust. He wasn't waiting for my answer, not really.

And I wouldn't have said no.

I cried out, and he held still inside me.

"Open your eyes, Gia. Look at me. I'm right fucking here."

I did, trying to move my hips beneath him but unable to.

"Hear me, Gia. You won't be able to change your mind. I won't let you walk away again. Do you understand me?"

I nodded, arching my back. "Please. I need—"

He pulled out and thrust again, I gasped, biting my own lip, tasting blood. *Blood*. With him, there would be blood.

"More," I said.

He smiled, pulled out, and impaled me again.

"You fucking left."

He was angry and furious and sexy as fucking hell.

"I won't ever let you walk away from me again. Fucking never."

I bit my lip again, harder, until I tasted more blood, and I came. I came with him watching me. I came watching him. My pussy throbbed around his cock, and he never even blinked until I'd squeezed every drop of pleasure from him, taking from him what he gave, knowing this sealed our pact, knowing that when he moved again, when he fucked me and I watched him come, that I was his.

I was his forever.

"What did you have to do with Angus Scava's arrest?" I sat on a stool at the kitchen counter peeling an apple, watching her as she made coffee. Although she had her back to me, I saw her stiffen.

"Nothing."

"Liar."

She poured two cups of coffee out of the old-fashioned machine and set one before me. She sipped from her mug and stood on the other side of the counter, her eyes on mine. I could see her thinking as she worked out how to answer. Did she think I hadn't realized the flash drive with the recording had disappeared when we'd left for my father's funeral?

I picked up my mug and waited.

"Nothing," she said again, turning away.

I sipped from the mug. "Christ. What is this shit?" I looked at the dark-brown water in my mug. That's exactly what it tasted like: fucking dirty brown water.

"Don't be a snob. The coffee machine was here when I moved in. It's fine."

She took another sip, but even I saw how she had to force herself to do it.

"You get used to it," she said.

"I'm not getting used to it." I stood and walked around the aisle to the sink and dumped my mug down the drain before taking hers and doing the same.

"What are you doing?"

"Let's go get some real coffee." I shook my head as she tried to argue. "You're Italian, for Christ's sake. You can't tell me you like that crap."

"I didn't say I liked it."

She grabbed her purse and jacket, and we walked out.

Once outside, we walked two blocks to a small café. Inside, we took a seat in a corner away from the windows. Gia ordered a cappuccino and I ordered a double espresso. After they came, I asked again.

"Gia, what did you have to do with Scava's arrest?"

She shrugged a shoulder and kept her eyes on

the flower design the barista had made out of her froth.

"I handed over the recording. I sent it anonymously."

I shook my head. "Do you think Scava won't know who sent it?"

"He'll think it's Victor."

"He might, but he might not. He will retaliate, you know that."

She met my gaze. "You'll keep me safe."

That took me back.

Yes, I would keep her safe, but I didn't expect her to say it, because saying it came with so much more.

"I couldn't just let him walk away scot-free, Dominic. Mateo died for that evidence."

"I know. But you put yourself in danger now."

"He's behind bars."

"He can run his entire organization from behind those bars. All he has to do is give the order."

"I couldn't not do it."

I drank from my cup. "I know. You'll come back with me today. You can't stay in your apartment."

"I have a job and school."

"You don't need a job, and you can take a semester off."

"I've already taken too many years off. I'm twenty-five, Dominic."

"If you're dead, you'll be taking the rest of your

life off, won't you? You're studying to be an attorney. Which do you think is the better option?"

"Shut up."

"I'm putting both houses on the market, my father's and Salvatore's. We'll move to the city."

"We're just moving in together? Just like that?"

"You never once struck me as a girl for a long courtship with flowers and romantic walks on the beach."

"I'm not. But it's fast, isn't it?"

"I want you with me. I thought I made that clear last night."

"So I'll always be an available piece of ass for you?"

I sat back, confused now. "That's what you think?"

She didn't reply but watched me through hooded eyes.

"Gia, you're a bright girl. Do you really think I came after you after eight months being apart, spilling my heart out to you, because I think you're a nice *'piece of ass'*?"

"Do you consider what happened last night, what you said, to be spilling your heart out?"

Again, I felt taken aback. "What do you want? I've never been a flowers and romantic walks on the beach type either."

"Maybe I am after all," she said defensively, averting her gaze from mine momentarily.

I smiled, still a little confused, but understanding. I leaned forward and took her chin in my hand, raising it so she looked at me. "I love you. Is that what you want to hear?"

She only stared as if she didn't believe me.

"I love you, and those eight months without you were like a little slice of hell worse than the seven years I'd lived before I found you huddled in the corner of that rotten cabin. I have never in my life wanted someone as much as I want you. And as much as I love fucking you, what I mean is that I want you in my fucking life, not just my bed. I don't want to let you out of my sight again. I want you safe and close and—"

She cried and smiled at once.

"What?" I asked.

"You are a romantic, in your own weird way."

She leaned forward and kissed my lips softly.

"You don't have the smoothest way with words, but you have a bigger heart than you think, Dominic Benedetti."

She sat back in her chair, her hands still in mine, clutching onto mine as I did hers.

I felt flustered looking at her. I felt...unsure. I'd never told any girl these things before. I'd never felt them or even bothered pretending I did. With her, though, I meant every word.

"Maybe we should just get married while we're at it." I said it before I lost my nerve.

Gia laughed, then wiped away a tear before returning her hand to mine. "Are you proposing?"

"Are you saying yes?"

"I don't know. Aren't you supposed to get down on one knee or something?"

I looked around at the other people in the place. No one was paying attention to us, but they would be in a minute. I shoved the table next to ours out of the way—luckily it was empty—and got on one knee, her hands still in mine.

"You already have me on my knees," I said.

"Oh my God, Dominic, I wasn't serious! Get up!"

She looked around and tried to pull me up.

"No. Gia Castellano, I love you, and I want you to marry me. I'm asking you to. Here on one fucking knee."

Everyone was staring now.

Gia's face flushed red, and she looked from them to me and smiled wide and cried and nodded her head. "I will."

I got up and drew her to her feet to stand with me, wrapping my arms around her and closing my mouth over hers as everyone in the place started to clap and whistle.

She broke our kiss and whispered in my ear.

"That was so embarrassing, Dominic."

"If you want romance, you're going to get over-the-top romance." I cupped her chin and tilted her head back to kiss her again, a long, soft kiss.

"I love you," she said. "For a long time now. I don't even know when it happened."

"I think it was the first time I saw your eyes. When they were glaring at me," I added, making her smile. "Let's get out of here."

IT TOOK ME TWO MONTHS TO DO THE ONE THING I needed to do to close the door on the past before I could move on with my future.

"You want me to come with you?" Gia asked from beside me.

We had just driven through the gates of the cemetery and pulled up near my family's plot.

I looked at the gated-off area, at the three largest stones.

"No. I need to do this alone." I squeezed her hand.

She nodded, and I climbed out of the sedan with the bundles of flowers. My breath fogged in the brisk morning air, and all I heard was the lonely sound of leaves crushing under my feet. I made my way up the hill and through the headstones of countless other Benedettis until I reached theirs.

Squatting down, I cleared some of the weeds, then lay the flowers before each of the stones. First, my mother. Then my brother. And finally, my father.

That was when I paused, traced his name and

the dates. I took a seat on a bench nearest his grave and glanced at the waiting car. With its tinted windows, I couldn't see inside and would have felt foolish for someone to see me, but I cleared my throat anyway and turned back to my father's grave.

"I should have done this when you were alive."

My eyes felt hot and damp. Death was so final and regret so permanent.

"But that night fucked with me, Paps. You telling me the truth like that, it fucked with my head. I wasn't like either of my brothers. Sergio felt duty bound, and Salvatore is just too good for this life. Me, I wanted it. Oh man, I wanted it so bad I could taste it.

"You're right, you know. What you wrote in the will about me being the most like you. You're right. Who'd have guessed it, huh, considering."

I wiped my hand across my face and stood, made a short turn, and kicked some pinecones away while I got myself under control. I didn't even hear her come up behind me until she slid her hand into mine and held it. Gia stood close but gave me space at the same time. This is what we'd become to each other. It was like we knew, like we felt each other's needs, and neither of us could stand the pain of the other.

Gia, a woman I'd hurt, one I'd been paid to break, had given me a part of her soul and stolen a piece of mine.

"Okay?" she asked quietly.

I nodded, and we walked back to the grave.

"I love you, old man. I miss you, and I wish I hadn't wasted the last seven years of your life. But you took care of me in the end, didn't you? You made sure I'd have the family's allegiance. And I forgive you for that night, for telling me like that."

Just then, a robin landed on my father's headstone.

Gia gasped beside me. The bird simply perched there, unmoving, and watched me for a long moment before it flew off and landed on a branch of the closest tree, still watching us. We remained silent until finally, it flew off into the sky.

"Wow," Gia said.

I exhaled a breath with a smile. "I don't think it's a sign or something."

"A robin symbolizes renewal, Dominic. Maybe it was your father—"

I touched the headstone one more time and turned to her, caressing her cheek, kissing the tip of her cold nose. "That's sweet, but it's just not really Franco Benedetti's style," I said with a short laugh.

I DIDN'T WANT GIA TO KNOW I WAS WORRIED. IF Angus Scava suspected Gia turned over evidence, he'd send men after her. He wouldn't need proof to do it. But I hoped with Victor coming forward as a key witness, he'd blame it all on his nephew. Victor would have had access to the recordings too, after all, and that recording was only a small piece of the evidence against Angus.

Gia quit her job, but she wouldn't quit school. So I moved in with her into her crap apartment for just over a month until I signed the lease on a condo in Little Italy. We fell in love with it the first time we saw it. It was charming with its exposed brick, reclaimed wooden floors, and huge windows. Gia and I had similar taste in furnishings: ultramodern, and it had nothing in common with any of the houses my family owned. Moving in together felt so natural, as if we'd lived together our whole lives.

Effie flew up to New York to visit. Isabella let her stay with us over the Thanksgiving break, and she and Gia hit it off from the start. I liked seeing Effie so at ease, and as much as I wished I could tell her the truth, I knew it wasn't the time. I saw Gia watching me with her, and I hated the look of pity she sometimes got. We never talked about it, though.

Ruling the Benedetti family came with its challenges. Now that I was boss, things were different than I'd always thought they were. I had no one I trusted. Salvatore didn't want to have anything to do with the family business, and the taint of Roman's betrayal still tasted bitter on my tongue. I retained

Henderson's services, but I had learned that everyone had their own agenda. I wouldn't be played again, not by anyone.

I married Gia over Christmas. We flew to Calabria, Italy, for the wedding. That house was the only one of the family homes I'd kept. I hadn't spent much time in it during my youth, and it didn't seem to hold the stain of betrayal in its walls. Salvatore and Lucia attended with all three kids. So did Isabella and Luke and their new baby girl, Josie. Effie was our flower girl, and Salvatore and Lucia stood as witnesses. Gia's mother and aunt attended, but that was all, and it was fine. I guess we were both loners. But together, just us, it didn't seem to matter.

I didn't show Gia the newspaper that arrived on our doorstep the morning of our wedding. I didn't tell her that Victor Scava had disappeared, along with all the evidence against Angus. I didn't mention the small box tucked inside the paper either. Angus Scava's wedding gift. A box containing Victor's tongue. Or what I assumed to be Victor's tongue. I guess it could have been Joe Blow's tongue, but I didn't think so. The card with it was addressed to the "happy couple" and wished us a long life.

I threw the box and the card into the fire.

This was mafia life. No rest for the wicked and all that shit. Both Gia and I had our eyes wide open, and we'd face whatever challenges came our way together. I'd keep her hands clean, though. I'd keep her pure and carry all the weight. All the blood.

I understood Salvatore for the first time in my life, then. I understood his decision to leave and respected it.

Dominic thought I didn't know about Angus Scava's release. He thought I didn't know Victor's disappearance most likely meant his death. I would let him believe it for now. This day was too important to spoil with talk of the Scavas. I was going to marry the man I loved. A savage beast of a man who'd been through hell and walked out on top of his world. I don't think he realized how lonely it would be at the top, not until he stood in his father's shoes.

But together, we weren't lonely. We fit perfectly, Dominic and I. It was almost as though we were the last two pieces in a puzzle, lost for years and found under the dusty couch. And once linked together, the empty space was filled and everything was complete as if it had never been empty at all.

When I was a little girl, I believed in fairy tales.

Not the ones Disney tells. No, I believed the real ones. The scary ones. The ones where not everyone got to meet their prince in shining armor or got their happily-ever-after. I learned too young how fucked up life could be, how pain and suffering and death lurked behind every smile. But I never stopped believing in the power of love, and I always loved the beasts more than I did the princes.

Dominic was my beast. And somehow, I was his princess.

I stood along with Effie at the entrance of the ancient, tiny chapel where we'd be wed. I wore the antique-lace wedding dress passed down from my grandmother, clutching roses so red they almost appeared black. Two men opened the doors, and the small gathering stood. The scent of incense and time poured from the open doors.

I met Dominic's gaze through the net of my veil, and my heart thudded against my chest. For a moment, I wished I had accepted Salvatore's proposal to walk me down the aisle, because suddenly my knees grew weak, and I wasn't sure my legs would carry me the distance between us.

But then Dominic smiled, and I saw how that dimple softened his face, giving him a younger appearance, an innocent one. *An angel of death.* That's how I'd seen him at the cabin, where he'd been sent to break me. Now I knew it was true. He was my angel of death. But he would slay all my enemies, and he would protect and love me.

The organ began to play the wedding march: a heavy, dark gothic piece I'd chosen. One Dominic had raised his eyebrows at but accepted without question. Effie walked ahead of me scattering bloodred rose petals in her wake. I took my first step, standing taller as I did, meeting every eye in the church, knowing that even though Dominic and I may never be accepted by some, it wouldn't matter, not anymore. We only needed each other.

Dominic took the last steps to meet me, and with his arm around my waist, he led me to the altar. We stood before the priest. The music stopped playing, and he began the service. I didn't hear much of what he said. I couldn't stop looking at Dominic, and he seemed unable to take his gaze from me.

I realized then I was wrong when I thought the love I'd find would be an ugly and twisted thing. I realized that love itself would bend any ugliness into its own—sometimes strange—sort of beauty.

Because it had been in those darkest moments that love had crept in and tethered us together, tighter than any chains could.

It had been in that darkness that beauty seemed to want to find us most.

I'd always preferred night to day, and I'd never been afraid of the dark. And as Dominic and I stood hand in hand, promising ourselves to each other, I knew this was exactly where I belonged, where we both belonged. We'd come from ugliness. Suffering had put us on the road to our destiny. But Dominic had been wrong about one thing. Even in our world, our love would last forever. He and I, we would make our own happily-ever-after.

WHAT TO READ NEXT

A SAMPLE FROM SERGIO: A DARK MAFIA ROMANCE

"Come here."

She hugs her arms, but moves toward me.

"Here." I hold one of the glasses out to her. She eyes it but doesn't reach out for it. "It'll calm you down."

"What is it?" she asks.

"Whiskey."

She takes it, drinks the smallest sip. Flinches when she swallows.

After draining mine, I pour a second glass and reach to turn on the lamp beside me. I sit back folding one ankle over my knee and stretching an arm over the back of the couch to get a good look at her. She was wearing makeup at some point but her earlier tears have smeared mascara across her cheek. Her eyes, a pretty almond-shape, are so dark, they're almost black. Her skin has a pale olive tone and she keeps biting her lower lip so it's bleeding a little. I can't tell how long her hair is. She's bound the dark mass into a messy bun.

"What did those men do?" she asks, surprising me.

I smile. "Don't worry about that." She's standing awkwardly and I'm thinking. "Do you know who I am?" I know she would have heard my name more than once.

She lowers her lashes and I wonder if she's contemplating lying, but then she nods once.

"Who?"

"Mafia."

"My name."

"Sergio Benedetti."

"Do you know my family?"

"Not really. I've heard the name, that's all."

"Drink your drink."

She takes another sip. "I have class tomorrow," she says.

I nod. Sip. Consider.

"What are you going to do?" she asks finally.

"I'm not going to do anything. You are. Get undressed."

"What?" She begins to tremble, shrinks herself as she hugs her arms tighter to her.

"Get undressed, Natalie."

"Why?" her voice is a squeak.

"Insurance."

"Why?" she repeats, taking a step backward.

"Because I need to make sure when I take you home later, that you're not going to tell any of your friends what you saw or heard." I wait. Watch her process. "It's the only way to keep you safe," I add on, not really sure why.

"Safe? How will that keep me safe?"

"Trust me—"

"And safe from who? You?" Her eyebrows knit together. "You said you wouldn't hurt me."

"I said I wouldn't hurt you unless you made me."

"I already told you I won't say anything. I promise."

She wipes fresh tears from her eyes. I finish my drink, set my glass down and get to my feet. She takes a step away from me when I come around the coffee table.

"Remember what you agreed to outside." I reach her, take hold of her arms, rub them. "Just relax, no reason to get so upset."

"No reason? This isn't—"

"Now, what's going to happen next is you're going to do as I say and take off your clothes and I'm going to take some pictures."

"Pictures?" She's panicking. "Why?"

"You repeat yourself a lot, you know that?" I pause but I'm not expecting an answer. "Like I said, insurance. You talk and the photos get sent to your parents, your friends, are posted along the walls at school, etc..."

"Etcetera?"

"Trust me, this is the easiest way for me to do this."

"What's the alternative?" she asks as she pushes out of my grasp.

"The alternative would be...painful."

She swallows. She's wringing her hands. "I think I'm going to be sick."

"You'll be fine. It's just a few pictures."

She shakes her head, rubs her face. "No."

I point to the bathroom, and when she walks out of the room, I resume my seat on the couch. She doesn't come back for a full ten minutes, but when she does, her fear seems to have lessened, or at least it's well hidden behind eyes of fire.

She's pissed.

"You want dirty pictures?" she asks, spitting the words.

I casually shrug one shoulder. It's sort of funny to see her like this. I wonder about the pep talk she must have given herself to get so worked up because she's so mad she's practically shaking. "You think you're going to blackmail me?" She takes a step forward, then back again. "Huh? Pervert?"

She's bouncing from one leg to the other like a boxer. I chuckle at the image but it only makes her angrier. She finally stands still, fists her hands at her sides, her face going bright red.

"Well you can try and make me."

I lean deeper into my seat, consider her, wonder if she's realized how much more interesting she's just made this. Taking my time, I unbutton the cuffs of my shirt, roll the sleeves up to my elbow before I reply. "You sure about that, sweetheart?"

"Don't call me that."

"Are you?"

"Fuck you."

"And you seemed so sweet," I say, standing.

She spins to run from the room, but I catch her easily, my hand wrapping around her arm to halt her. I pull her into my chest. Cock my head to the side. "I was thinking I'd get a slow strip tease, but this will be much more fun."

"Let me go!"

I lean in close, inhale the scent of her. Smell the fear creeping back up to the surface. Make a point of doing so. "Just remember, you chose this. It could have gone easier."

Available at all retailers. One-Click now!

THANK YOU

Thanks for reading *Dominic: a Dark Mafia Romance*. I hope you enjoyed it and would consider leaving a review at the store where you purchased the book.

Want to be the first to hear about sales and new releases? You can sign up for my Newsletter here!

Like my FB Author Page to keep updated on news and giveaways!

I have a FB Fan Group where I share exclusive teasers and interact with readers. It's called The Knight Spot. If you'd like to join, click here!

ALSO BY NATASHA KNIGHT

Ties that Bind Duet

Mine

His

MacLeod Brothers

Devil's Bargain

Benedetti Mafia World

Salvatore: a Dark Mafia Romance

Dominic: a Dark Mafia Romance

Sergio: a Dark Mafia Romance

The Benedetti Brothers Box Set (Contains Salvatore, Dominic and Sergio)

Killian: a Dark Mafia Romance

Giovanni: a Dark Mafia Romance

The Amado Brothers

Dishonorable

Disgraced

Unhinged

Standalone Dark Romance

Descent

Deviant

Beautiful Liar

Retribution

Theirs To Take

Captive, Mine

Alpha

Given to the Savage

Taken by the Beast

Claimed by the Beast

Captive's Desire

Protective Custody

Amy's Strict Doctor

Taming Emma

Taming Megan

Taming Naia

Reclaiming Sophie

The Firefighter's Girl

Dangerous Defiance

Her Rogue Knight

Taught To Kneel

Tamed: the Roark Brothers Trilogy

ABOUT NATASHA KNIGHT

Natasha Knight is the *USA Today* Bestselling author of Romantic Suspense and Dark Romance Novels. She has sold over half a million books and is translated into six languages. She currently lives in The Netherlands with her husband and two daughters and when she's not writing, she's walking in the woods listening to a book, sitting in a corner reading or off exploring the world as often as she can get away.

Write Natasha here: natasha@natasha-knight.com

Click here to sign up for my newsletter to receive new release news and updates.

NATASHA KNIGHT

www.natasha-knight.com

Made in the USA
Monee, IL
01 February 2025

11325286R00208